Stefanos Metadorakis would make being in love intoxicating....

Molly squared her shoulders. She didn't need to be thinking such thoughts.

Stefanos looped a hand over the headrest of her seat, brushing her bare shoulder gently. She absorbed the wondrous shiver moving through her. She ought to be ignoring it, she told herself.

He turned off the car's inside light. In the semidarkness he felt even closer. The hand near her shoulder touched her chin softly, and her eyelids began to close. He put his hand around her neck, drawing her even nearer.

Stop him! a little voice in her mind cried frantically. *It'll just make things worse.*

But she couldn't stop him. His parted lips brushed against her mouth, warm and moist, and heat pooled in her like hot wax under the flame of a candle. Molly leaned toward him. How wonderful to be held again....

Dear Reader,

Welcome to another month of fine reading from Silhouette Intimate Moments. And what better way to start off the month than with an American Hero title from Marilyn Pappano, a book that's also the beginning of a new miniseries, Southern Knights. Hero Michael Bennett and his friends Remy and Smith are all dedicated to upholding the law—and to loving the right lady. And in *Michael's Gift*, she turns out to be the one woman he wishes she wasn't. To know more, you'll just have to read this terrific story.

The month continues with *Snow Bride*, the newest from bestselling writer Dallas Schulze. Then it's on to *Wild Horses, Wild Men*, from Ann Williams; *Waking Nightmare*, from highly regarded newcomer Alicia Scott; *Breaking the Rules*, Ruth Wind's Intimate Moments debut; and *Hear No Evil*, a suspenseful novel from brand-new author Susan Drake. I think you'll enjoy each and every one of these books—and that you'll be looking for more equally exciting reading next month and in the months to come. So look no further than Silhouette Intimate Moments, where, each and every month, we're proud to bring you writers we consider among the finest in the genre today.

Enjoy!

Leslie J. Wainger
Senior Editor and Editorial Coordinator

Please address questions and book requests to:
Silhouette Reader Service
U.S.: 3010 Walden Ave., P.O. Box 1325, Buffalo, NY 14269
Canadian: P.O. Box 609, Fort Erie, Ont. L2A 5X3

HEAR
NO EVIL

Susan
Drake

Published by Silhouette Books
America's Publisher of Contemporary Romance

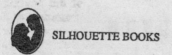 SILHOUETTE BOOKS

ISBN 0-373-07588-X

HEAR NO EVIL

Copyright © 1994 by Susan Ward Dunn

SUSAN DRAKE

has always loved writing and traveling and has haunted stationery stores and libraries from an early age. She counts among her travels one trip to Hawaii, one trip to North Africa and five trips to Europe, including a year of study in Spain and a stint living in a farmhouse on a Greek island. Though she now has enough hearing loss to qualify as "deaf" on her state income tax, she once taught Spanish in high school and junior college and is still very much a part of the hearing world with her job as a computer programmer at a local university. She lives in New Orleans with her husband of fifteen years, one cat, three bikes, five computers and a front lawn that needs lots of tender loving care.

To Sue, Patty, Bob, Robin, Laura,
Anna and Maureen for offering insights
and encouragement.

To Jim B. for showing me his spy camera.

And to Riley for dragging me back to Greece.

Prologue

"Will you do it?"

Stefanos Metadorakis let his hand slide off the cold glass of the window, knowing he could never agree and wondering why he couldn't say so.

Behind him, the clink of ice cubes against glass told him his old colleague must be getting a refill on his scotch. Stefanos turned and glanced across the hotel suite at Leo Rollins. He and Leo had worked together at NATO before going their separate ways. Leo was still doing security work, something he himself had never gotten involved with.

"I'm offering you a chance to get even, Steve."

Get even? Excitement fizzed through him, but Stefanos ignored it to return his gaze to New York's night skyline. "I'm surprised you'd even consider me after the way I messed up in Lidacros."

"You did a great job two years ago, Steve, and you know it."

Stefanos looked at his hands. Scar tissue ridged his palms, testifying to the torture and reconstructive surgery he'd endured over the last two years. He jammed his hands into his trouser pockets and turned his back on the steamy July night outside. "Right," he said in a self-mocking tone. "I did a great job."

"Your hands were a mess, but you got out alive," Leo said, leaning forward. "And saved a kid's life, too."

"And managed to get a lot of men killed as punishment for my escape," Stefanos said.

"You could get revenge for those men. And for the little boy whose family was killed."

He *had* been trying to vindicate their deaths for the last two years, Stefanos thought, running a hand through his thick, brown hair. He'd met with little success so far.

"Okay, think about it." Leo levered his beefy frame out of his chair.

It was going to be hard to do anything *but* think about it.

"So how's your grandfather doing?" Leo asked when they reached the door of his hotel suite.

Stefanos raised an eyebrow. His grandfather had been hospitalized with a heart attack a few days before, but he didn't think the news had been circulated. "I guess I shouldn't be surprised you know why I had to rush to New York," Stefanos said.

Leo smiled. "No, you shouldn't."

Stefanos laughed. "He's going to make it."

"Glad to hear it." Leo shook hands and left.

Wearily Stefanos stripped off his clothes and slipped between the covers of the bed, trying to remember the last time he'd been this exhausted. It had been on the mountain. He'd been carrying Nikos for what seemed like forever and—

Stefanos rolled over, burying his face in the pillow, but the past would not leave him alone. In his mind's eye he saw again the darkness of the cell-like room his kidnappers had put him in, heard again the rasping of metal against metal, felt the same hopelessness that had washed over him each time he'd heard that sound.

Then the dream came.

The night shadows of the mountain swallowed the path ahead of them like a black fog. The boy crept along beside him, both of them being careful to stay hidden behind the rock outcrop.

"You will follow the path." Nikos stopped and pointed to a row of dark pines along the ridge in front of them. "It is not far now. The border is close."

Stefanos opened his mouth to answer when the shadows came closer, darkened, and took on the shape of a man with an automatic rifle.

An explosion of gunfire ripped the air. The boy fell, and suddenly the soldier disappeared. In his place stood Stefanos holding the rifle in his own hands. All of the old men of the village appeared then, and all of the young men, too, standing in a line in front of him. He began to shoot them, one after the other....

Stefanos jerked upright in the bed, his heart hammering in his chest, a silent shout of outrage choking his throat. He stared into the semidarkness of the hotel room. After a moment he realized where he was and forced himself to loosen his death grip on the sheet.

He swung his feet to the floor, pulled on a robe, and walked to the window, where he braced a hand against the cold steel of its support. Would he never be free of this dream?

Maybe not. It held enough of the truth to fester inside him forever.

Stefanos found his cigarettes, lit one, and thought about the two landscape paintings he'd bought the evening of his arrival in New York. He'd never met the artist, but she'd come looking for him. Because she had, Leo had, too, and they'd both come for the same reason—his contacts at Meta-Hellenic Shipping, the Metadorakis family business.

He would help Leo, but he'd keep his family out of it as much as possible. If something went wrong, he'd pay for it. He didn't want any innocent people hurt this time.

Chapter 1

A red light flashed off her rearview mirror. Molly Light glanced up from the road to see an ambulance practically on top of her bumper. Why hadn't he put on his siren yet?

Molly pulled over to the side and adjusted the volume of her hearing aid. The vehicle sped past and now the wail of the siren pulsed over her. Through the back window Molly caught a glimpse of a paramedic bent over someone, and Molly's stomach tightened in sympathy.

She rather felt she was an emergency herself or would be soon, what with her hopes and dreams crashing to pieces all around her. She checked the mirror, absently smoothed a few wisps of blond hair away from her face, and turned her minivan back onto the street, once again the quiet, shady thoroughfare of an elegant New Jersey suburb.

The late afternoon sun glinted off the chrome of the steel blue Jaguar behind her as its driver also pulled back into traffic. She'd seen that car on the parkway a few minutes earlier. It wasn't as if she'd never seen a Jag, but—

Molly gave herself a mental shake. She didn't have to be paranoid. The car behind her was a coincidence, just like the man she'd thought had been following her in New York City the other night.

She turned her attention to her driving, and within minutes the wooden sign proclaiming the entrance to Newpark School of Art appeared ahead, stark white against the phthalo green of the spruce trees behind it. Molly turned into the driveway that led to the redbrick colonial building and wondered what she could say to convince Roger McCauley, her friend and mentor, to postpone selling the school.

She'd finished teaching her summer classes several days ago, and the parking lot stood empty except for Roger's sedan. This might be the last time she'd have any reason to be here and the thought made a lump of sadness lodge in her throat. Molly parked and turned off the ignition. Maybe she would get Roger to agree. She'd try, anyway.

Inside the school's office, Roger stood behind a cluttered desk dressed in his white-shirt-and-khaki-pants uniform, one hand resting across the top of an open packing box, the other holding the phone receiver to his ear. When he saw her, he rolled his eyes and mouthed, "Wait. My wife."

Molly nodded and walked to the window. She couldn't understand what he was saying so her watching him wouldn't have been eavesdropping. Still, she thought it more polite to give him privacy.

Outside the window, lengthening shadows marched across the broad sweep of lawn. She focused on the grassy spots still lit by the sinking sun. Roger hadn't done anything about putting in gardens, but if she got the school, she'd do some planting—beds of nasturtiums, larkspur and bachelor buttons, bold strokes of color nestled in the green.

If she got the school, she reminded herself.

A movement beside her made her turn. Roger stood next to her, his gray brows pulled into a scowl. "Don't look so harassed," Molly teased. "You're lucky to have her," she said, thinking of his wife.

"I know," he said aloud, then continued, moving his hands in Ameslan or American Sign Language patterns. "But this cross-country marriage is ridiculous."

Because of the quiet in the building, Molly could understand his speech without the help of signs this afternoon. She would have stopped him, but Roger had gotten in the habit of using them and she liked him to be comfortable when he talked with her.

Molly dropped her bag onto Roger's desk and pushed one of the packing boxes next to a chair. "You're going to end that long-distance arrangement pretty soon, and you're right to."

Roger handed her a stack of books, then signed, "You didn't think so before."

"I've always thought so." Molly piled the books into the box.

"If I were married, I'd want to be with my husband."

"You'll marry again."

"I doubt it," she answered, wishing she didn't sound so wistful.

"Give it time," Roger signed. "You're only twenty-eight. But you'll never meet anyone if you turn up your nose at men."

"I don't turn up my nose at men."

"You could've fooled me."

Molly laughed, more out of self-defense than amusement. She appreciated her friend's concern. He didn't think she met enough men, or tried to, but meeting them wasn't the problem. She'd never told Roger the reason her ex-husband had left her, or even that he'd been the one doing the leaving. It seemed pointless to get into that now, though, and they needed to talk about something else. "Roger?"

He handed her more books and raised his eyebrows in question.

"Do you think you could put off making a decision about the sale?" she asked as she packed the books. "For another eight weeks?"

"Eight weeks?" he asked, looking at her incredulously.

Molly winced. He made it sound like years, and she felt selfish. If he agreed to her plan, he would have to come back from St. Louis to negotiate the sale, and it wasn't as if she hadn't been working months already to get the necessary funds.

"You know I wouldn't ask if it weren't important. I talked to a loan officer at another bank today after lunch." She pulled a business card from her wallet and handed it to Roger. "I know the other bank and the government agency turned me down, but this man thought my prospects were good for a loan."

Molly didn't mention not getting the artist's commission offered by Meta-Hellenic Shipping. That had been a shot in the dark, the last gasp of a desperate woman.

Roger studied the banker's business card. Molly twisted the loose ends of her single braid around her fingers, feeling the way she had when she'd tried to get one of the best portrait brokers in New York to take her on. Getting the school was much more important by far.

"What if I wait and you don't get this loan after all?" Roger finally asked.

"I have to get it. My life will be a big fat zero without the school . . . without the kids"

"That's not true," Roger said and shook his head. "You have a good reputation as a portrait artist. You might like the idea of owning the school, but I don't think you really want all the headaches that go along with running it."

"You run a school, teach kids, have control over what you do with your time and life." Molly held out her arms and smiled. "Why not me?"

Roger gestured to the telephone.

Molly knew what he meant. Talking wasn't a problem, as she'd learned language before developing the hearing loss and could hear her own voice when she wore her hearing aid. Understanding other people's voices *was* a problem. If she ran the school, she would use the telephone relay service, but she would also need to have normal phone access to be successful.

"Your secretary said she'd stay on with me to handle calls. I've been here three years, and it's getting so I need to come and be with the children. They get so excited. Being around them takes me out of myself."

She'd had a hearing impairment from the age of six, but she'd been adventurous and optimistic both as a child and as a teenager. Because her portrait work necessitated long hours alone, she'd let her life revolve in smaller and smaller circles until she was practically afraid to meet new people. Teaching at Newpark had forced her to interact with the world. As a consequence, she'd grown more confident.

Roger put an arm around her shoulders, then backed away to sign. "I'd give you more time if I could, but I've got to take this offer if we can finalize the details. Newpark isn't the only site the college guys are looking at."

"I didn't realize you had to make a decision with them so soon." Molly sank onto a corner of the desk and suppressed a sigh. It would be emotional blackmail to let Roger see how much she felt this loss, and she utterly refused to use that ploy on anyone. "When do you meet these people?"

"They said they'd send someone in the next day or two. He could even come today for all I know."

The lump came back to her throat. No! She would not cry.

Roger gestured to the almost full packing box and was about to say something—probably that they needed more boxes—when the telephone rang.

"I saw the packing supplies in the foyer. I'll make some boxes while you're on the line," she said. She could use the opportunity to get her emotions under control, too.

Roger nodded, and Molly left the office. She lectured herself silently about the uselessness of self-pity, then started taping a box together. She'd almost finished when, from behind her, the foyer was flooded with light.

Molly glanced over her shoulder. A man stood silhouetted in the school entrance. She set the box down to greet him. He closed the door, eliminating the backlight, and now she could see something besides his general shape.

She automatically cataloged her impressions: navy jacket, yellow shirt, a strong, tanned neck, brown hair burnished with touches of burnt sienna, intent brown eyes, brown eyes that captured her gaze and held it.

The dust motes dancing in the sunlight that came through the transom seemed to stop and so did the air coming into her lungs. She felt weightless and strangely, but pleasantly, disoriented.

He broke the spell when he lifted a hand to straighten his yellow-and-navy-striped tie, which had snagged on a button. Molly followed the movement, catching the flash of gold from his watch. She couldn't help taking in his trim waist and broad shoulders. Along with his tanned face and hands, they suggested an athletic life-style.

"Hello," she said. She took a step closer to him, then decided she didn't want him to introduce himself. People's names were hard for her to understand even when the other person spoke clearly. Besides, he'd no doubt come to meet Roger. With the summer session over, she had no official reason to be at the school.

Molly indicated Roger's office. "You'll find Roger McCauley in there."

The newcomer glanced at the office door, then back at her. She gave him an encouraging smile, wondering if he was the buyer Roger expected. With his impeccable clothing and restrained gestures, he certainly looked like an administrator of some sort.

The stranger didn't return her smile, and she felt let down. How could she be disappointed when she didn't even know him? She gestured toward the office again. "He was on the

phone a minute ago, but he might be off now. Why don't
you knock?''

Molly watched the stranger's mouth for his response. He
had a long, rather thin mouth with only a slight indenta-
tion in the upper lip. It somehow didn't seem to fit the rest
of his face with its dark ridge of brown brows and straight
nose. He said something she didn't understand.

"It's really all right for you to knock even if Roger's not
expecting you. I'd do it for you, but I won't hear through
the door if he answers.''

Suddenly the office door opened. Roger came out and
extended a hand to the stranger. Molly watched them a second, then reluctantly pulled her gaze away. She couldn't remember ever seeing a man as dramatically handsome as
their visitor, but she still didn't need to stare. "I'll go start
packing in one of the classrooms—"

Roger caught her eye. "Wants to meet you," he signed.

"Wants to meet...me?" Molly looked up at the well-
dressed man beside her. Something about this tall, dark-
haired, dark-eyed man made her edgy, though she couldn't
figure out why.

The visitor smiled, and the curve of his lips seemed to go
on forever, almost meeting the dimple creasing one cheek.

Molly felt a quickening inside her. The dimple gave his
face an entirely different aspect, that of a man who enjoyed life. It would probably be the feature she'd play up in
a portrait, along with those mesmerizing eyes. She stuck her
hands in the pockets of her jeans, wishing she hadn't
changed out of the slacks and silk shirt she'd worn when
she'd met with the bankers.

"Go on," Roger signed, gesturing toward his office and
giving her a wink. Her heart sank. He must have seen her
staring. As soon as this guy left, Roger would be on her case
again about meeting men.

"Okay, thanks," she said and turned her attention to the
visitor, undeniably curious about him. "We can talk in
here.''

She stepped toward Roger's office, accidentally brushing the man's sleeve. Little sparks of awareness skittered along her nerves. Interesting, thought Molly. Dark men weren't usually her type.

"You must have introduced yourself to Roger, but I'm afraid I didn't get your name. I wear a hearing aid and—"

His head tilted slightly, his gaze traveling quickly over her as if he was looking for evidence of it. She lifted her left hand to her aid, wondering how he'd missed it. He'd been standing more or less on her right, though. The right ear was hopeless. It had a complete loss of hearing so an aid couldn't help it.

"I need to see your mouth when you speak to me," she continued explaining as she watched his wide mouth. "And perhaps you could enunciate?"

"Yes," he answered. "I can do that."

"Good." She smiled. "I'm Molly Light," she said, sticking out her hand.

When he grasped it, the warmth and feel of his skin startled her. It was as if she'd never shaken hands with a person before. That was silly, of course. Molly looked up, her gaze colliding with the man's warm, brown-eyed one.

Suddenly she realized they were still holding on to each other. "Look, I—"

He released her, and she quickly stuffed both hands into the pockets of her jeans. "I'm afraid it's a mess in here right now." She scanned the jumble of books and odds and ends heaped on every surface. "I'll clear a chair if you want to sit."

He shook his head.

A little surge of relief rushed through her. Apparently he didn't expect this conversation to take long. "What can I do for you?" she asked.

He pulled an envelope from his pocket and showed her the address on the front. Her pulse quickened. He held the envelope she'd left two days before at the Louis Stadler Hotel for Stefanos Metadorakis.

Molly regarded her visitor. She'd been led to believe Stefanos Metadorakis was an older man. This guy couldn't be past thirty-five, and she didn't see any gray strands in his rigorously disciplined reddish brown waves. "You're Mr. Metadorakis?"

He nodded, then raised an eyebrow as if to cue her to continue.

She hadn't wanted to meet him dressed like this, she thought, standing straighter. She looked up at him, realizing what she really wanted was a pair of heels. The man stood only about six inches taller than her own five-six, but it suddenly felt more like two feet.

Stefanos Metadorakis slipped her note into his jacket pocket. Molly watched his tanned and ringless fingers close the flap and smooth it down, almost missing his next words because of her distraction.

"Did I wait long? Is that what you asked?"

He nodded. "At the hotel."

"Oh, a while." Actually she'd sat in a chair in the lobby long enough to incite all sorts of solicitous attention from the bell captain and registration clerk. They had probably thought she was a detective the way she'd scrutinized everyone who came into the lobby.

"It was nice of you to come looking for me. I'm flattered." She was surprised, too. In the note she'd left him she'd asked only for a few minutes of conversation. She'd certainly never expected him to come looking for her.

He smiled, and the burnt sienna chips in his brown eyes glowed like beads of dark amber. She swallowed against the sudden tightness in her throat. What was wrong with her? She'd analyzed plenty of people's faces without experiencing this physical uneasiness.

"I like—" he said slowly and looked at her expectantly.

Molly shook her head. "I didn't understand that last thing you said. Could you repeat it, please?"

Stefanos Metadorakis retrieved a small leather-bound notebook from his inside jacket pocket, wrote something in it, then turned it so she could see.

She leaned closer, catching a faint citrus smell. It reminded her of sunny afternoons in the Mediterranean and suited his being Greek, or at least part Greek. When her gallery had mentioned selling to him, she'd found out he worked for the State Department. He probably had to be a U.S. citizen for that job.

"Shall I write this down?" he wrote.

Molly glanced up at him. "Do whatever is easiest for you."

"Okay," he wrote and smiled. "According to your note, you want to talk about the commission my family is awarding. I think your art would be perfect for the new company offices."

"I'd hoped you would say that. I thank you for purchasing my paintings, and I appreciate your driving out to talk with me today, but I'm afraid it's too late. I saw in the paper this morning that Meta-Hellenic is making the award privately. I haven't heard anything, so I assume I didn't get it."

He shook his head, then wrote in his notebook, "As I understand it, the company hasn't awarded it yet. They just want more time to think about it."

"Really?" She moved a box, perched on a chair and looked around the room. It would be so good to call this "her" office. She still had a chance to do that if she could convince this man to champion her cause.

Stefanos sat in the companion chair, as much at ease as if he were in his own living room. His relaxed posture made him seem less threatening.

Threatening? The thought brought her up short. Roger must be right. She really was out of practice with men, but she needed to concentrate on the school and the art award right now. "When will Meta-Hellenic make a decision?"

"I'm not sure, but I think it will be soon. I can't promise anything until I talk with my cousins at the company, of course, but perhaps they will listen to me." He lifted his notebook again and wrote, "Why don't we talk about this over dinner?"

"We can talk about it now, can't we?"

"I was planning to eat before driving back. I would enjoy your company, and we could continue our conversation. What do you say?"

She hesitated.

"You have another commitment?" he wrote.

"No. It's just that..." Molly glanced around the office as if she could find the words to express what she felt. Trouble was, she didn't know exactly why she was stalling.

"I'm not married and my family is busy," Stefanos Metadorakis said. He smiled, his dimple teasing her. "Believe me, I'd much rather have a charming companion to share dinner with than eat alone."

A little curl of anticipation tightened in her stomach.

He raised one brown eyebrow. "Then your answer is yes?"

The scrape of metal on metal echoed in the long, empty hallway as Molly Light jiggled her key into the lock of her apartment door. She was nervous, Stefanos thought, watching the way her one thick blond braid fell over her shoulder, catching in the loose collar of her yellow T-shirt.

"The apartment's kind of a mess," she said and flipped the braid back over her shoulder.

Her subtle floral scent drifted over to him. She liked perfume, and he bet she liked only expensive perfume. While her apartment house seemed pretty mediocre, he suspected she was just biding her time until she could move into more luxurious digs. He'd read the dossier Leo had given him— he knew the type. It would be easy to hate her, but he had to be sure she didn't see anything but casual interest.

He waited for her to open the door, bracing a hand on the door frame in a relaxed pose.

Molly Light glanced at him. "You sure you wouldn't rather wait in the lobby?"

Why was she stalling?

She'd asked about his Jaguar when they'd walked out of the school to their cars, and he'd admitted he had been behind her on the street. He'd said he hadn't seen the school sign because a blue minivan—hers—had turned in front of it. She'd seemed to accept the implication that he'd been looking for the school, but maybe she doubted his explanation now that she'd had time to think about it.

Stefanos hoped not. He couldn't tell her he'd seen her leave her apartment building and had followed her. After all, he wasn't supposed to know what she looked like or what kind of car she drove.

She continued to look up at him, and Stefanos realized he hadn't answered her earlier question about waiting in the lobby. "No, I don't mind," he said.

Molly's mouth tilted up on one side, then suddenly the smile framed both sides of her oval-shaped face and brought a sparkle to her blue eyes.

He returned her smile. Apparently she didn't suspect his real reasons for seeking her out, but he'd have to remember how observant she could be. Thick brownish blond eyelashes swept down to hide her eyes. She sure knew how to use those blue eyes to good effect. He'd give her credit for that.

"Don't say I didn't warn you." She opened the door.

He followed her inside and looked over her shoulder at the room. The setting sun shone through several bare picture windows. Stefanos squinted against the glare and picked out the sofa and wing chair grouped around a black lacquered coffee table. A pair of pink terry-cloth slippers lay in the center of the thick beige carpet.

Molly strode into the room, scooped up the slippers and lifted a filmy white garment from the innards of the wing chair. Stefanos watched her ball the gown in her hands, unable to suppress a surge of masculine interest.

"Make yourself comfortable," she said. "I won't take long."

"No hurry." He watched her walk across the room. She was pretty in an unsophisticated way and definitely had a nice walk, especially in those jeans. He could see what a man would like about that walk, what he liked about it. "Take your time," he said.

She turned at a doorway—to the bedroom, he presumed. "Did you say something?"

He repeated his remark. A furrow puckered her forehead briefly, then she smiled and disappeared. He stared at the place she'd been standing before he closed his eyes and rubbed the bridge of his nose. He needed to keep his focus here, he reminded himself, and went back over what Leo had told him about Molly and her involvement in espionage.

A U.S. defense contractor was developing a new plane for the navy. Somehow the specifications were winding up in the hands of Topolac, a military dictator. This dictator and his army chiefs had already received three transmittals of data. According to Leo's contact, there would be at least one final handoff—probably before the NATO conference meeting in Athens next week. That's where Molly Light came in.

The chief suspect was a man named Julian Silver, an engineer for the defense contractor, and he was a friend of hers. Leo thought she wanted Meta-Hellenic's commission award as a cover for her trip to Greece to deliver the last installation to Topolac. The traitor was using microfilm to pass on the engineering information. Stefanos wondered if Molly had the last roll somewhere in her apartment now.

He surveyed the elegant though well-used couch and armchairs. He opened the back of the brass ship's clock and a drawer in the table beside the door, but found no microfilm. The clock, some oriental nesting tables, and a crystal paperweight suggested a craving for quality that made sense considering Molly's background.

After living in a number of foster homes as a teenager, she'd married an up-and-coming young attorney. They'd divorced in short order. She'd continued her ambitious climb, going on to art school and finessing her way into the stable of a prominent portrait broker. She'd done very well for herself, but she wouldn't get what she wanted in this case. Not if Stefanos could help it.

Beyond the living-room furniture stood several large worktables, one with a slanted surface, and an easel, which held a finished portrait in oils. The top of a set of white storage drawers sported several metal cans and rags and a scatter of brushes and pencils. Pulling open a few drawers, he saw they were filled with more art supplies.

Stefanos propped his hands on his belt. Her apartment wasn't what he'd expected. Molly Light wasn't what he'd expected.

For one thing, Leo had failed to mention her hearing problem. He himself had never had anything to do with someone hearing impaired. At first, his inexperience had made him apprehensive as to whether they'd be able to understand each other. He was still anxious about her misunderstanding him.

He slipped a hand into his pocket and wrapped his fingers around a lighter, letting the smooth metal soothe and cool his nerves. Molly had been very resilient, though. He couldn't help admiring her no-nonsense attitude about her loss. His grip on the lighter tightened. He didn't want to admire anything about her.

Stefanos crossed the living room and switched on the light in the dimly lit kitchen. A glass sun catcher hanging in the window caught his eye, its blue almost the color of Molly's eyes. His gaze dropped to the Early American table over which it hung, taking in the dirty dishes still there. Only one place setting, he noted, and moved to the adjacent counter, where a row of miniature African violets bloomed under a grow lamp. Stefanos rubbed a fingertip across one furry petal.

The domesticity and hominess of Molly Light's apartment closed around him like a warm blanket. He allowed himself to absorb the comfort of it, telling himself he did so only because of its novelty. After a moment, he shrugged off the feeling and returned to the living room.

The portrait on the easel drew his attention again, and he walked over to Molly's studio area. The painting depicted an older woman in a red dress, with her hands clasped in her lap. Molly had portrayed the woman's face so vividly, Stefanos had the feeling he would recognize this woman as soon as he saw her enter the room.

It must be one she'd done on commission, he thought, pulling his gaze away and checking his watch. Something about this place bothered him. Her coconspirator, Julian Silver, might be there, but he'd heard no voices or unusual sounds from the bedroom. Stefanos decided he'd better find a way to get a look inside that room just to make sure.

His muscles remained tense, as if a threat hovered close by. Becoming restless, he glanced around. The canvas bag she'd carried into the apartment rested on a nearby table, and a wire-bound sketchbook spilled out of it onto the tabletop. Stefanos opened the book and had just started to peruse its drawings when his sixth sense told him he wasn't alone.

Molly Light stood in the bedroom doorway watching him. He noted her bare feet curling into the carpet, then lifted his gaze to take in the green sleeveless jumpsuit with the rhinestone belt. It showed her small waist to advantage, and made him think of mermaids or sirens. She lured him like one, too, he thought, his blood pounding a little harder.

"Hi," he said, pleased he sounded perfectly in control.

She anchored a loose tendril into the twist atop her head, and Stefanos found himself wishing she'd left her hair down. It would look lovely flowing around her shoulders.

She took several steps into the room. "I didn't hear you—I mean—of course, I didn't hear you, but I was worried—" She stopped, noticeably flustered. "Maybe you'd like a cup of coffee or something while you wait?"

He felt her nervousness, heard it and saw it. If he was going to get any information out of her that he and Leo could use, he obviously had to get her to relax with him. Stefanos strolled over to her, carrying the sketchbook. Her delicate scent played like a fragrant melody over his senses, but he ignored it. "Is there a problem?" he asked aloud.

"No. I just thought you might want something."

"No, nothing." *Except to know what's really bothering you,* he added silently. He held up the sketchbook.

She frowned, then shrugged. "I keep in practice. Faces fascinate me."

He glanced again at the pencil portrait of a small boy. She'd really caught the child's smile. It reminded him of Nikos's grin. Revenge for Nikos was one of the reasons he was trying to gain this woman's trust. He placed the sketchbook on a table, and Molly followed his movements like a hawk. He'd have to be careful not to make a misstep. "You're very talented," he said.

"You flatter me."

"If I'd wanted to flatter you I would have told you I'd come to New Jersey because the hotel clerk had mentioned how pretty you are. I am surprised you want to do landscapes."

She seemed to be hanging on every word. He wondered if he should go back to using his notebook, but she'd been understanding him ever since they'd come into her apartment. She tilted her head and took another step toward him.

"I am surprised—" he started to repeat.

"What did you say?" she asked.

He laughed. They'd both spoken at the same instant. "Sorry." She glanced away as if he'd insulted her. He touched her arm to get her attention. Her soft skin beneath his fingers sent that unwelcome masculine reaction spiraling through his body again.

Molly turned toward him. "I didn't realize you were going to speak."

Stefanos pulled out his notebook. "I didn't realize you were going to speak, either. Sorry I laughed. I suppose I was a little embarrassed," he wrote.

Was he really saying this? It was working, he realized, noticing the way the corners of Molly's mouth inched upward.

"I'm surprised you want to do landscapes," he wrote.

Molly raised her blond brows. "You mean for the commission? They're a nice change."

"But don't you do portraits?" he pressed.

"Most of the time. It's harder to make a living as a landscape painter, though I enjoy that more, actually."

Stefanos nodded. "Would you be planning to go to Greece if you got the commission?"

She expelled a breath. When she spoke, she gazed at his chest, unable, he supposed, to lie to his face. "I don't see how I could do a very good job of the landscapes otherwise. The two paintings you bought I did from old slides, but I haven't many, and none of boats and ships. I presume Meta-Hellenic Shipping will want nautical subjects?"

"I would think so. What did you have in mind for this trip?"

She hesitated, sliding the glittering belt with its rhinestone buckle from side to side and drawing his gaze to that part of her anatomy. Probably intentionally, he warned himself. In a low-key way Molly Light flirted quite well, making a man feel he was discovering her assets. He slipped his hand into his pocket, wrapped his fingers around the cold metal of the cigarette lighter again and reminded himself his job didn't involve an appreciation of her feminine attributes.

"It wouldn't be a long trip." Molly made a vague gesture and caught his gaze, but only briefly. "Say a week or two.

I'd make some sketches and take some photographs, then do the final paintings here. If I get the commission, I'll need a portion of the award in advance to cover expenses.''

The money she would make from selling defense secrets wasn't going to be enough, huh? Bitterness churned in Stefanos's stomach. He doubted she intended to do any painting at all. She'd probably be basking in Switzerland, instead. Hadn't Julian Silver, the man involved with her in this illegal scheme, recently bought property there?

''I don't know anything about artistic commissions,'' he wrote. He walked over so he was standing next to her. ''Is it customary to give an advance?''

''With the award programs I know of, the whole amount is presented when the award is announced,'' Molly answered.

''My family has never commissioned art before. They do not know the rules of the game.''

She repeated his last sentence in a voice that sounded worried. ''It's the usual procedure.''

''I see. Thank you for explaining.'' He braced a hand on the doorjamb and glanced into her bedroom. From his position he could see only a nightstand beside the bed, and had absolutely no way to determine if she was hiding anything—or anyone.

He sensed her beside him and reluctantly averted his gaze. She stood squarely in the doorway watching him, her arms crossed. ''Did you want to make reservations at the restaurant before we leave?'' she asked. ''They may be crowded on Friday evenings.''

''That would be a good idea.'' He took a step toward her again and smiled, confident his agreement would make her feel less defensive. ''Is the phone in the bedroom?''

''Yes, but you'll probably want to use the one in the lobby.''

What he really wanted was to get a good look around her bedroom. ''It'll be easier from up here and—'' Stefanos started to brush past her but found her hand on his chest, her fingers splayed against his shirt.

She stared at him.

Stefanos told himself to step back. He couldn't move a muscle, not even when he saw the bewilderment in her blue eyes change to wariness.

"If you don't want to call from the lobby," she said softly, dropping her hand, "then maybe we'd better forget about dinner altogether."

A sigh rolled through him. What was it about this woman? He ought to be able to control her easily, and he'd always been able to control his reactions—except when he hadn't planned them ahead of time. That was the trouble with Molly Light. He hadn't planned far enough ahead.

He stepped back. "I'll use the lobby phone. Meet me there when you're ready."

Chapter 2

Molly watched the apartment door close behind Stefanos and felt her shoulders relax. As she turned back to hunt for a pair of shoes in the closet, she chastised herself for refusing to let him use her phone. If she wanted his help in getting the commission, she would have to be friendlier.

Being friendly wasn't usually a problem. Was it just because she hadn't wanted to draw any more attention than necessary to her hearing disability?

She glanced at the telecommunications device where it sat on her dresser. With its keyboard, adding-machine roll, and two rubber cups, her TDD didn't look much like a phone. She would have had to explain how to use it and how calls were made through the relay service.

Explaining would not have been the problem. Standing next to him to do the explaining would have. Stefanos Metadorakis had a way of making her feel he stood too close even when he looked at her across the room. She did have to be within a few feet of a person in order to have a chance at understanding him. Her good friend, Julian, usually stood close to her when they talked, though, and she didn't feel the least bit threatened. Of course, she'd known Julian a long time.

Stefanos wasn't the sole cause of her discomfort. She didn't want to think about returning to Greece. The trip was sure to bring back memories she'd rather not face. Well, she would have to confront that prospect if she got the art commission. Hadn't she told herself the same thing when Julian had first urged her to apply for it?

Maybe Roger was right. Maybe she was out of practice with men. She and Warren had divorced eight years ago, and she really shouldn't keep thinking every man used the same tactics. Stefanos Metadorakis didn't, anyway. If he had, he would have given her some highfalutin reason for coming out to see her. He'd merely told her the truth.

He liked her paintings. He didn't like dining alone. Just wanted some company.

She could sympathize with that, she thought, fastening on a pair of earrings. Giving herself a once-over in the full-length mirror, she noticed that the buckle of her belt sat off center. She slid it back into place and rubbed her bare arms.

Stefanos, with his Greek blood, wore a tan as if it was second nature. Next to him she would look as washed out as an old rag. Quickly she put on blusher and poked around on the dressing-table top for her lipstick, trying to remember the last time she'd worn any.

She pulled the cover off the tube but paused to gaze at the snapshot stuck in her mirror. It pictured one of her children's classes at Newpark School. Her students stood in the yard grinning proudly as they held up their masterpieces. As always, the photograph made her smile.

The children. The school. They were the reasons she was going out to dinner with Stefanos Metadorakis. She wasn't looking to impress him with her beauty—if that was even possible—but with her professional abilities.

Molly recapped the lipstick without applying any, found her black clutch bag, slipped her wallet and hearing-aid batteries into it and left the apartment.

Through the glass-paneled security door separating the lobby from the first-floor hallway, she saw Stefanos standing by the pay phones, the receiver at his ear. He stood with his weight on one leg and a hand in his pants pocket. It was a common male posture, but one she'd always thought attractive because it spoke of confidence and self-assurance.

She could be confident, too, couldn't she?

The restaurant where they ate dinner turned out to be a confection of shimmering light, from its chandeliers and the shiny strips of satin in the beige-patterned wallpaper to the glow of the table candles reflected from lustrous, silver-plated flatware.

Stefanos Metadorakis had turned out to be a charming conversationalist, surprising her yet again. She'd thought he'd been flattering her earlier when he'd talked about wanting her company, but he actually seemed to enjoy it. He'd been very interested in her art, and it was obvious he'd read her application for the award. She'd had no trouble stressing her professional qualifications for the commission.

Setting her dessert plate aside, she relaxed, confident he had accepted her hearing loss as just another personality trait, not a handicap. In fact, they'd hardly mentioned it after she'd asked him to talk to her instead of write.

"That was a lovely dinner," she said now. "You should have had some of the chocolate mousse."

His wide, sensual mouth moved in speech.

Molly took a sip of coffee, thinking about what he could have said. She'd been reading him pretty well until now. "Would you repeat—" she turned up the volume on her aid "—would you repeat what you—" She didn't finish, still unable to hear her own voice. "Wait a minute. I've got to replace my hearing-aid battery. Will it bother you if I do that here at the table?''

He shook his head.

Molly swallowed her chagrin and unzipped her purse. Her battery would have to die on her just when she needed to appear as "normal" as possible. She should have changed the battery before leaving the apartment, she supposed, but she hardly thought about the aid unless it stopped working.

She quickly found her replacement batteries, took one out of the package and slipped her aid off her ear. A ripple of awareness flowed over her. She glanced up and connected with Stefanos's dark gaze. "I'll be back on the air shortly," she joked. "One moment please."

He smiled the way she intended him to, thank goodness. Molly closed the battery chamber and looped the aid back over her ear. She tucked her purse into her lap and leaned forward. "Now, after that brief station break, we can get back to what you said."

Interesting, she thought. This was the sort of thing she usually said to put people at ease, but she hadn't used humor with Stefanos before. Probably because she hadn't been relaxed enough, she thought. She didn't really feel relaxed now, but he'd been watching her intently, so she'd had to say something.

"Will your hearing loss be a problem on a trip to a foreign country?"

She waved a hand. "I've managed before." Molly knew she ought to say something to derail this line of questioning, but she couldn't think of a thing that wouldn't sound defensive.

He leaned toward her. "It must cause some difficulty for you, I am sure."

"I'm used to it," she answered.

"Have you always worn a hearing aid?"

Molly regarded the candle on the table as she thought about his question. "Not until ten years ago," she said, reaching out to feel the warmth of the glass chimney. "I probably should have worn one as a child, but no one ever bothered to find out exactly what I needed."

"You only wear one?" he asked, hooking his fingers through the handle of his coffee cup.

"Yes. They haven't invented an aid that will help the other one. It's completely gone."

"I'm sorry." Sympathy in his brown eyes underscored his words.

She gave a little laugh. "It's not your fault."

A burst of noise from the patrons at a nearby table made her turn her head. Her gaze still lingered on them when Stefanos brushed his fingers lightly across the back of her hand. Heat flowed from his touch, curling through her at an alarming rate. "What is it?" she asked.

He frowned, and Molly grimaced. Had she been sharp with him? He'd touched her quite a lot, and she hadn't minded before. She did the same thing herself when she wanted to get a person's attention or encourage him to look at her when he spoke. "Did you want to say something?" she asked and raised her eyebrows.

"You heard that laughter?"

She smiled at the typical question. "Yes. I hear sounds with my hearing aid because I have some residual hearing."

"Then you hear me? You're not just lip-reading?"

"Under most circumstances I both hear and speech-read and put them together. In a really quiet place, I can usually hear most everything someone says."

"But you can't understand me?" He looked at her with what she thought must be disbelief. She pressed her lips together. Her explanation would no doubt feed his doubts about her coping abilities. He leaned forward. "Did you understand me?"

"Yes. I was thinking about how to explain this to you. Sometimes I can't understand you, you're right. I still hear you, or some of what you say. Because I don't know what I'm missing, though, what you say doesn't always make sense to me." A furrow plowed between his straight brows.

"It's one of those situations where you have to be there to believe it," she said and hoped the topic was now closed.

"You don't get everything I say even lip-reading, do you?"

"That's true," she replied, sighing inside. She might as well get all his questions answered now, she told herself. "I don't understand everything you say. Speechreading is not a hundred percent thing. I wish it were."

"And your friend Roger?"

"Roger?" What subject were they on now? "The director of Newpark School?"

"He was making hand movements to talk with you, wasn't he?" Stefanos wiggled his fingers in imitation.

"Yes. American Sign Language, otherwise known as Ameslan. I have trouble understanding Roger's voice. It's deeper than yours, and no matter how slowly he speaks, I can't seem to understand him. Some people—like you—have more of an instinctive knack for phrasing than others."

Stefanos nodded, but he studied her silently while they finished their coffee. Molly got the impression she'd taken some sort of oral test. Later, as they drove along the parkway, the notion lingered. She wondered what conclusions he'd reached about her. She looked at him, visually tracing his long, straight nose and determined chin. "I enjoyed myself tonight. Thank you for the dinner."

He reached across and clasped one of her hands. Molly looked down at their joined hands in her lap. The rough texture of his palm seemed to assert his maleness, as did the seductive weight of his hand against her most vulnerable place. She closed her eyes and leaned back, relishing the fact that he found her attractive. She hadn't felt this way since— Molly stiffened.

The memory of another first date and another man came back to her, and Molly slipped her hand free. She couldn't let herself get carried away here.

Stefanos glanced over at her, probably wondering if he'd misjudged her. Molly swallowed uncomfortably. She had allowed his hand to stay in her lap a few moments, hadn't she? She might have touched him an awful lot, too. Because of that, he might already have gotten the impression she'd be willing to sell her favors for his help. No doubt when she corrected him he'd count her resistance as another strike against her.

The silence in the car pressed around her like a heavy cloak. Maybe she'd already struck out with him. Well, it couldn't be helped. She adjusted her air-conditioning vent and waited anxiously for them to reach her building.

Eventually the green turn-signal light blinked on the dash. They pulled off the street and into a slot near the door to her building. With relief, Molly unfastened her seat belt. "I appreciate your time and interest tonight. Anything you can do to help me would be appreciated. If you can't do anything, I'll understand. I do hope you enjoy the paintings you bought for yourself."

He held up his hand. Molly turned toward him, little impulses of distress skittering along her nerves. He pulled out his cigarette case. She could almost see him trying to decide how to phrase his next words. Would he refuse to help her? She clasped her hands tightly in her lap and wished she'd told him how much the school meant to her. No, that would have been an emotional plea. His cool manner and something else she couldn't name told her he might not recognize the importance of emotions.

"You don't mind if I smoke, do you?" he asked after he'd offered her one.

"No." She watched his long, elegant fingers flip back the lid of the lighter, thinking how out of place smoking seemed for him. His tanned skin and vigorous walk suggested a sports-oriented life-style she wouldn't have associated with smoking.

He turned on the dome light and said with a sardonic twist to his mouth, "It is a nasty habit."

"Why do you smoke, then?"

He shrugged.

She waited for him to say something. When he didn't, she looked out the windshield at the couple entering the lobby. The man draped his arm around the woman's shoulders, and she smiled up at him, obviously very much in love.

Stefanos shifted. Molly looked over at him again, watching him roll the wheel of his lighter and bring the flame to sudden life. The warm light softened his features. She remembered the dimple in his cheek and the vibrancy of his smile. Stefanos Metadorakis would make being in love intoxicating, as intoxicating as it was for the woman she'd just seen.

Molly squared her shoulders. She didn't need to be thinking those kinds of thoughts. "Listen," she said, "it's getting late. Why don't I get in touch with you tomorrow? At your hotel?"

He shook his head and stubbed his cigarette out in the ashtray.

"Well, then…" She stared at the dashboard. What more could she say?

He looped a hand over the headrest of her seat, brushing her bare shoulder as gently as a butterfly. She absorbed the wondrous shiver moving through her. She ought to be ignoring it, she told herself.

"I don't know how much longer I will be at the hotel," he said slowly. "I will get back to you. Here?"

"All right. I'll give you my number. May I borrow your pen?" Molly pulled out a business card, wondering if this was another variation of "Don't call me, I'll call you." She took his pen, careful to avoid touching him. "I'll also give you the number of the relay service for the deaf. Are you familiar with how to use that?" When he shook his head, Molly briefly explained how the relay worked, then handed him both card and pen.

Stefanos put them in the console tray and turned off the inside light. In the semidarkness he felt closer. The hand near her shoulder touched her chin softly, as softly as the last glow of a sunset fading into twilight. Her eyelids began to close. He slipped his hand around her neck, drawing even nearer.

Stop him! a little voice in her mind cried frantically. *It'll just make things worse.*

She could no more stop him than she could have tuned a musical instrument. His parted lips brushed against her mouth, warm and moist. Heat pooled in her like hot wax under the flame of a candle, and she raised her free hand to his chest, sliding it over the soft fabric of his shirt. She liked the hard feel of his muscles underneath just as she liked the way his hand pressed against her rib cage now. Molly leaned toward him. How wonderful to be held again.

His mouth found hers again. How wonderful—

The gearbox banged her shin. Molly stilled. What was she doing here? "I think we better stop," she muttered, trying to ignore the warmth and softness of his lips. He released her instantly and sat back. Molly leaned against the headrest, both pleased and disturbed by his speedy retreat. "What was that for?" she asked. Her voice sounded too breathy, so she straightened and tried again. "What was that kiss for?"

His mouth pulled up in a grin, and his dimple winked at her. Molly swallowed her embarrassment. He shrugged. "A thank-you for being such a pleasant dinner companion."

His compliment touched her, and she smiled even as she noticed how skillfully he'd handled the question. This man was nothing if not experienced with women. "I forgot to mention something," she said.

He lifted an eyebrow.

She considered the best way to phrase her next request. She didn't want to imply that she'd be too busy to handle this commission. Yet if she got it, she would purchase the school and soon be involved with planning the fall classes.

"I suppose it's premature to discuss travel plans, but—" she paused "—if I was accepted, do you think there would be any delay in receiving the commission and award? I've already got a valid passport, and I'd like to go to Greece right away.''

He dropped an arm over the steering wheel. ''Why?''

''I understand the ferries to the islands run more frequently in the summer,'' she said, using a perfectly good reason she only now thought of.

He nodded. Though he did it no differently than he had all evening, the gesture now seemed cold and formal. She wondered if he really would help her get the commission. If she didn't get the Meta-Hellenic award, she would have to admit she'd lost the school. It wouldn't do any good to get a bank loan after Roger had sold the place.

After opening her door, Stefanos accompanied her to the building entrance, opened the door for her then left without another word. Molly watched him walk back to the car, her expectations deflated by his abrupt departure. She smoothed the wisps back from her forehead and opened the lobby door.

Everything that needed to be said *had* already been said, she told herself, walking past the security guard's office. Besides, casual conversation with her was difficult for some people. Maybe Stefanos had gotten tired of the effort. If that was the case, she understood completely. She felt a headache coming on herself.

She rubbed her forehead for relief, blocking from view the man coming toward her down the first-floor hall. He was almost on top of her before she looked at him. The navy pants, navy windbreaker with clipped-on ID tag, and black-rimmed glasses told her he was an ordinary mechanic or repairman.

She averted her gaze, not wanting to be caught staring, then looked at him again when what she'd seen registered in her mind. A little circular scar marked the man's cheek near his glasses, a scar small enough that most people wouldn't have noticed. She did, and she suddenly found herself gasping for air. There didn't seem to be any in the hallway.

The man who'd followed her in New York had had a scar exactly like that. Was this the same guy? She took a closer look.

The stranger stared back at her, his watery blue eyes holding her transfixed. In New York he hadn't worn glasses or a uniform, but she remembered those eyes. Her pulse pounded. He was like a cat hypnotizing its prey before pouncing. Her mind froze.

She managed to keep walking and reached the elevator without being accosted. Once the doors slid shut, she sank back against the wall, her heart hammering. She was safe now. Or was she? He might really be a tradesman, but the coincidence chilled her. He could easily have followed her out to New Jersey and waited for her to come home. Her pulse tripped into double time, and she clutched her hands together to keep them from shaking. When the elevator opened on her floor, Molly hurried down the hall.

She had her key ready when she reached her apartment, but the door swung open as soon as she touched it. Molly paused. Had she been in such a hurry to join Stefanos in the lobby earlier that she hadn't closed it properly?

She couldn't remember, but she couldn't stand out in the hallway thinking about it, either. Two steps into her apartment, she stopped and gaped at what she saw. Her living room lay in shambles.

A hand closed around her arm. She felt herself being forced away from the door. "Wha—" Molly twisted against the intruder's grip.

She had only the vaguest impression of a hard face before the man wrenched her back against his chest. An overpowering smell made her senses swim. She fought desperately for air. Suddenly, blackness blotted out everything.

Molly opened her eyes. Everything appeared blurry. She rubbed her eyelids and tried again. This time she could focus. She pushed herself to a sitting position and stared at the contents of her purse, scattered around her on the beige carpet.

Something slipped off her lap, and she looked down to see one of the pink washcloths from the bathroom. Why had she been holding her washcloth, for Pete's sake? An irritating smell drifted up to her. She tensed, remembering what had happened, and darted a glance at the front door. It was closed. Molly let out a breath she hadn't realized she'd been holding, rubbed a hand across her face and looked at the crumpled washcloth on the floor again. Her assailant must have used that to knock her out.

She rose unsteadily to her feet. A sick feeling swept through her, sending her staggering to the bathroom. She managed to relieve the worst of her nausea, then splashed water on her face and stumbled back into the disheveled living room. She felt sick all over again, but this time it was from shock.

Cushions lay scattered about; drawers gaped open. Mrs. Hart's portrait remained the only untouched item. She should be thankful for little things, she supposed, except that the portrait wasn't a little thing and it was due to be delivered next week.

In the kitchen, a trail of broken crockery stretched across the floor, illuminated by the glow of the counter light the burglar must have turned on. The bedroom hadn't fared any better. The intruder had dumped her clothes from the closet onto her bed and the contents of the top of the dressing table onto the carpet.

Feeling an icy chill pass over her, Molly rubbed her arms. Who would have done this?

That was for the police to decide. She looked around the room, searching for her telecommunications device. It lay on its side against the floorboard. With shaking fingers she picked it up and plugged it in again. The red light for the connect tone didn't appear. She checked the socket and tried again. Still nothing.

The security guard in the building could call for her, but she didn't like the idea of going down to the lobby. Standing and shaking in the middle of her bedroom wasn't going to accomplish anything, though. Molly took a deep breath. Her burglar wouldn't be hanging around the scene of the crime, anyway. She ought to be able to get to the security guard's office all right.

No one followed her downstairs. In fact, no one seemed to be around at all. The guard was in his office, though, and she had him call the police.

When the police officer arrived, she told him about the man she'd seen in the hall. She hadn't heard him coming up behind her, since the directional microphone on her hearing aid eliminated most background sound. He probably had followed her upstairs, though, and into her apartment. She'd been so shocked at the state of the living room, she couldn't remember whether or not she'd closed the door behind her.

A search turned up no trace of her assailant. The back door of the building had been forced, though, and they decided the burglar had left that way. Back in the guard's office Molly watched the cop fill out his report and wished she hadn't been so uptight with Stefanos. She could have invited him upstairs for coffee. He would have protected her. Molly didn't know how she knew that. The fact that he worked for the State Department might be part of it, but he'd impressed her as being very capable, if a bit nosy.

While the building guard secured the broken entrance, the policeman accompanied her to her apartment and wanted to know if anything had been stolen. She didn't know. "Call us if you discover anything missing or remember anything else."

"I'll do that," she said and thanked him.

The security guard assured her the lock on her own door would be replaced as soon as possible, and she reluctantly went back inside the apartment.

She hated the thought of being in the apartment alone now, but apparently it was safe. Besides, the longer she took to clean up the chaos, the longer it would take to start putting the event behind her. Life went on, and in this case, she felt fortunate she still had a life.

She started cleaning, thankful she wouldn't have to stop and meet Julian Silver for their usual Saturday brunch. He'd said he had something else to do this weekend, and she'd gotten the impression he'd be meeting someone else.

By morning, Molly had taken care of the kitchen. She had just made a pot of coffee when there was a knock on her door. It was Julian. He looked the picture-perfect fashion plate in his Gucci loafers, plaid slacks and navy polo shirt. Before she could open her mouth, he stepped past her into the apartment.

"I've been waiting at Voltaire's over an hour."

"Oh, no." She lifted her hand to her mouth. "I thought— well, never mind what I thought. I'm sorry." She'd misunderstood Julian before but had never inconvenienced him. "I hope you at least ate some—"

Julian had been staring at the living room, and he now gave her a look of disbelief.

"Write this down, will you?" She looked around, spotted the notepad and pen she usually kept near the door and retrieved them. "I've been up all night and can't concentrate too well right now."

"You threw a wild party and didn't invite me!" he wrote.

She knew he meant it as a joke, but she didn't feel like laughing. Instead she gave him a summary of what had happened as she straightened the room.

"You didn't get a look at him then?"

"Just enough to know he was a man and not a woman. Who would do such a thing?"

Julian shook his head. "There have been some other random burglaries in the area, you know," he wrote on the pad.

"No, I didn't." She propped her hands on her hips. "How do you know about the burglaries in my area?"

"One of your security guards told me about them last week."

Molly slipped her hands into her jeans pockets. That sounded reasonable. She still wished she wasn't always the last one to find out things. Most of the time it didn't matter, and people did have to go out of their way to inform her of something someone else could overhear. If she'd known about the other burglaries, though, she definitely would have had Stefanos Metadorakis walk her to her door last night.

She shrugged mentally. That was water over the dam now. Stefanos's image lingered in her mind for a moment, and she wondered if she'd ever see him again.

Julian had been wandering around the room for the last few minutes, but he rejoined her now.

"I guess the guard let you go through just now?" she asked.

"He knows we're friends. He told me to tell you there's something for you downstairs."

"What now? She rubbed her forehead tiredly.

"A courier's waiting. Wants you to sign for something."

"You could have done it, Julian."

He tossed the notepad on the table beside them and said something.

Molly sighed inwardly. Julian could be so considerate about some things, but he could never seem to slow down enough for her. Stefanos Metadorakis had. Stefanos had been calm and patient about everything.

Her friend gestured for her to precede him out the door, then followed her. Presumably he'd said something about coming with her. "You don't have to come. It's probably only the delivery of the oil paints I ordered."

The courier didn't have the paints, though. Instead he handed her a brown envelope. The return address made her pulse quicken. She tore open the flap and pulled out a letter written on Meta-Hellenic Shipping's letterhead. Eagerly she hurried back up to her apartment, Julian following behind.

Molly sank onto the couch and read the letter through quickly, then leaned back, took a deep breath and read it again.

Julian sat beside her. "Are you all right?"

She laughed and scanned the letter in her hand. "No, I'm not."

"Bad news?" he asked, speaking slowly enough for her to understand.

"Great news." She handed him the letter. "I'm just in shock. They're offering me the commission. Can you believe it?" She felt as light-headed as if she'd drunk too much champagne. "I thought that my hearing problem had put him off and that he would hold it against me like those bankers did."

"Who are you talking about?"

"Stefanos Metadorakis," she answered.

Julian screwed his mouth to one side. "We talked to some Metadorakis guys at the reception, but I don't remember that name."

He was talking about the reception he'd gotten invitations to, the one where she'd met the shipping company execs.

"We didn't meet him at the reception. I had dinner with him last night."

Julian lifted his chin. "So that's why you weren't home."

"Did you come by?"

He paused, then shook his head. "No, but when you were talking about the burglar, you mentioned you'd been out. You don't usually go out after dark."

"I know. But he asked, and well, I did want him to do a favor for me. It wasn't going to hurt me to go out to dinner with him—at least I hadn't thought so at the time. It would have been worse if I had been home, though." She shuddered at the thought of what might have happened to her in that case.

Julian was frowning at her.

Why? He was the one who'd suggested she apply for the commission in the first place.

"What's going on?" Julian wrote. "Where does this Stefanos guy come in?"

"You remember I had to go into New York on Thursday," she explained. "Well, I stopped by the gallery to see if anyone had expressed interest in the Grecian landscapes I had there."

Molly crossed her legs and ran a palm over the coarse denim of her jeans. "Anyway, my broker told me about this Stefanos Metadorakis buying both of them. He's related to the family giving the commission. I decided to go around to his hotel and try to talk to him."

"Why is he staying at a hotel?"

"I don't know. He's with the State Department. I guess he doesn't work in New York."

Julian scribbled furiously, "Getting involved with this guy doesn't sound like a good move."

Molly stared at him. "Why not?"

"This strange man shows up and claims to be a certain someone. He wants to take you to dinner, and you don't have any proof he's who he says he is."

"He had the note I left for him."

"He could still have been anyone," Julian insisted.

"You've been watching too many TV police shows." Molly glanced at the handwritten note attached to the Meta-Hellenic letter.

"Uh-oh. This is a note from Stefanos." She handed it to Julian. "If I want the commission, I have to leave tomorrow night and fly back to Greece with him. It's one of the conditions on which they're offering this award. I know I told him I wanted to go as soon as possible, but with the portrait to finish and the school to buy—"

She rubbed her forehead. "How am I ever going to make this flight?"

* * *

Late Sunday afternoon, Molly stood in the New Jersey gallery of Sykes and Sims. She was trying not to fidget while the well-dressed woman in front of her assessed the portrait on the stand.

She and Mrs. Hart had already had a similar meeting once before, and at that one her client had wanted changes. Molly hoped the woman would be satisfied today. She'd be back from Greece in a few weeks, but Mrs. Hart wanted the portrait before then.

Molly glanced at the clock on the wall. If she didn't leave soon, she'd never even get to Greece. She'd never see Stefanos Metadorakis again, either, another part of her mind said.

Mrs. Hart smiled, and Molly relaxed. "This is going to be fine," the woman said.

"Thank you. I hope your husband will like it, too."

"I think he will."

"Good. Thank you for coming in on a Sunday. I appreciate it." Molly gave the woman her card and gestured to the manager who had met them there. "Mr. Sims will see about getting it wrapped for you." He'd also see about getting the payment, thank goodness. She hated handling that part of the business.

Mrs. Hart turned to Todd Sims, and Molly made a quick exit. Once on the road, she switched her thoughts to the upcoming trip and glanced at the dashboard clock. Stefanos Metadorakis had probably already left for the airport. He looked like the type who would arrive early, prepared for anything.

Her grip tightened on the steering wheel. She certainly wasn't prepared, at least not for seeing Stefanos Metadorakis again. What could she expect from him? Had he volunteered to escort her because of her hearing problem? He'd been pretty curious about it.

She didn't like his thinking she needed a baby-sitter, but maybe, just maybe, he was accompanying her because he felt the same attraction she did. What then? Did she want to pursue it or was that asking for heartache? She had too many questions, she told herself with a laugh, and not enough answers.

At her apartment building, she found Julian's Mercedes parked near the side exit. Good. Julian had agreed to drive her to the airport. She was surprised he had the time. As an engineer for a company designing a new plane for the navy, Julian often worked on weekends. He went into New York sometimes, too, and Molly suspected he had a girlfriend who worked at the UN.

Collecting the hangers of some dry cleaning from a few days before, she hooked them over her shoulder before hefting a portable easel she didn't want to leave in the car. She wasn't just surprised about Julian's having the time; she was glad, too. He'd picked up some last-minute necessities from the drugstore for her this afternoon, and yesterday he'd taken over cleaning her apartment so she could meet Roger and the real estate agent.

That had been a scary meeting. Since the Meta-Hellenic award check wouldn't arrive for a few days, she'd had to make the down payment for the school from her own account. The check she'd written had pretty much wiped her out. She'd have the money from Meta-Hellenic by the time she returned from Greece, she assured herself as she stepped out of the elevator. Julian was waiting for her beside her door.

"You're going to miss the flight," he said.

She smiled. "I hope not. Here—" she shifted the items in her arms so she could hold out the keys "—open the door, will you?" Julian did so, and once inside the apartment she put the easel in the corner and walked into the bedroom. "I've got to finish packing. Just a few things left," she said, hanging the cleaning in the closet.

Julian had followed her into the bedroom. Molly took the drugstore bag from him now and packed the items. When she transferred her travelers checks and passport to the small purse she planned to take, something fluttered to the floor.

Julian retrieved it. After a glance, he frowned and wrote on a notepad he carried. "I thought you were going to deposit this expense check?"

"No, I have to talk to Stefanos about that," she answered. She'd thought the company would have issued the check, but Stefanos had written it on his personal account. Asking him for a favor was one thing, taking his money was another.

She pulled a navy cotton sweater from the closet, tossed it onto the bed, then got out a denim jacket and held it up in front of her. No, the sweater would be better, she decided. She glanced down at her leather flats. They looked better than her tennis shoes, but weren't as comfortable. Which should she—

Julian came up to her and showed her what he'd written. "You're nervous, aren't you?"

"Yeah, I guess so," she admitted.

"I know you're probably thinking about the last time you were in Greece. When you were with Warren."

Actually she'd been thinking about Stefanos, but at Julian's remark, memories of that earlier trip seeped into her mind. Molly slammed the door on those thoughts. "Let's not talk about Warren."

"I'm not talking about him. I'm talking about you. Are you going to be able to handle this trip?"

"I think so." She'd have to be able to handle it. "Stefanos Metadorakis is not a Hollywood producer."

"Warren wasn't into movies when you met him."

"I know, but he already had the mind-set and was planning on going to California even then." Molly quickly focused on her packing again, squeezing the tennis shoes into the side pocket of her art supply bag. Picking up a spray bottle of cologne, she caught Julian's frown in the mirror.

"I hope you're not trying to impress that Greek guy," he wrote. "I found out about him."

"Oh?" She misted some of the cologne onto her wrists. It was one of the few luxuries she allowed herself, so she ignored Julian's comment. "What did you find out?"

Julian made a vague gesture. "He sounds like Warren."

Her jaw tightened. Warren again. She put the bottle down. "Stefanos Metadorakis hasn't used me. He's *helped* me."

"So far. If I remember correctly, Warren was nice to you in the beginning, too."

Molly wondered if maybe she hadn't deposited Stefanos's check because he subconsciously reminded her of her ex-husband.

"Metadorakis is very smooth, isn't he?"

Yes, he had been, she thought—until after the kiss. No, even when she'd noticed the confusion in his gaze, he hadn't expressed or acted upon it. "Just stop, okay? I'm already nervous about being around him again."

"Because you don't know what his motives are!"

"That's not it." Molly crossed to the bed and closed the carry-on bag full of painting supplies. "I want him to like me. I know I told you I never wanted to feel that way about a man again, but—"

"Then don't." Julian patted her arm. "If you didn't have to leave today, I could fly over with you. I'm going to come over as soon as I can, anyway."

Molly straightened and stared at him. Julian hadn't taken a trip anywhere outside the New York City area in the last two years. "You don't have to do that. You've already been a big help."

"I thought you'd be pleased," Julian wrote, his mouth pulling into a rueful smile. "You're always telling me I need a vacation."

"That's true. You do need one. You sometimes even work weekends."

"I was thinking you might want some company," he suggested. "To keep any stray memories at bay."

She'd probably be too busy coping to have much time for memories, pleasant or unpleasant, but if Julian needed an excuse in order to take a vacation, then she didn't mind giving him one. It was the least she could do for him.

"Sure." Molly slung her roomy canvas bag over her shoulder and picked up the small purse and camera. "It would be fun to have some company. We better get out of here now, I think. Stefanos has been a nice guy so far, but I'd hate to cause him to miss his flight."

Chapter 3

Stefanos waited for Molly to pocket her change. She just stood at the counter staring at the money in her palm. He had to fight the urge to check the time, glancing instead at the other travelers streaming past in the airport concourse.

They never should have stopped at this newsstand. They wouldn't have if she hadn't taken him by surprise. He needed to be prepared for surprises, naturally, but he also needed to get Molly on that flight—the flight that was being held for them.

He surveyed the passing scene again. Even if they weren't in a hurry, he wouldn't want to hang around. A man had come to the hotel yesterday asking for him. It might have been someone from the shipping company. Leo Rollins was checking to make sure, because it could just as easily have been someone with less friendly motives.

Come on, Molly. Stefanos hefted her two carry-on bags and his briefcase and took an expectant step toward the exit.

Molly glanced at him. "Wait a minute," she said and handed the ten-dollar bill back to the clerk. "I think you meant to give me a five."

Stefanos frowned at Molly. What was with this honesty gimmick? Was she playing a role? He knew criminals could be virtuous about the most unexpected things. Maybe this was just another example. Maybe he was too edgy, as well.

The clerk checked the receipt for the magazine, then looked relieved. "You're right." She gave Molly a five in exchange for the ten. "Thanks for catching that."

He shifted his weight restlessly, watching Molly stuff the bill into her wallet. She smiled. "All set."

Finally. They had no time to lose now. Stefanos rushed her to the boarding gate, past a relieved flight attendant and onto the plane. "This is us," he said slowly, stopping her from entering tourist class. "Do you want the window?"

Molly raised her blond brows, her blue eyes wide. "Oh? This is us?" she asked, obviously only now understanding the situation. "You don't mind the aisle?"

He shook his head, and she stepped past him, brushing him with her soft fragrance. After stowing the bags, he settled beside her, trying to ignore the way the perfume reminded him of all her feminine attributes.

The attendant stopped by. "Don't forget to buckle your seat belt, sir."

He glanced at Molly to repeat what the woman had said, but she'd already fastened hers. She bent forward to push her bag under the seat now, and a long strand of hair worked loose from her braid to fall over her cheek. He lifted his hand to tuck it back but caught himself in time. He watched, though, as her slim fingers anchored it behind her unencumbered right ear.

His mind conjured up the image of her bending over *him*. He was sinking his hands into her hair, letting the heavy golden strands slide across his fingers.

What was a woman like this doing with Julian Silver? He'd seen Leo's suspect in the flesh for the first time when the man had dropped Molly off at the terminal. Thank goodness Molly had done enough talking to make it unnecessary for him to say anything more than hello. Even with his diplomatic training, he wasn't sure he could have been civil.

Stefanos ran a hand through his hair. What was with him? He never got emotionally involved in his job. He was this time. This time he had a personal stake in the outcome. Perhaps he'd succumbed to Molly Light's attraction because his emotions sat so close to the surface. That would explain why he'd kissed her Friday night in the car. Otherwise, his action made no sense, especially since he'd already decided *not* to kiss her.

He glanced at her. There was nothing particularly alluring about Molly's well-scrubbed, girl-next-door looks. Even her clothes—a long-sleeved white shirt and tan slacks—were unremarkable. Yet, she attracted him. He didn't usually go for women of slight build, preferring instead a more rounded figure in a woman, a figure like the one Kristi had.

Stefanos closed his eyes and tried to conjure up Kristi's image. Last night he'd tried to do more than use his imagination, but when he'd called Kristi, she'd been unavailable. She was getting married, of all things. He'd given her his best wishes but had felt regretful, too. What he'd appreciated most about Kristi was that she'd accepted their relationship for what it was, with no strings attached.

The plane taxied away from the terminal, and Molly studied the emergency card as if she intended to memorize it. When she finished, she got out her guidebook, blatantly ignoring him. After a twinge of wounded male pride, Stefanos regarded her thoughtfully.

His first goal was to get to know Molly. Leo had suggested seduction as a possible means. Stefanos mulled the idea over again now. No, he needed to forget the man-woman stuff. He could accompany her to Greece and find out when and where she'd pass the classified information over to Topolac's man without getting involved sexually.

The plane roared down the runway and lifted off the ground. Molly looked up, her blue gaze connecting with his brown one. For a moment, they stared at each other, then she looked out the window, watching the world below tilt away from them. Stefanos touched her arm, and she turned to look at him again.

He let his gaze linger on her mouth, wondering if she remembered the kiss they'd shared on Friday night. Better to leave that unspoken, he told himself.

"Did you say something?" she asked.

He took a small notepad from his inside jacket pocket. "No, I wanted to get your attention. Are you okay?"

She lifted her eyebrows. "Sure."

"Not afraid of flying then?"

"No." She looked at him curiously. "Are you?"

"It's practically second nature. I did a lot of it as a kid."

"Really? Why?" She propped her chin in the palm of one hand.

Stefanos hesitated. He didn't want to reveal any more about himself than was necessary. Her blue eyes studied him with interest, though, and he felt compelled to respond. "I went to school in New York, where I lived with my mother. In the summer, I would go to Greece to visit my grandfather and my father's family. I guess I liked airports and airplanes because they meant escape."

"You wanted to escape from Greece?"

Stefanos nodded. "When it was time to go, yes. My father married against my grandfather's wishes and the old man hated my mother."

Molly leaned forward. "You're kidding."

"No, and it was mutual."

"In a situation like that," she said, nodding, "I can see how you got used to negotiating and developed a talent for it."

"Perhaps." He'd never considered why he'd gone into a diplomatic career. That she'd immediately understood the implications of his past bothered him. He smoothed his tie.

This conversation wasn't working as planned. She was supposed to be revealing something to him, not the other way around.

She opened her mouth as if to speak, but closed it without saying anything.

Stefanos lifted his notepad and wrote, "Go ahead. You were going to say?"

Molly retrieved the guidebook, which had slipped off her lap, and clung to it as if to a life preserver. "I was going to ask about your father, but it's none of my business."

No, it wasn't. He looked at her, wondering what might lie behind her remark, and noticed the tightness around her mouth. He made an offhand gesture, hoping to put her at ease. "My father died when I was six. He wasn't around when this tug-of-war was going on." Molly gazed at him, her eyes limpid pools of blue. He could feel her sympathy reaching out to him. Stefanos touched Molly gently on the cheek. "He married an American woman, so that's why I'm American."

"Your mother?"

"She's remarried and lives in San Francisco," he wrote, grimacing. If only she'd married that guy a few years earlier, his teenage years would have been a lot more bearable.

"Sorry. I didn't mean to be nosy."

"No problem." His mother just wasn't one of his favorite topics. He hadn't meant to tell Molly half as much as he had. Hell, he hadn't planned to mention anything about his family, but his revelation might prove useful. Maybe now she'd be more open when he asked *her* personal questions.

Molly looked up from his notepad and smoothed the halo of blond wisps away from her face. "I might be able to hear you here. Why don't you try talking to me?"

"Can you understand me now?" he asked aloud.

She blinked.

"C-a-n-y-o-u-u-n—"

"Understand me?" she finished for him, giving him a brilliant smile. "I didn't know you could finger-spell."

"Learn-ing," he said slowly as he tried to spell out the letters. "I thought it would be useful," he said aloud and dropped his hand. "I'm not very good yet. Perhaps you could help me?"

She repeated part of his question. Stefanos heard interest in her voice and pulled from his briefcase the sign language book he'd bought yesterday.

She glanced at the book, then at him, then back at the book again. "You really want to? It won't embarrass you?"

"It does not embarrass me," he said.

"I'll bet nothing does."

He raised an eyebrow. "Why would you say that?"

She frowned. "I didn't get that. Maybe we should start those lessons?"

"Yes." He nodded his hand in the sign for yes.

Her face lit up with a smile. "You already know some signs, too!"

"Not many." He opened the book to a marked page and showed her the diagrams for the letters.

"Not yet, you mean." She went through the alphabet with him, making him imitate her hand positions. They'd reached the letter *r* when she suddenly stopped. "What happened to your hands?" she asked.

Stefanos gave her what he hoped was a rueful look, trying to act casual, and displayed his palms.

"Oh, my!" she exclaimed.

He saw the concern in her face. Admittedly, the puckers of scar tissue weren't pretty, but surely she'd felt the roughness of his palm when he'd held her hand on the drive home from the restaurant.

"Was it from a sports accident?"

"No, not a sport." Though it had definitely been an accident—one of misjudgment. He rubbed at the palm of one hand with the thumb of his other.

"Do they hurt?" she asked, leaning forward.

"Sometimes."

"Do you want to stop then?"

"No," he signed.

"Hey," she said, smiling, "you're doing great."

In spite of himself, Stefanos let himself bask in her praise.

"I noticed you're having trouble with the *h,* though. We'd better straighten that problem out right now. The *h* is made this way." She held up her hand in the correct position.

He tried to imitate her.

She shook her head. "The best way to remember it is..." She took his hand, and Stefanos instantly tightened against the contact. She tried to flex his fingers. "Hey, loosen up."

He let them go limp and gazed at the top of her head as she bent over his hand. Her hair would be silky, as silky as the sensations her touch evoked.

"The hand is held sideways so that the top is flat," she was saying. She moved her palm across his hand formation to illustrate her point. "I think you've got..." The brush of skin against skin tantalized him almost beyond endurance. "I think you've got it," she whispered, glancing at him.

The sound of her voice, low and tinged with the night, moved through him, matching the mystery in her eyes, so clear and yet so unrevealing. He wanted to know that mystery, needed to know it. He lowered his head, stopping a breath away from her lips. A primitive need urged him to finish what he'd started. His mind protested. She'd gotten to him, it warned.

A jolt suddenly went through the plane. He lifted his head and dropped his hand. The plane lurched again. This time the pilot's voice came over the PA system.

Stefanos let out a breath and settled back into his seat. That had been a close call.

Molly sank back against her seat and closed her eyes, trying to calm her pounding heart. She'd almost let him kiss her again. Even with her own vague doubts, she'd paid little attention to Julian's earlier advice about Stefanos's character. Maybe she should think about those warnings now. The man positively hypnotized her.

He glanced at her now and slowly spelled out the word "turbulence."

Definitely, she thought ruefully. There was turbulence both outside and inside the plane. She tightened her seat belt and tried to figure out how they'd come to this, especially since she'd been so anxious during most of their conversation. Ever since they'd gotten on the plane, she'd expected him to criticize her for arriving late. Once she'd finally decided he wasn't going to, she'd begun to relax.

Maybe that was why she'd asked about his hands. She usually respected someone else's privacy. His evasive answers had disappointed her. Of course she had secrets from him, too, things he would never learn about unless they got to know each other better—much better.

Under the present circumstances, getting to know him better would probably never happen, yet she was thinking like a woman who *wanted* something more from him than a casual acquaintance.

Stefanos's consideration pleased her. Not many people had the desire to use signing or the patience to learn it. She couldn't believe he'd bought the signing book just to make a pass at her. Julian would probably think so. He'd warned her that Stefanos Metadorakis was of the same ilk as Warren Flint, her ex-husband.

If Stefanos really was a playboy, he would have taken advantage of her attraction to him. He wouldn't have stopped before kissing her, or would he? Could Stefanos be stringing her along the way Warren had? If so, she'd better set the record straight.

She'd been staring out the window even though there wasn't anything to see. Now she pulled down the shade and turned around. "Stefanos—"

He was looking at her. Beyond him an attendant stood in the aisle also looking at her. Stefanos asked if she wanted a drink before dinner.

"The bumpy ride is over?"

He nodded and Molly saw that the seat-belt sign had gone off.

She agreed to a glass of wine and watched Stefanos continue speaking to the woman. He wore his tousled hair just long enough for waves to form. One fell over his temple, and she noticed the shadow of a new beard already showing on his cheeks. His white shirt and navy suit, an unremarkable combination on some men, added drama to his tanned features and athletic build.

His palms attested to past suffering, suffering he'd learned to cope with. Conquering pain was always a struggle and yet his polished exterior gave no hint of that inner drama. She'd caught an intriguing peek at his private life already.

That was really important, wasn't it? she asked herself sarcastically. What she ought to be thinking about was whether or not she was coming across as too familiar. If only she knew what constituted normal conversation.

The flight attendant moved on to the next passenger, and Stefanos smiled at her.

"Listen, Mr. Metadorakis—" she started, using the formal manner of address to try to create a businesslike atmosphere.

"When you call me that, you make me feel like my grandfather."

She watched his long, elegant fingers form the letters, finding it hard to believe he'd held hers. She could still remember every sensation, though.

"Perhaps you do not want to be friendly?" One corner of his mouth lifted, creasing his cheek with that dimple.

"I'd like to be friendly." She hesitated then added, "Stefanos, I noticed at the boarding gate that we're flying via Rome."

"Yes, we connect there. There were no seats on any direct flights," he said.

"You probably could have gotten tourist class."

He gave her an amused look. "No, not even that."

She smiled. "I appreciate your help in getting the commission. I don't know how you managed to get back to me so soon."

"I can be persuasive." He was spelling out nearly every word, and she showed him how to make one movement for each word. He signed the sentence again.

"I noticed," she said. "You did a pretty good job of talking me into going out to dinner with you the other night."

He took out his cigarettes and lit one. "I thought you enjoyed yourself."

He turned the lighter over in his fingers. She got the distinct impression he did it so he wouldn't touch her. She should be glad, but she liked him touching her. It had been so long since she'd received these little attentions from a man. "Yes, I enjoyed myself. How could I not?"

"Did your friend mind my taking you out?"

She frowned. "My friend? Who are you talking about?"

"The man who brought you to the airport."

"Julian?"

Stefanos nodded. "Is he your boyfriend? Fiancé?"

"If he was, I wouldn't have accepted a date with you."

He crushed out his cigarette. "Dinner at Michael's wasn't a date," he said, spelling out the name of the restaurant.

Then why did you kiss me?

Stefanos caught her gaze and she knew he could tell what she was thinking. She ought to look away instead of challenging him like this, especially after what had almost happened a few minutes ago. He wouldn't retreat, either, and the tension spun out between them.

Finally Molly looked down and traced a seam on the upholstery. "Anyway, when I asked for your help in getting the commission, I didn't expect to be traveling with you."

"No, probably not. My accompanying you on the flight was one of the stipulations for the company's offering you the commission."

"That's unusual." She kneaded the armrest. Though she wanted him to practice signing, their conversation went slowly, giving her plenty of time to agonize over the implications of his words. "Is it because of my hearing problem?"

"Partly. My cousin—" Stefanos gestured as if to say that was life "—wants to be sure you get there all right."

She frowned, wishing she hadn't asked.

"I still don't understand why we had to leave in such a hurry."

He raised a dark eyebrow as if her question surprised him. "I thought *you* were in a hurry."

"Isn't it inconvenient for you to drop everything and make this trip?"

He smiled, showing his dimple. "I didn't drop everything to make this trip," he said slowly, spelling each word. "It was the other way around, actually. I work in Athens, you know."

"No, I didn't know. I assumed you worked in Washington."

He seemed to consider that a moment. "It's a normal assumption, I suppose. Someone else was supposed to take some documents over to the ambassador."

Molly glanced down at the briefcase at his feet. A movement in the aisle made her glance up at the attendant. Would anyone else know he was carrying important State Department documents? She hoped not. She wanted nothing more than to blend into the background.

Stefanos continued, "It turned out the other guy wasn't available after all, and so when I called to say I could leave New York now—my grandfather's been ill, but is out of danger now—they asked me to take them. I made a request that they try to get another seat, and, voilà, they did."

"Amazing what a little clout will do for you, huh?" Molly shifted, suddenly uncomfortable. "I hate to think of taking this seat away from someone else."

"Why?" That dark eyebrow rose again. "It's paid for."

"Speaking of money..." Molly took her small leather purse from her canvas bag and found the check Stefanos had written on his private account. "You remember when I spoke to you about an advance for expenses?"

"Yes."

"I suppose I made something of an issue of it, but I didn't expect you to give me a personal check." She held it out. "I can't accept this."

He waved it away with a vague gesture. "Why not?"

"Because this commission isn't a personal transaction between us." Stefanos folded his arms. "You bought my paintings from the gallery, but *you* got my paintings," she said heatedly in response to his act of disapproval. "I'm doing *this* work for Meta-Hellenic. It doesn't seem right to take money from you personally."

The hearty sound of his laugh danced over her. Had that really been a laugh she'd heard? Yes, the curve of his mouth told her so.

She ought to be indignant and yet she found herself more curious than anything else. "What's so funny?"

"You're worried about how I spend my money," he answered aloud.

"I thought the company would issue the check. After all, they're the ones offering the award."

He smiled and turned his hands palms up as if he were blameless. "You do remember it was Friday night when we talked about your getting the award," he said, and reached across to touch the back of her hand with a finger.

Molly drew her hands into her lap, then immediately felt annoyed with her defensive action.

"I had very little time in New York," Stefanos explained, speaking and finger-spelling in spurts. "The next morning I spoke with my cousin in charge of the award selection. He doesn't have anything to do with the disbursement of funds. Saturday is not normally a working day, either. We could not find the controller at home. We were lucky to find a secretary to type the letter."

Why hadn't his cousin in the New York office written the check? she wondered. She was about to ask when he leaned forward.

"You did say you needed money for expenses."

"Yes, I did."

"That wasn't true?" He raised one expressive brown eyebrow.

"I was thinking mostly of the expense of the plane ticket." She folded the check and tapped it against her thumbnail. "Since I won't be making the final paintings until I return, I can buy most of the art supplies later."

He propped his elbows on the fold-down tray and steepled his hands. "I see."

What exactly did he see? He apparently wasn't going to say, so she got out her travelers checks. "You must let me pay for my plane ticket."

He shook his head. "It's already paid for."

Lord, he could be stubborn! She ought to accept the check as Julian had suggested, but she couldn't. In the past, people had made her feel indebted to them on purpose and she'd fallen into their trap. Now when someone tried to do it, she felt tight inside, as if she were being put into some sort of cage.

Molly stiffened. "Look, I'd feel better if you would get the company to take the cost of the ticket out of the award check."

Stefanos looked at her, his brown eyes flashing. Why was he forcing this check on her—his check? She raised her eyebrows to indicate she was waiting for an answer. When he gave her none, she tore the check in half and put the pieces back into her purse.

Molly stretched to relieve the cramp in her shoulder and glanced around the boarding lounge in Leonardo da Vinci Airport outside Rome. About fifteen other passengers had also been stranded there since the day before, first by a mechanical problem with their plane, then by a general strike.

Stefanos sat a chair away, practicing some of the signs from the signing book. She couldn't believe his diligence, but she supposed it took his mind off the tedious waiting. They'd been delayed for what seemed like centuries, but a check of the date on her watch told her it was still only Tuesday.

Her guidebook and the magazine from the New York airport lay on the seat beside her. She'd been doing a lot of sketching up to now, so she picked up the newsmagazine. Turning the pages, she thought about her argument with Stefanos over his expense check.

She hadn't planned to destroy it, and her impulsiveness made the action even more frightening. Usually she was able to control her anger, but she had been pretty upset with Stefanos.

They hadn't mentioned the check or her tearing it up again, but she'd noticed he hadn't minded going dutch on all the meals they'd shared here. She should have felt better once she'd cleared the air, but she hadn't. Her curiosity was working overtime, she supposed, and she'd really like to know if Stefanos had been insulted. She hoped not.

Molly turned the page. A photograph in the center of the next one grabbed her attention. She stared at the image of the smiling man and felt the old frustration burn through her. So vivid was the feeling, the man in the picture could have been sitting across from her now.

People were all around her, but she felt alone, just as she had so often when she'd been married to Warren Flint. Molly closed the magazine. She stared at the cover, trying to blot out the hurt her ex-husband had inflicted on her. It didn't work, and she found the page again to read the caption accompanying the photo.

He was starting work on a new film, seeking locations, though it didn't mention where. The item went on to hint he needed a hit movie after the last two box-office bombs. He was still famous enough to get a mention in this national magazine. That should make him happy.

She certainly hadn't been able to make him happy—not in any way that had mattered to her. She tried to keep her mind from going back over the events of her short marriage, but she could see them as if a movie played in her head. Molly stood, noticing out of the corner of her eye that Stefanos glanced up at her.

She ignored him, not feeling up to saying anything polite, and paced to the windows to stare out at the tarmac. When that didn't shut down her thoughts, she stuffed her hands into her pockets and took a deep breath. It was probably exhaustion that was making the sight of Warren's photo so traumatic.

Stefanos joined her. She nodded to him and hoped he wouldn't suspect how upset she was. The last thing she needed to do right now was unburden herself to a man. Laying out her emotions to a man whom she didn't trust emotionally would be even worse.

Outside, several deserted planes shimmered in the hot Italian sun. She tapped on the glass with her rolled-up magazine. "They look odd just sitting there without anyone doing anything to them. I never really noticed how big they are. Always running to catch a flight," she said, trying to joke. She laughed, but sounded anything but merry.

Stefanos's gaze found hers and she swallowed. His brow furrowed with concern. "You okay?" he signed.

"Yeah, sure." She glanced away, knowing she didn't sound very convincing.

Stefanos stepped in front of her and put his arms around her.

"Really, I'm okay," she said. She felt like a kid, but as a kid she'd learned never to lean on anyone emotionally. The only time she'd broken that rule had been with Warren, and look where that had gotten her.

Stefanos's arms tightened, and Molly couldn't resist laying her head on his shoulder. As long as she kept things in the proper perspective she could let herself absorb the warmth of his hands and the solid hardness of his chest. His hands stroked over her back, and one part of her mind warned her he might be making a play for her.

Was she so insecure that she couldn't accept a simple, comforting gesture from him?

"I guess maybe I'm tired." She eased back and regarded him. He'd long ago shed his jacket. He'd taken off his tie, too, and the unbuttoned collar of his white shirt bracketed the hollow of his strong neck. Lifting her gaze, she noted the fatigue etched on his face. "You must be tired, too."

"Something upset you," he said, ignoring her remark.

"I saw a picture of someone I used to know in the magazine I was reading."

He raised his brows and indicated the magazine she held. She handed it to him and watched him flip through it. "Who?"

Was he really interested? Molly turned the pages to the "People" section and pointed out Warren's photo. "My ex-husband, Warren Flint."

Stefanos barely glanced at the photo, and unless he was a speed reader, he couldn't have had time to read the caption before he closed the magazine and handed it back to her. She took it with a twinge of regret for even showing it to him. Apparently he'd only pretended to be interested.

"It upset you to see him?"

Molly regarded him. "We don't have to talk about him if he doesn't interest you, Stefanos. Goodness knows, I don't want to talk about him."

As soon as she'd spoken the words, she knew they weren't true. It felt good to admit her frustration aloud. She chewed her lower lip and caught Stefanos's gaze.

"I don't want you to get the impression that I'm criticizing him," she blurted. "Warren is just Warren. Besides, if I hadn't approached him in the first place, I never would have gone out with him. Or later married him. But with him I always felt inadequate." She made a gesture of helplessness.

"That was a long time ago and I don't understand why it should upset me now. Lost dreams, maybe. I always end up getting angry at myself when I let those memories get to me. I know I have a handicap, and—"

"It's not something you should be ashamed of," Stefanos said, signing at the same time the three or four words he knew.

"Thanks," she muttered.

He stepped back and pulled a cigarette from his case. Molly almost envied him the vice. It looked like a wonderful way to divorce oneself from a situation or change the subject. After all her heavy emotion just now, she figured that was exactly what he wanted to do—change the subject.

She'd told Stefanos her own reaction had angered her. It still annoyed her. It had been eight years since she'd last seen Warren in the flesh. Eight years was a long time. She'd thought herself totally recovered from the debilitating relationship with her ex-husband.

Maybe she'd never assimilated emotionally what had happened with Warren. Therefore she'd never really gotten beyond it. She hadn't had any serious relationships since then because until she'd met Stefanos no man had interested her.

Her hearing loss seemed to be both a barrier and a bridge between them. She almost thought his interest in her handicap was one of the things that had convinced Stefanos to help her get the commission. But that was crazy, wasn't it?

Chapter 4

Maybe he should just kiss her and get it out of his system. Stefanos took a drag on his cigarette and studied Molly while she examined his cigarette case. His gaze honed in on her pink lips. The memory of her warm body against his telegraphed renewed longing. No, kissing her wasn't a good idea. He might not be able to stop. Would Molly even allow it?

"I've never seen one like this. Except in the movies. It's antique, isn't it?" she asked, avoiding his gaze to watch his hands.

"Yes."

He moved closer to the window and farther away from Molly, who continued to study the cigarette case, rubbing her fingertips over its engraved surface. He needed to step back emotionally, too. And gain command of the situation. He hadn't felt in control since the ridiculous way he'd acted about the expense check.

The check had served its purpose, which had been to get her on a plane to Athens. He supposed he'd tried to force her to keep it in order to prove to himself he was in control. That wasn't like him. It wasn't like him to be in a situation he couldn't handle, either, not since his kidnapping in Lidacros. As long as he stayed calm and uninvolved emotionally, he'd be able to stay on top of the situation.

"It's lovely," Molly said. She handed him back the silver case, looking fresher than she had any right to be, her blue eyes bright. She'd slept, he reminded himself, while he'd watched.

Stefanos pocketed the case. "Thanks. You were right." He signed the whole sentence, using a sign he'd just learned. "You were right about being tired. Sorry we're stuck here."

"It's not your fault."

"Yes. Well, they thought the strike—" he spelled the last word "—might be over by now."

"Really? I don't know about you, but I'm ready to get to Athens."

"I'm ready." *Way past being ready,* he added silently. Putting space between him and Molly was getting to be his number one priority.

He rubbed the back of his neck, knowing he couldn't give in to a personal goal here. His job was to stick with her— and find out her plans once she arrived in Athens. They hadn't discussed Athens. In fact, he'd been avoiding all conversation with her, and he needed to remedy that.

"Anyway," he said and continued signing, "the flight from here to Athens is short and we won't have a meal." He waited for her nod of understanding. "Besides, it's nearly noon. Maybe we should get something now."

"Good idea." She followed him back to their seats. He put the sign language book away. "You're really doing great with your signing," she said.

He glanced up from locking the briefcase. Her gaze shone with real pleasure and for a second he wanted to forget who she was and why they were traveling together. He shrugged mentally, telling himself he was just glad she seemed to have recovered from her distress.

He might have been able to learn more about her motivations if she'd continued to talk, he thought, and he needed to learn about those. Disgust made him look away from her a moment. His job didn't preclude offering comfort when it was needed, did it?

She was still smiling about his signing progress, and he realized he hadn't responded. "You think so? I feel strange, as if I'm leaving something out. A long sentence sometimes works out to be only three or four movements."

"I know." She put her magazine in her canvas bag and shouldered it. "But I can usually tell what you are trying to say because of the context."

Her gaze connected with his, setting his pulse to beating faster. By now he should be prepared for the effect those blue eyes had on him, he thought, giving her a nod.

They started down the concourse toward a stand-up food bar with table service. On the way, Molly stopped at one of the souvenir carts. The vendor gave her an ingratiating smile. Stefanos scowled. Why couldn't this guy have gone on strike?

"What do you think?" she asked and held up one of the small stuffed donkeys.

"You want a souvenir of the thirty hours we've spent here?" he asked aloud, forgetting, in his surprise, to sign.

She laughed. "No. I mean as a gift for a little boy."

Stefanos took the plush toy from her and squeezed it. He only knew one child, and at ten Nikos was probably past the age when he'd want something like this. He wasn't a particularly active boy, though. And whose fault was that, huh? With an inner grimace, he gave the toy back to her.

Molly stepped closer. "Did I say something wrong?"

He frowned and signed, "What are you talking about?"

"You looked terribly unhappy just now."

Great. She could be so damned perceptive at the worst times. Stefanos indicated the stuffed animal. "I suppose I was making a comment about it."

"You don't like it? I can imagine a child cuddling something like this. You know, like a teddy bear."

"You sound as if you'd like to have children." Stefanos smoothed his tie, not understanding why he'd said that. He always avoided talk about children.

"Sure," Molly answered.

He thought he caught a wistful expression on her face when she put the toy back in the display, but she smiled at the vendor.

The merchant took the opportunity to bombard her with a stream of questions, all in Italian. Molly told him patiently about her hearing problem—in English, of course. Unfortunately her reply only encouraged the man to say more.

Stefanos shifted his weight, watching Molly examine some of the other items—plastic replicas of Mount Vesuvius, silver teaspoons, postcards. He picked up one of the volcano replicas, weighing it in his hand. That would appeal to a ten-year-old. He didn't want to encourage Nikos to like him, but Nikos didn't have a family to buy him a gift, and it was close to his birthday. He didn't have to be around to hand it to him, anyway.

Molly touched his arm, her soft fingers gliding over his forearm. "Do you have someone to buy for?"

"I know a kid. Sort of." He glanced at the display, noted the price in both dollars and lira and paid the man.

"Yours?"

"I'm not married." He took the bag from the man and steered her away from the cart. "I told you that."

"You could have been."

"You think so?"

She stopped. "Isn't there a woman who fits your standards?"

Stefanos twisted his mouth. How had they gotten onto this topic? He regarded Molly. Somewhere along the line he'd reverted to speech. She seemed to be understanding him, though, so he continued speaking. "I don't have any standards for them to fit."

"I don't believe that."

He pushed a hand into his pocket and wrapped his fingers around the lighter. "Molly," he said. "It's not an issue, is it?"

She glanced away. Stefanos resisted the urge to put his hands on her shoulders. She didn't need comforting this time. Her gaze settled on him again. "No, of course it's not an issue."

She bit down on her lower lip, leaving a sheen on it when she released it. Stefanos thought about the near kiss on the plane and about the real kiss. She started walking, breaking his train of thought, and he fell into step beside her.

They reached the food bar. Stefanos guided her to a table where they ordered sandwiches and coffee.

He disliked being unable to get past the sexual attraction he felt for Molly. If he analyzed his reactions, he could probably rid himself of it and get on with his job. He needed to. He was beginning to think about her as just Molly, not Molly Light, Julian Silver's comrade in espionage. He didn't like it, either. It was making him feel as if he were being backed into a corner—a very small, dark corner.

Later that Tuesday afternoon, Molly walked out of the Athens airport customs area. They'd finally arrived.

She hitched up her shoulder bag and watched Stefanos tuck his red diplomatic passport into the breast pocket of his jacket with more than a twinge of regret. They'd soon be going their separate ways.

He noticed her gaze and gave her a smile, bringing his dimple to life. Even in the state of exhaustion he must be in, he looked dangerously handsome.

Suddenly a woman came flying up to him, threw her arms around his neck and kissed him on the cheek. Stefanos dropped his brown leather bags and held the woman away. He smiled at her, but when he glanced at Molly, he buttoned his jacket again as if he was embarrassed by the woman's public display of emotion.

"This is Claire Green." He spelled her name then continued signing. "She's my assistant at the embassy." The brunette, nearly as tall as Stefanos, looked elegant in a blue suit with a blue-and-green-patterned shell and a neat, short haircut.

Feeling dumpy and dirty beside her, Molly rubbed her hand down her hip before holding it out. "Hello. I'm Molly Light."

Claire Green shook hands then started speaking to Stefanos again. Molly concentrated but couldn't hear her very well. Passengers from another flight began to trickle past them and the din grew louder. Stefanos stepped out of the path of traffic, surprising Molly by taking her arm and guiding her back out of the way, too.

"Why don't you give me the name and address of my hotel?" Molly asked now that she had his attention. "I can get there on my own."

Claire Green nodded her agreement, but Stefanos, taking the woman's hand off his arm, said something about "the car." Claire gave her a strange look, then left.

"Look," Molly began. The last thing in the world she wanted was to be a fifth wheel, especially with a man like Stefanos who made her want to be marooned on a desert island alone with him. "I'm just in your hair now."

He held up his hands. "You are not in my hair," he said slowly. "Claire has gone for her car. You must let us take you to the hotel. I want to—"

"Be sure I get there all right," Molly finished for him. Probably his cousins at the shipping firm had specified this duty, too.

He inclined his head, causing the heavy wave he combed sideways to fall forward over his brow. "It is decided?"

"Sure." She'd offered to separate only in order to accommodate him. If Stefanos didn't want to be accommodated, it was okay with her. She watched him help a porter load their bags onto a handcart, then walked with him toward the exit. "I see an exchange booth." She indicated a small office to the right of the building exit. "I'd like to change some money. Do I have time?"

Stefanos glanced that way, pursing his mouth in thought. "Of course," he finally said and nodded.

"I'll only be a minute," Molly called over her shoulder, already halfway to the exchange booth. She took a position in one of the lines and took out her travelers checks, wondering how much money to change.

A vague sense of danger seeped into her mind. She looked around. None of the people in the lines were looking her way. Then she saw him.

A medium-size man of slight build, with black hair and mustache stared at her from outside the booth. He caught her gaze before she could look away, tapped on the glass, and lifted his chin a couple of times as if to gesture her to come out.

The last thing she wanted to do was fend off some unwanted attention. He was either flirting with her or had mistaken her for someone else. In either case she should ignore him. Molly turned her body to block the man from her line of sight but could still feel his gaze. She was probably going to have to get used to being noticed in this country, but she tightened her grip on her purse, anyway.

Her turn at the counter came at last. Folding the drachma notes into her small purse, Molly hoped the dark-haired man had gone on to greener pastures by now. The guy was probably harmless, but she'd prefer not to be bothered.

Stepping out of the way of the next person in line, she accidentally collided with someone. "Oops, sorry. Excuse me." She glanced up and her heart stopped.

A big, red-haired man with a well-trimmed beard smiled down at her, his blue eyes laughing at her. "It's me," he said—or she thought that was what he said.

Molly tried to catch her breath. There was no reason for her to be out of breath—except from the surprise of seeing her ex-husband, Warren Flint, in the flesh. It had to be him although physically he'd changed. He'd gained weight, and he wore his hair long and curly rather than short and neatly cut. Otherwise, he looked the same. From his expensive watch and soft silk shirt to his stylish, Italian loafers, he wore exactly the kind of clothes she would have expected him to wear.

She needed to play this cool, she decided. "Hello, Warren. This is a surprise, but I'm afraid I've got to hurry right now," she said all in a rush and turned toward the exit. Warren stepped around her to block her path. Irritation perked through her, but Molly tamped it down. If Warren noticed her annoyance, he'd find a way to use it against her. "Well, maybe a couple of seconds." She paused and looked around Warren. She couldn't see out into the lobby far enough to locate Stefanos. "You're looking well."

Warren was about to say something when another customer trying to leave bumped him with an airline bag. Warren shoved the Japanese gentleman out of his way and muttered something that twisted his mouth into an ugly shape.

Molly moved over to a side counter, hoping to draw Warren out of the traffic path. She would have left, but she knew Warren would follow her until she listened to what he had to say. He raised his bushy red eyebrows and said something.

"I'm sorry, Warren, my hearing's gotten worse—"

"Never was any good," he said slowly and unmistakably.

Molly looked down then folded her arms, angry that she had to explain this to him. He *knew.* "With all this noise I can't understand you."

"You just did, didn't you?" His blue eyes looked at her slyly.

"Yes. You were speaking slowly enough."

Warren lifted a hand and tucked a strand of loose hair behind her ear. She almost batted his hand away. He had no right to touch her. It wouldn't surprise her, though, if he assumed she was still at the same point of emotional development as when he'd left her. At that time, she'd not only lapped up his interest; she'd sought it.

Molly tucked another strand of hair behind her ear. She lifted her chin defiantly but he spoke first. "What are you doing here?" he asked.

"Changing money." She realized now that she didn't want Stefanos to see them and moved farther from the door. If he joined them, Warren might make a joke about her inabilities. That would hurt, especially since she felt she'd finally earned Stefanos's friendship and respect.

Warren put a hand on her arm.

She tried to gauge his attitude. "What are *you* doing here?" she asked, gently pushing his hand away.

"Had to bring someone out to catch a flight," he answered, though she wasn't sure how she understood. He continued talking, moving his hands. She watched his hands automatically, but he didn't use signs and his gestures only distracted her from watching his mouth.

"I didn't get that," she said simply, proud she offered no apology this time.

He screwed his mouth to one side then gestured for something to write on.

"I really do have to go, Warren."

He motioned again, and she handed him a tablet from her canvas bag. "I'll let you go in a minute. Tell me what you're doing in Athens."

"Painting."

He gave her a long look and printed, "Come on."

Molly stiffened. "It's true. I'm doing a commission for a company. Frankly I'm surprised you're interested in anything I'm doing."

He spoke now, saying something that sounded like, "Come on, Molly, I spent two years of my life with you."

"I'm painting some landscapes for a shipping company," she offered, wondering how she could cut this conversation short and get out of there.

"Weren't you thinking of doing portraits?" Warren printed.

"Yes, and I do them, but Julian—" She bit her lip and watched Warren carefully. According to Julian, he and Warren had disagreed about something and never spoke to each other anymore.

"What about Julian?" he asked, not even blinking.

Molly shrugged to suggest her answer was of no consequence. "He happened to find out about a commission. Suggested I could get it." She smiled, unable to hide her pride. "I did get it, and now, if you'll excuse me." She took her tablet from him. "Someone is waiting for me."

"Who?" he asked.

"A friend. I have to meet him now." She turned to leave.

Stefanos stood in the doorway, his arms crossed, his eyes intent on her. Beside her, Warren gripped her arm. Molly frowned at him. "Introduce us," he said distinctly and pushed her in Stefanos's direction.

Molly studied Stefanos's expression but could see nothing of what he thought. "Sorry about the delay here," she said and hoped she sounded more casual about this encounter than she felt. "I've run into an old—"

Warren extended his hand and spoke, cutting her off. She watched the two shake hands, wondering what they were saying. Warren gave Stefanos his business card, and they exchanged a few more words before Stefanos glanced at her. She clutched the handles of her canvas bag more tightly. What *was* Warren saying to him?

"Do you want to meet him later for dinner?" Stefanos said slowly.

Molly stared at him, sure she'd misunderstood. Stefanos knew how she felt. "Do I want to meet him later?" she repeated.

"Yes," he signed.

She suddenly realized he'd only been translating what Warren had said. "I don't think so." She turned to address her ex-husband. "I'll be pretty busy—"

Warren interrupted to ask Stefanos a question. Stefanos answered him and Warren looked stunned. If she didn't know better she would have thought Stefanos had been abrupt with Warren. He might well have been, though. She could feel the tension in Stefanos's fingers as he all but dragged her away from the exchange booth and out of the building into the sun and wind.

She'd braided her hair again on the flight from Rome, but the usual wisps and strands in the front had come loose. She held them back from her face now. "You're angry," she said, hoping he wasn't. She would have known sure if she'd heard the conversation, but now all she could do was ask.

Stefanos glanced at her, then scanned the automobiles at the curb.

Molly propped a hand on her hip. "If you want, you can tell me the name of my hotel, and I'll take a taxi. I've got Greek money now, and there seem to be plenty of empty ones."

He looked down at her, his dark eyes flashing. "I am not angry with you, but at your ex-husband," he signed, stumbling over some of his letters. "I can see why his photograph upset you. He said—"

"He said what?"

A muscle in the corner of Stefanos's mouth twitched. "He said something that wasn't very nice."

"About me? I don't mean to be paranoid. Well, maybe I am being—"

Stefanos signed no three times. "I don't agree with what he said."

"Well—I—" Molly dropped her hand. Stefanos had shown a lot of consideration for her up to now, but his attitude still amazed her. She smiled. "Thanks. I'm sorry

Warren made you mad. Did he say what he was doing here in Greece?'' she asked, wondering why she even cared.

"Making a movie, or about to."

The knot of tension in her stomach suddenly loosened. "Oh, that's right. In the magazine article about him it said he was starting a new movie. It didn't say anything about Greece. Does the movie take place here?''

Stefanos shrugged. "He's looking for something . . .''

"Something what?''

"Mediterranean,'' he spelled.

Molly nodded. Running into Warren here made sense then. He certainly knew what Greece looked like.

Stefanos's assistant pulled her car to the curb. Stefanos helped the porter stow the luggage in the trunk and tipped him. Molly waited on the busy curb. She was anxious to get settled, she thought, glancing around.

Beyond Claire's car sat two yellow taxis and then a black car. The man she'd seen flirting with her stood at the open passenger door of that car. He gestured to her.

Molly clenched her jaw. This man was on the verge of leaving, and he was still trying to pick her up one more time. She really doubted he thought he remembered her, so he had to be flirting. Besides, she'd heard that Greeks considered themselves the best lovers in the world.

Stefanos climbed into the back seat after her. She smiled at him and propped her bag in her lap. She'd expected Stefanos to sit in front with his assistant. From the glance Claire gave him now, Molly could tell *she* wanted him to sit up there.

He stretched his arm along the back of the seat. She felt the heat of his hand behind her shoulder. He smiled at her and brushed his fingers across her shoulder. Was he trying to reassure her? About what?

He couldn't know about the man who'd flirted with her. She wasn't going to tell him, either. It would only suggest to him that she needed a chaperon. It was going to be bad enough with Julian tagging along later. She didn't need a whole troop of people watching over her.

About a half hour later, four-thirty local time, they pulled up in front of the Ithaca Hotel. Stefanos unloaded his luggage as well as hers. "Are you staying here, too?" Molly asked.

"No, but I will catch a taxi home. Claire needs to get back."

Molly waited while Stefanos spoke to Claire. His assistant drove off, and they entered the lobby. At the registration desk she asked about her reservation. The clerk raised his eyebrows, checked his listing and shook his head.

"But—"

Stefanos laid a hand on her arm and spoke to the man behind the desk—in Greek, she assumed. The hotel employee disappeared into the back room.

Molly crossed her arms and looked at Stefanos. She wished she didn't have to depend on him for a translation. Depending on him made her feel too much like the way she'd felt with Warren, who'd kept her at a disadvantage most of the time. "What's going on?" she asked.

"He's finding out if someone else knows anything," Stefanos said, signing the words he knew.

The clerk returned with another man, perhaps a manager, who spoke with Stefanos. "Someone goofed," Stefanos signed, repeating the gesture for "mistake." "They don't have a reservation here for you."

"But—" Molly clutched her bag, worried and tired and a little edgy. Stefanos had impressed her as being prepared, and that should have meant double-checking everything. "Did Meta-Hellenic make a reservation someplace else, do you think?"

"I don't know." He rubbed a hand across his mouth. Probably embarrassed, Molly thought. His gaze caught hers. "Why don't you come stay with me?"

She stared at him. Had she heard him right? "I can probably find something."

"There's going to be an international conference in town in a few days. And this is the summer tourist season. I don't want you to have to sleep on the roof of some hotel because you can't find a room anywhere."

Molly considered his offer. Could she trust him?

She wouldn't even be asking herself that if she hadn't run into Warren. The issue from the beginning with Stefanos had been whether or not she could handle traveling alone, though. Besides, she still didn't want to feel obligated to him for any favors.

Molly opened her mouth to decline his offer when she felt the sensation of being watched. She turned slightly and froze at the sight. The man from the airport, the flirting Greek, stood across the room watching her. He had a distinctive face with a lower jaw slightly out of alignment she would have recognized anywhere. Was he staying at this hotel?

Stefanos touched her arm. Molly tried to pretend everything was normal even while tension coiled through her.

"You can look for another hotel tomorrow," he said, and signed "tomorrow." "After you get caught up on your sleep."

Molly surveyed the lobby again, but the dark-haired man had vanished. Had he gone to his room or was he waiting somewhere out of sight to learn where her room was? She was not interested in finding out. She was interested only in getting back on track so she could return home—to the school.

"You're probably right," she said, accepting Stefanos's hospitality. "It would make things easier for now. Thanks."

Stefanos steered them out of the hotel and hailed a taxi. When they were underway, he glanced over at Molly. She looked out the window as they passed the Parliament building where the *evzones* in their short white skirts and tasseled hats watched over the Tomb of the Unknown Soldier.

Stefanos studied the way the afternoon light burnished her dark blond eyelashes. He wondered how he could have thought her only passably pretty before. Molly appeared calmer now, but she hadn't been calm a moment ago. If his instincts were right, she'd been afraid. He didn't like it, and he didn't like the hotel staff's not knowing anything about a reservation in Molly's name. Making those arrangements was supposed to have been Leo's job.

Something had gone wrong, and until he knew what, he needed to keep a close eye on Molly. He wondered why she'd come with him. Was she getting cold feet about her involvement in the espionage or was she afraid to run into her ex-husband again?

Anger surged through him when he recalled the man's insulting remark about Molly. Ten years ago Flint would have been better-looking, but his personality would basically have been the same. His ego shone like a neon light, and Stefanos couldn't believe Molly had married someone like him.

When he'd first seen her talking to a man at the exchange booth, he'd thought the guy might have been her contact. Then he'd recognized Flint from the photograph in Molly's magazine. Though Molly had acted pretty cool at the airport, she'd sounded unhappy when they'd talked about Flint before. One of those times she'd been covering up, probably the one here in Athens. Besides, Flint had given him a plausible reason for being in Greece. He'd said he was looking for movie locations.

Molly turned, and their gazes caught. "Is it far?" she asked.

He looked past her, picked out a few landmarks and shook his head. "No," he signed. "Not now."

The taxi pulled into the quiet, tree-shaded neighborhood in which he lived and, in another moment, stopped in front of his house. He paid the driver, and they got their luggage.

"This is it?" she asked, stopping on the front walk.

"Yes." He eyed the big, ordinary-looking stucco with the jasmine vine cascading down its facade, wondering why she sounded so awestruck.

"The jasmine smells heavenly."

He nodded absently, letting his gaze travel around the garden. The approaching evening filled it with shadows, but he noticed nothing unusual.

"It's beautiful, Stefanos."

Something leapt inside him just as it had the first time she'd used his given name. He could have suggested she call him Steve like everyone else, but he rather liked the sound of his Greek name on her lips. She pronounced the *s* on the end, but that wasn't important. It wasn't important that she used his given name, either, he reminded himself as he led her inside.

His housekeeper, Eleni, came out from the kitchen. She hugged him as usual. He introduced Molly, gave Eleni some instructions, then led Molly up the stairs to the guest room. Standing behind her, he tried to ignore her velvety fragrance. He'd always liked the clean, neat, uncluttered lines of contemporary furniture, but she might find the room too bare. He wondered if she'd be comfortable here. He did want her to be comfortable, too, even though he'd be anxious and watchful with her in the same house.

He shifted his weight restlessly now. Molly finally moved from the doorway, walking over to the small replica from the National Archaeological Museum. He watched her run a finger along one of the statue's outstretched arms. A streak of heat went through him as if she'd touched his skin and not the bronze.

He tried to resist the need growing inside him. Stepping past her, he accidentally brushed her arm as he set her cases down. Unbidden, the memory of her body leaning against his earlier that day melted through him. That embrace in Rome played so vividly in his mind, it could have happened a moment ago. He probably shouldn't have held her then, but she hadn't minded. Would she mind now?

She dropped her shoulder bag on the bed, and he walked over to her. "This is better than a hotel room." She said, smiling at him.

And the service is great. Stefanos watched a strand of blond hair fall from behind her hearing aid. No matter how often Molly redid her braid, this lock always worked loose. He reached to tuck it back and found himself twining it around his finger, instead. "Glad you like it."

Her blue eyes widened, then softened, and he slipped his arm around her waist, pulling her closer. There couldn't be any harm in touching her just a little. He'd let go in a second.

He didn't let go. He bent his head to cover her mouth with his. She yielded to him, reaching up to encircle his neck with her slim arms. In his hands she felt slender and supple like the tendrils of the jasmine vine, soft as the petals of its fragrant blossoms.

"I've been wanting this, too," she murmured, her voice growing husky. "Ever since the last time."

A tiny warning flashed through his mind, disappearing like a spark fizzling out on the ground.

He planted kisses down her throat and farther down, loosening the top buttons of her blouse. She smelled warm and female, and he felt her fingers in his hair. Tightening his arms, he moved his lips along the swell of her breast not covered by her brassiere. The rest of the world was about to fade into nothingness when he heard a sound behind him.

He broke away from her, turning in the direction of the noise. Eleni stood in the doorway, her arms laden with towels. He took them from her, feeling embarrassed, angry—and confused. He didn't want to think Molly had deliberately enticed him, but had she?

"Why did you let me kiss you?" he asked aloud when the housekeeper had left them. He'd been signing and speaking interchangeably based on how well Molly seemed to understand him, but he didn't know if he had the patience to sign now. "If Eleni hadn't walked in, you'd be half-undressed by now."

Molly, who'd sat down on the bed, shot up, her eyes full of fire. "You make it sound as if that kiss were my fault. I can't imagine you doing anything against your will. You're too strong to let someone else control you."

"Let's just forget it," he signed, knowing it was an inadequate answer. He could not chance saying more, not until he had his emotions under control.

"Forget the kiss? It's a little late for that." A smile played across her mouth. "At least for me. Maybe...it wasn't..." She looked at him, her expression one of dismay. "Maybe you didn't feel anything...special?" she glanced away.

He knew what she was asking. She wanted to know if she had misinterpreted his enthusiasm. Stefanos lifted a hand to brush the backs of his fingers along her cheek, realizing too late they still stood too close together. "Why don't you shower and change clothes? Then we'll go out and eat."

"You want this last piece?" Molly held the plastic bread tray out toward Stefanos.

"You take it," he said, giving her a smile.

He glanced around the outdoor taverna she'd suggested for dinner. She hadn't volunteered how she knew of this place. The food had proved good, though, and light bulbs strung between the eucalyptus trees gave the little restaurant a festive air. Too bad he didn't feel like partying.

He'd learned nothing yet about the snafu at the hotel, but the gun pressing into his back gave him a measure of confidence he hadn't had at the airport or hotel. It made him feel in control. It also didn't hurt that the lights from the tobacco kiosk on the corner made it easy to see anyone approaching from the street.

The night breeze shifted the leaves above, cooling his face and neck. He wished it could cool his anxiety, too. Tom Wilson, the agent who'd delivered the gun, was at this very moment trying to contact Leo Rollins back in the States.

Tom was also calling the number on Flint's business card to substantiate the man's story. In the meantime, he would keep an eye on Molly.

Across from him, Molly pulled on her cotton sweater. In the stark lighting she appeared fragile. He needed to stop thinking of Molly as vulnerable. It only added to his confusion. Trouble was, he'd thought of her as delicate from the beginning. Was that because of her hearing loss?

The breeze carried the scent of violets, Molly's scent. He remembered the tray of African violets in her kitchen, remembered testing their soft, furry petals. Molly's mouth had been soft. So had her throat, and the swell of her breast. She'd threaded her fingers through his hair almost greedily, letting him take what he'd wanted. Maybe it was just his male ego, but he didn't think she'd been pretending her response when he'd kissed her awhile ago. But why would she encourage his interest unless she meant to use him in some way? He ought to be on his guard with her, unless she was innocent . . .

She looked across the table, catching his gaze, and smiled.

"You're quiet tonight," he said, speaking slowly.

"I don't like conversation all the time. It's tiring for me." She folded her arms on the table. "I'm not complaining, but I can amuse myself."

Stefanos rubbed his thumb across her knuckles. She'd known loneliness, too. She hadn't mentioned the episode in the bedroom again. He'd replayed it at least a million times, trying to anesthetize himself to its effect. Every time he thought about it, though, the images became more vivid. Now his skin heated immediately, and he could think only of how he wanted to slide his hands over her bare skin, of how he wanted to slide his own bare body over hers, into hers.

His whole body tightened. Stefanos let out a breath and settled back in his chair. He probably should have apologized for coming on to her back at his house. From what

Molly had told him in the Rome airport, he'd acted exactly like her ex-husband.

"Stefanos..."

He raised an eyebrow in answer. She tugged on her hand, and he let go. "Forgive me. I didn't realize I was still holding your hand."

She reached for her canvas bag. "Would you excuse me?" she asked and pushed her chair back.

Surprised and instantly alert, he stood, too. "Where are you going?"

"Well..." She glanced around the outside dining area. "I think I'll try to find a ladies' room here."

He blinked. Oh, that was where she was going. "There must be a washroom inside."

"Fine," she said, frowning. "I'll just be a minute."

Stefanos watched Molly walk across the flagstone terrace. She was definitely tense now, but she'd seemed relaxed earlier in the meal. What had made her nervous again?

He needed information, and the agent at his house might know something new by now. Stefanos glanced at the magazine kiosk on the corner. The vendor would have a phone. It would only take a minute to call and find out.

Chapter 5

Molly felt Stefanos's gaze as she walked through the tables of the outdoor dining area. He might have seen through her ruse, but she didn't care. She needed to put her reactions into perspective, and a sigh of relief escaped her when she stepped into the empty inside dining room.

The way she felt when he touched her or held her hand or just looked at her made it impossible to think about anything but the way he'd kissed her. Even now she imagined his mouth on hers, seeking, tasting, then trailing tantalizing sensations down her throat and under her collar.

Molly leaned back against the door of the rest room. She couldn't remember ever feeling as warm, as absolutely liquid, as willing as she had when Stefanos had kissed her. She'd been upset when he'd tried to lay the blame for the kiss on her. The kiss had been mutual. That was the problem. She hadn't refused it and she should have. She could even have told him she wasn't interested.

Molly loosened her braid and got her brush out of her bag. She would have accepted another kiss from him, too. Why? Did she want to pursue a relationship with him?

It would be so easy to fall for Stefanos, she thought, pulling the brush through her hair. He fascinated her. Every time she turned around, she discovered some new aspect of his personality. Tonight she'd found out he enjoyed eating outdoors because he liked the night and the fresh air. When she'd asked why, he'd told her how beautiful the night could be with its millions of stars. It was the sort of thing she would have imagined a boy of ten or so saying, not a man in his middle thirties.

And the way he treated her! She'd never met such a patient, considerate man, a man who made sure she understood what was happening, a man who made her feel strong and a man who didn't see strength as a drawback in a woman.

Until tonight he'd resisted the attraction. In fact, even though the housekeeper had interrupted them, she knew Stefanos would have stopped. Stefanos would do nothing unless he wanted to do it. Also, when he'd held her hand just now at the table, she'd found it difficult to believe he hadn't realized he did. So was he deliberately teasing her? Had he intended to unsettle and confuse her from the very beginning?

Maybe he did, and maybe he was more like her exhusband than she'd originally thought. She started to rebraid her hair. Julian had told her she didn't have the experience to handle this sophisticated man. Her friend might be right, but Molly felt she could trust Stefanos. That was why she'd accepted his invitation to stay at his house. He'd been genuinely concerned about her—or was she fooling herself as she had with Warren? Would Stefanos turn out to be someone entirely different, too?

Fastening the French braid she'd just finished, Molly tried to put the idea to rest. Her body ached with exhaustion, and no doubt her mind felt tired, too. Even if any of this hysterical speculation were true, she'd be leaving his house to-morrow. Her heart skipped a beat at the thought of leaving him. Going out on her own, she corrected. Well, she'd miss him, too, but they each had their own life, and hers was back in New Jersey with the school.

Molly skirted some glass-doored refrigerators on her way back, then paused a moment when she pushed aside the long plastic strips hanging in the dining-room doorway.

The little restaurant with its tables scattered amongst the trees was exactly as she remembered it from ten years ago. Though she'd come with Warren then and wanted to avoid the possibility of running into him again, she really liked the festive and friendly atmosphere of the place. She smiled to herself, glad she'd resisted the urge to stay away.

She stepped outside under the canopy of tree branches. A movement caught her eye. Maybe a waiter? She stepped to one side, but whoever it was deliberately bumped her ten-nis shoe. She swiveled to find a dark-eyed, dark-haired man smiling at her. Fear skittered along her nerves. This was the flirt from the airport. No mistaking his off-center jaw.

Her heart pounding, she stepped backward and stum-bled over the stone border at the bottom of a tree. His hand shot out to steady her, and he said something. In English, maybe, but she wasn't sure.

She tried to free herself, but his grip tightened. "I don't—" Molly shut her mouth, wary of telling this stranger about her hearing problem. She darted a glance toward Stefanos.

Oh, no. Stefanos wasn't at their table. The man holding her arm continued speaking, and Molly made herself look at him, telling herself to act calmly. He stopped talking, but before she could say another word, a waiter came through the doorway with a tray full of food. Molly jerked her arm free and hurried past the other tables, hoping the man would be distracted long enough for her to find Stefanos.

She cast a frantic glance around. Stefanos had to be here somewhere. Afraid to look back, she wove her way through the tables to the edge of the outside dining area. Suddenly she saw Stefanos at the magazine and tobacco kiosk on the street corner.

He waved to her, pocketed his cigarettes and met her halfway. The stark illumination from the streetlights shadowed his eyes and sharpened the planes of his face. She shivered. This was Stefanos, silly, she told herself.

Molly took his arm. The hard strength of it underneath his jacket reassured her. She still didn't want to linger. "If you've paid the bill, I'd like to go, please."

"What's the matter?" Stefanos signed.

"Have you paid?" she repeated.

He frowned down at her, his gaze intent. Molly jammed her hands into her pockets. Stefanos looked as if he thought she were crazy. His expression reminded her of her ex-husband. Warren had always insinuated that she read the worst meaning into a situation because she couldn't hear everything and didn't understand.

"I don't know if you noticed, but a man was flirting with me when I was in the exchange booth at the airport."

"Are you talking about your ex-husband?"

She shook her head. "Before I ran into Warren. This same man came into the hotel where you thought I had a reservation, and he just showed up here now."

Stefanos stiffened. Molly watched him survey the restaurant. "Where?" he signed.

Taking hold of his arm again, she peered around. "He was at the doorway when I came outside, but I don't see him now," she said. Her hammering heart slowed, and she took a deep gulp of air.

Stefanos removed her hand from his arm. "We'd better find out who it was."

"No." Molly tensed. "Let's just go home. Okay?"

"I want to talk to the owner," he signed, completely ignoring her request.

"Why ask for trouble? The man's gone, Stefanos. What can you hope to do now, anyway?"

Stefanos quickly squeezed her shoulder. "The family that runs the taverna should know about him," Stefanos said aloud, spelling a word here and there when she stopped him. "They won't want him bothering the other customers."

"No, I guess not." A sudden loud sound startled her. She caught Stefanos's arm. "What's that?" she asked.

"Sounded like a car backfiring."

"Backfiring? Is that what it sounds like?"

He nodded and steered her back to the inside dining room. They found the proprietor. Molly described the man, but a search of the premises failed to turn him up.

"Why is this guy following me?" she asked.

Stefanos raised an eyebrow. "You tell me."

Molly repeated his words. What did Stefanos mean? That he wanted her to come up with an explanation? She shrugged, bewildered. Was this another way he was making her feel off-balance? He continued to regard her as if he expected an answer. She didn't have to answer him, she told herself, annoyed. She glanced around the taverna, then back at him. He hadn't moved. "I have no idea why he's following me," she said through gritted teeth. "What will the restaurant owner do?"

"I don't know." He pulled several notes from his pocket to pay for dinner. "I'm not sure he would recognize him from your description."

"Maybe it wasn't the same man." Molly rubbed her forehead. Had this stranger really been the same one from the airport? She had been thinking about him, and maybe she'd superimposed the man's features on this person. Even to her befuddled brain his following her to the taverna seemed pretty farfetched. "I'm tired, I guess."

Stefanos led her to the car, and they drove back to his house. Unlike earlier today, this time she felt no relief at the thought of going home with him. The episode with the man had changed Stefanos. He seemed stiff, as if he'd put on a mental suit of armor. It scared her that he'd seen her alarm, too.

Molly surreptitiously rubbed her sweaty palms on her jeans, hoping Stefanos wouldn't notice. He could use her fear against her only if she let him, but the sooner she got away from him, the better. In that respect, nothing had changed.

Everything had changed, thought Stefanos, turning north on Vasilissis Sofias and maneuvering into the middle lane.

Molly had talked about a man bothering her tonight. He didn't know if it was just a story, or if a man really had made a play for her. She'd been nervous, and she might have overreacted to a simple gesture. He still didn't know why she'd been tense when she'd gotten up to go inside. She might have planned to meet someone at the taverna but gotten cold feet.

Her voice came to him now from across the front seat, confident and forceful, almost too loud for the inside of the car. "I thought I'd look for a hotel tomorrow morning."

So much for the cold feet. Stefanos looked over at her.

Molly held his gaze for a few moments, then glanced out the windshield, twisting the handles of her canvas bag. "Stefanos, you're going to drive off the road if you keep looking at me."

Stefanos turned his attention back to the street and gripped the wheel a little more tightly. He thought about pulling over to the curb to talk, but he'd have better control over the situation at home with the other agent around.

"I haven't got a lot of time here," she continued. "And I need to get started on my sketches."

It sounded as if she planned to go ahead and hand over the microfilm to one of Topolac's men. If so, she didn't have a lot of time, as she'd said. Leo thought Topolac expected to have all the technological information in his fat, sticky hands before the international conference. It would convene on Saturday, only four days from now.

A sigh of exasperation swelled in his chest. Molly was intelligent. He didn't understand how she could be so stupid as to get involved with someone as dangerous as Topolac—or as dangerous as Julian Silver, for that matter.

Out of the corner of his eye, he saw her weaving her slim fingers through the handles of her canvas bag. That must be where she was keeping the microfilm. She never let it out of her sight.

At his house Stefanos parked in the driveway. They got out and Molly started toward the steps to the kitchen. He waved to her to follow him around to the front. Leo's agent, Tom Wilson, would probably still be in the kitchen with his housekeeper and her husband. He'd have to speak to Tom as soon as he could, but Molly didn't need to know the other man was in the house.

"Eleni will bring us coffee," Stefanos said in the front hallway, signing what he could. "I'll go ask her."

"Coffee? I'd just as soon call it a night." Molly walked to the staircase.

Stefanos stopped her with a hand on her arm. "If you go upstairs, I'll have to come up after you." Her gaze caught his, wary and curious at the same time.

He explained, "I don't know if I can trust myself to be with you in your bedroom again."

She raised her blond eyebrows, then looked away. "Is that an apology or a threat?"

Stefanos took her by the shoulders. She looked up at him. She did not back away, he noted. "We need to talk." He let her go. "Do you understand?" She nodded warily. "Not about what happened in the bedroom." He wouldn't apologize for kissing her. It hadn't been one of his smartest moves, but he *had* meant to kiss her. "Not about us, exactly. Will you oblige me?"

"Just for a few minutes, I suppose it's okay."

In the living room, he switched on a few lamps and gestured her to the couch. "Let me speak to Eleni."

He hurried to the kitchen, greeted his housekeeper and her husband and explained to Tom about the man at the taverna. "She might be throwing up a smoke screen, but I want to be sure no one followed us home. Would you look around outside?''

In the living room, Molly was looking at his photograph of Nikos. Stefanos came up behind her. She didn't hear him, so he moved to one side to catch her attention. She nodded at the picture. "He's the one you bought the present for in the Rome airport, isn't he?"

"Yes," he replied, watching her, not surprised she'd figured out the connection.

"What's his name?"

"Nikos." he said, spelling out the name.

"Nikos?" she asked. "Who is he exactly?"

Stefanos lifted an eyebrow, wondering why she had to know. "That's not important."

He warmed with the rush of affection he always felt toward the child who'd saved his life. He didn't have to wait long for the guilt to follow, guilt for the needless deaths of Nikos's family and friends.

Stefanos rubbed a hand over his mouth. *The bad guy always gets his in the end,* he told Nikos silently. At least he hoped so. This time the good guys might win, only if Molly helped him, though.

Molly moved from beside him, her tennis shoes making soft sounds on the wood floor. It was almost too quiet, he thought, tensing and glancing up to find her at the French doors. He joined her and tested the handles. Locked. Good. He wanted no more surprises tonight.

She peered through the panes into the night. "Where does this go, Stefanos?"

"They open onto a terrace," he said, feeling her gaze on his mouth.

"What's past the terrace?"

Did she plan on meeting someone? The man from the taverna, maybe? "Just the neighborhood," he answered.

She nodded absently.

Had she understood? She usually had him repeat if she hadn't heard him very well, but tonight she hadn't been acting as normally. He had no idea what she'd do, and he wanted to be sure she understood him.

"Can you hear me okay?" he asked.

"Your house is probably quieter than the restaurant or street, isn't it?"

He raised his eyebrows. "You can't tell?"

"I have ringing in my ears," she said, hitching the handles of her bag higher on her shoulder.

A gentle sympathy seeped through him, but he curbed the urge to express it. Under other circumstances he might extend it to her, but right now he wasn't sure whose side she was on. He wanted her on his side, but he'd have to get her to come clean first. Just then his housekeeper appeared with the coffee, eliminating any need for a response to Molly's remark.

"*Efharisto,* Eleni." Stefanos thanked the woman in Greek as she placed a tray with the pot and cups on the coffee table in front of the sofa. "You and Manos ought to go now," he added.

Eleni and her husband normally lived in the back of the house, but they had arranged to stay with relatives for a few days. There might be trouble, and he wanted them out of harm's way.

Molly sat on the sofa and smoothed her hand over the brown-and-cream-striped upholstery. He remembered those hands sliding through his hair. Stefanos swallowed. "Help yourself." He indicated the coffeepot.

She poured herself a cup and doctored it with sugar. "What did you want to talk about?" Her face reflected nothing but casual interest. Playing it cool, was she?

Feeling anything but cool himself, he undid his tie and the top button of his shirt, catching Molly's gaze. "Just a little warm. Hope you don't mind," he said.

She shook her head. "This is your house, but if you're hot, maybe we should be drinking iced coffee."

"I doubt Eleni's ever heard of it," he said, and wondered how to broach the subject of the espionage. He could tell her about his hands. That story would reveal to her how determined Topolac and his followers could be. Stefanos felt around for his cigarette lighter in his jacket pocket and gripped it tightly. He hated talking about his hands.

A noise came from the back of the house. Eleni and her husband would have left before now. Stefanos tensed, listening for something more.

Molly was looking at him curiously. "Is something wrong?" she asked, her voice rising a pitch.

No other sounds came from the back rooms. Stefanos poured himself some coffee. "Everything's fine. Why?"

She hesitated a moment. "I guess I'm still keyed up over what happened at the restaurant."

"You don't have to worry. I'm here." He took a couple of swallows before putting his cup on the table and shifting to face her. "You realize what you are doing is dangerous, don't you?"

"Dangerous?" She sipped her coffee, looking as calm as could be. "Did I understand you correctly?" she asked.

"Yes. You are doing something dangerous," he repeated and signed both.

Molly laughed and tilted her head. "What's so dangerous about taking photographs and making sketches?"

Stefanos almost smiled. She didn't back down easily. "You didn't really come to Greece to paint, did you?"

Molly set her coffee cup on the table. "Well, I probably won't make the actual paintings here. I'll make sketches and take photographs. I thought we talked about this before."

"What about the real reason you're here?" He didn't want to explain what he knew because she might decide to play along with him and still hide something important, something that could prove deadly.

Molly leaned toward him, frowning. She looked about to touch him but lowered her hand to her lap again. "Are you all right?"

"Of course," he said, one corner of his mouth pulling up. Clever of her to turn the spotlight back on him.

"Then why are you asking me—"

"Why did you want the art commission?" he asked, holding her gaze.

Molly smoothed her hair back from her face with both hands. "I know we talked about this before, Stefanos, and I'm too tired right now to play games."

"This isn't a game, Molly."

She stared at him hard before shifting closer to the end of the sofa. "What is your problem, Stefanos?" He said nothing. "Okay, we'll go over this again if you want. I wanted the art commission for the prestige and the money."

"Money can't buy happiness. I know." He felt his mouth twist with the disgust he was trying to keep inside. "I've seen people try that."

"It can make a lot of things happen."

"Like a place in Switzerland, a fancy car, plenty of clothes. Is that what you need?" *He could give that to her.* Stefanos slammed his mind shut on that thought. "You said you didn't love Silver."

"Didn't love Silver?" Molly repeated, frowning. She smoothed her hair back from her face. "Is that what you said? It doesn't make sense."

She was very good at the bewildered look, Stefanos thought uncharitably. Why should he be charitable?

Molly rubbed her palms on her thighs and darted a glance around the room. He saw a look of determination come into her eyes, and she stood.

Stefanos rolled to his feet.

"I don't call this talking." She lifted her canvas bag from the floor. "If you plan to continue badgering me I'll find someplace else to stay tonight."

"No." Stefanos tried to grasp her shoulder, but she shrank back from him. "I don't want you to leave," he signed, forcing himself to be patient. "I want you to tell me what happened at the restaurant."

"I told you before," she said, an edge to her voice.

"So you did."

Her hands trembled, and Stefanos watched her slip them into the pockets of her jeans. He wanted to take them, take her into his arms, but he couldn't hold her and talk to her at the same time.

If she would only realize he was doing this for her own good! If she helped them out by confessing what she knew, she might be able to get off easy. He was now sure she really had no idea what she was involved in.

"Should I have believed you, Molly?" he asked, softening his voice.

She took a step back. Stefanos froze. He hadn't realized he'd taken a step toward her. Sweat beaded on her upper lip, and as she wiped it away, he saw fear cloud her blue eyes. Fear of him? His gut twisted, and he lifted a hand. She recoiled from him. Stefanos dropped his hand, wondering what he'd been trying to do. Wipe that look from her face?

"He scared you," Stefanos said, referring to the man she'd spoken of at the taverna.

"Yes, and—" She bit her lip as if she wanted to keep from saying anything else and took two more steps away from him.

"And?" he prompted.

"I'm okay now. Anyone would have been frightened under the circumstances." She paused, regarding him. "I guess you're never afraid."

Stefanos started to say he was a little afraid of her when a muffled noise broke the silence. It came from either the terrace or the yard and he turned toward the French doors. The glass reflected the room's interior, and he couldn't see through them. Tom Wilson might still be outside, but he shouldn't be making enough noise to be heard in there.

Stefanos checked his watch, and his chest tightened. The other agent should have come inside by now, but he hadn't heard the back door open and close. Stefanos went back to stand directly in front of Molly. "I have to go check on something," he said, speaking as distinctly as possible. "Wait for me here."

Molly rubbed her arms. "I think I should find a hotel for tonight. Really, I don't want to—"

He made a calming gesture and said firmly, "Do not leave. Do you understand me?"

"You don't want me to leave, but—"

"I'll explain later," Stefanos said and strode out of the room.

He didn't want to leave her by herself, especially if something was happening outside, but he had to check on Tom. Stefanos slipped out the kitchen door, locked it behind him, and descended the steps to the driveway. He let his eyes adjust to the darkness then peered into the shadows. "Tom?" he called softly.

The darkness echoed his own voice back to him. Stefanos pulled out his gun, quickly releasing the safety. The sound he'd heard had come from the back of the house. Halfway around the house, he found Tom sprawled on the ground near a hedge, holding his shoulder.

"What happened?" Stefanos dropped to a knee, took Tom's hand away and swore as warm blood spilled over his fingers. He folded back the tail of Tom's jacket and applied pressure to try to stop the bleeding.

"Someone was out here already. Guess I startled him. Jeez—" Tom pressed his own hand to the wound. "I don't know where he went."

"Keep up the pressure," Stefanos commanded. He glanced toward the terrace, but shrubbery blocked his view.

The crash of breaking glass suddenly tore through the night. He shot to his feet and rushed toward the sound. A man stood outside the living room, his hand thrust through a hole in one of the French doors. *"Stasi!"* Stefanos yelled. He leapt up the steps to the terrace. "Stop!" he repeated in English.

The figure whirled. To Stefanos, everything seemed to be happening in slow motion. The man had a gun; he was pointing that gun now. Stefanos's mind snapped back and he ducked to the right, falling into the sharp branches of the hedge as he heard a high-pitched ping. His heart hammering, Stefanos steadied himself and fired at the advancing figure.

The man froze, then pivoted and ran. Stefanos fired again, then followed, running as fast as he could. The man disappeared into the shadows. Stefanos stopped, telling himself to be cautious. He took a small step forward. He heard the sound of running feet growing fainter all the time.

Stefanos sighed. He wouldn't be able to catch him now. He set the safety on the gun and went back to Tom.

"Where's the woman?"

"She's still inside, I think." Stefanos knelt beside him. "Can you get to your feet?"

"Give me a hand." Tom's voice sounded thready. Stefanos helped him sit, but Tom groaned.

"Hang on a few more minutes," Stefanos said. "We'll get you to a doctor."

He went back to the terrace, where the door yielded to his touch. The prowler had shot out the lock. He quickly entered and scanned the living room. The coffee tray still rested on the table in front of the sofa, but Molly's bag beside it had disappeared. So had Molly. Where was she?

He tightened his grip on the gun and strode across the room.

She had to get away from him. Molly ran through Stefanos's dark kitchen and tried to block from her mind the image of the man at the windows. She didn't have much time. He would break inside any minute.

She tried the knob of the back door. *Please don't let this one be locked, too. Please!* She tugged on it again, fumbling for a lock to release. The overhead light came on, momentarily blinding her. Molly's heart slammed into her chest. He'd found her.

She cast a frantic glance around, looking for something to use as a weapon—a skillet, a bread knife, anything. The counter lay bare, and her throat closed up. She drew her canvas bag up to her chest and turned slowly, expecting to see the dark man with the off-balance chin.

Stefanos stood in the doorway.

Relief swept through her. Her knees nearly buckled and she braced herself against the counter.

Stefanos's chest rose and fell as if he was trying to catch his breath. "Are you all right?" he asked and walked toward her.

"I'm okay—" She stopped, her throat suddenly dry, her gaze riveted to the mean black gun he held. Had he been carrying a gun all night, and she hadn't known it?

"It's all right," he said slowly. Stefanos slipped the automatic under his jacket and behind his back. The action exposed the large crimson stain on the front of his shirt.

Molly gasped.

"What is it?"

She lifted a hand but couldn't bear to touch his wound. "You're bleeding."

"No." He feathered his fingers across her cheek, the expression on his face so tender, her heart nearly stopped. "But a friend of mine is hurt."

"The man at the window—"

"Got away. Will you help me? I have to get my friend to a doctor."

Molly leaned forward. Surely she'd misunderstood. "Help?"

He nodded and started opening drawers.

Someone was hurt, Molly told herself, trying to dispel the sense of unreality she felt. Stefanos held out a flashlight. Molly took it and asked, "What do you want me to do?"

"Come outside," he answered, then grabbed a stack of clean dish towels. He pulled a key from his pocket and unlocked the door. Molly switched on the flashlight, took a deep breath, and followed him out.

Stefanos checked their surroundings before pointing down the driveway. Her flashlight beam picked out the large bulky shape of Stefanos's friend, and they started toward him.

Blood shone wetly on the man's dark jacket, and Molly gritted her teeth. The guy was so far gone he didn't even open his eyes when Stefanos slipped a folded towel underneath his jacket lapel and against the wound.

She didn't want to look but couldn't help watching Stefanos check the man's pulse with his free hand. Her gaze shifted to take in the man's short, dark hair cut in a military style and his rather unremarkable features. The cold light of the flashlight picked up the grooves etched across his forehead and a little circular scar on his cheek.

That scar. Terror clutched at her. This was the man who'd followed her in New York, the man who'd broken into her apartment. She started to shake, watching helplessly as the beam of the flashlight danced over the shrubbery along the drive.

A voice spoke—a steady, male voice that she knew tried to soothe her. How could she calm down when she felt so clammy and cold? The voice came again. Molly took several deep breaths and directed the beam back to the two men below her, one lying, one crouching.

"What's wrong?" Stefanos signed.

Molly focused on the man on the ground. "He's very dangerous. How could—"

Stefanos shook his head. "Friend," he signed.

She froze. Her burglar was a friend of Stefanos's? One part of her brain yelled for her to get out of there fast. But where could she flee?

Beyond the car in the driveway, darkness shrouded the street. The man who'd tried to break in, the man who must have shot this "friend" of Stefanos's, was still out there somewhere.

She'd gotten a pretty good look at him and knew it had been the same one who'd grabbed her at the taverna. He might be watching her this very minute, waiting for another chance. A shiver slipped down her spine, and she glanced at Stefanos.

She didn't know if she could trust Stefanos to get her out of this mess in one piece, but at least she could understand him. That was better than nothing.

Chapter 6

"What are you doing here?" Stefanos signed, his brows drawn into a scowl. "It's not safe."

"Not safe?" Molly scanned the *cafenion* downstairs from the doctor's office where Stefanos had brought the wounded man.

Even now, at eleven o'clock at night, a number of Greek men sat drinking coffee from the distinctive little white cups all cafés in Greece seemed to use. The men paid no attention to her, nor had they earlier, though she'd kept an eye on them.

"I didn't want to wait upstairs." The doctor's apartment with its ornate Victorian furniture and heavy drapes had made her feel imprisoned. "What about your friend?"

"We got the bullet out."

Bullet? She swallowed. Guns, bullets—how had she stumbled into this situation?

Stefanos pulled a notepad from his inside pocket, careful to keep his jacket buttoned across his bloodstained shirt; he wrote something and handed the pad to her. "I think we should be having this discussion somewhere in private."

She looked up at him, and he pointed to the stairs near where she sat at the back of the room. He meant the doctor's upstairs. "Is this man really a doctor?" she asked.

"He's a doctor—from Cincinnati," Stefanos wrote. "Expatriate. His wife is Greek."

She toyed with the handles of her canvas bag. That probably made sense. "But why didn't you take your friend to a hospital?"

"This doctor is capable," he wrote. "If we'd taken him to a hospital, we would have had to report the gunshot wound. You and I would have had to give statements as witnesses."

Her pulse tripped into double time. "That's a problem?"

"Maybe. If you don't want to talk upstairs, we can go to my office at the embassy." He held the notepad so she could read it.

Molly clutched her bag and wished he wouldn't stand right over her. "Are you really with the embassy?"

"You saw my red passport, didn't you? All U.S. personnel attached to embassies carry one like that."

She studied his neat printing on the pad, wanting to believe him but needing him to convince her. Molly frowned. "How do I know it's yours?" Stefanos pulled out his wallet and showed her his embassy ID card. The photo on it matched him perfectly. Molly handed it back to him. "Well..." He gestured toward the stairs. "But I have some more questions."

His brown eyes regarded her almost cynically. She was about to ask why when he lifted his hand. "Fine," he signed resignedly. "I'll answer them if you'll come upstairs."

She stood and gripped her canvas bag firmly. "Okay."

Upstairs in the doctor's living room, they settled on the overstuffed couch decorated with lace antimacassars.

"Who is this man who's wounded? Does he really work with you at the embassy?" Stefanos said nothing, merely massaged the back of his neck, studying her thoughtfully.

Molly crossed her arms. "You did say we'd continue this conversation, Stefanos."

"You remember out in the driveway, you were afraid?"

Molly gave a little laugh, then rubbed her arms. Even through the thick cotton knit of her sweater she felt cold. "I remember vividly."

"Why?" Stefanos signed. "Were you afraid the intruder—" he spelled the word "intruder" "—would come back?"

"No. I recognized the wounded man." She gestured to the room where Stefanos had taken him when they'd arrived. "Not at first, of course. He was wearing glasses and a navy jacket and khaki pants the last time I saw him."

Stefanos raised an eyebrow. "Are you sure it was him you saw?"

Molly stiffened. Was he trying to put her on the defensive? Well, if she'd learned anything in her marriage it was that she didn't want to be put on the defensive. She clasped her hands and placed them precisely in the middle of her lap. "I'm a portrait painter. I have to remember faces to be successful. Will you tell me who he is?"

Stefanos ran a hand through his hair, crossed to a chair and sank down. "He works for the Department of Defense. He's an investigator," Stefanos spelled out.

Molly crossed her arms again. "I don't believe that."

"Why not?"

"You have to have a warrant to search someone's house."

Stefanos frowned. "What are you talking about?"

He looked as though he probably wouldn't believe her. She might as well try, though. She squared her shoulders. "He knocked me out and ransacked my apartment, or rather the other way around."

"No." Stefanos shook his head. "I'm sure he didn't search your apartment."

She glared at him.

He returned her gaze with a steady, forthright one.

Molly looked across the room to the filmy curtains at the window. The green and blue neon of the *cafenion* sign outside gave them an eerie glow, she thought absently, wondering if she could be mistaken about this "friend" of Stefanos's.

She hadn't gotten a good look at the man who'd mugged her in her apartment, but she'd had plenty of time to observe the man in the hallway. She'd thought they'd been one and the same. But maybe they weren't? Molly turned back to Stefanos. "Who searched my apartment then? And why?"

"I don't know." He pushed his hands into his pants pockets.

"Well, I did see your friend." She nodded in the direction of the doctor's office. "Why don't you ask him if he saw me?"

He hesitated. "Will you stay here?"

"Yes."

Stefanos left the room. When he returned a few minutes later, a frown pulled his dark brows together. "Tom did see you that night after I brought you home. He was wearing a disguise in order to be accepted by the public and any security guards. After you passed him in the hallway, though, he left by the side door. He was in your building because he'd followed Julian Silver there."

Molly shook her head. "Julian? Why? Besides, Julian wasn't even there."

"How do you know?"

"Because he told me so." Molly explained about her and Julian discussing that very thing. "Why would your friend be following Julian, anyway?"

Stefanos's dark gaze found hers. "Why didn't you report the break-in to the police?" he asked, ignoring her question.

"I did." She walked over to stand directly in front of him. "The apartment security guy called the cops and they came almost immediately."

Stefanos stared at her then turned away.

Molly studied his back, annoyed and hurt. What was going on here? His shoulders slumped. Suddenly she realized the situation might be frustrating for him, too. "Is something wrong?" she asked softly. He turned, looking totally wrung out. Molly's heart turned over. "You look exhausted," she said.

He waved away her concern. "I'm sorry you were mugged, but why didn't you tell me about this break-in before? Like when you got to the airport?"

"You know we didn't have a chance to talk then."

"What about later? On the flight?"

Why was he interrogating her? Molly wondered why she just didn't get up and leave. But with the luck she'd been having, she'd probably run smack into the man who was following her. Besides, her things were still at Stefanos's house. She would like to retrieve them once she'd decided what to do.

"Why does it matter to you, Stefanos?"

He sank onto the couch. "I've got a problem to solve. You could help me by answering some questions for me."

"You mean more questions."

"Whatever. How well do you know Julian Silver?" he asked, speaking slowly.

"He's a friend."

"How good a friend?"

"I don't know what standards you're using. We meet for breakfast or lunch about once a week. He gets me out of the apartment to art openings or to the mall. Sometimes we run errands for each other. It's useful to have a friend like that, don't you think?" she asked, realizing Julian was the only friend she did these things with.

Stefanos shrugged. "How did you meet Julian?"

"He was a friend of Warren's and used to come over for supper a lot. He was fun, and I enjoyed his company. Warren was away a lot at night trying to build up his law practice then—he didn't go into the movie business until later. When Warren and I split, I lost track of Julian until about a year ago when I happened to run into him at a shopping mall. Is that what you wanted to know?" His questioning was starting to make her very nervous.

Stefanos had been turning his cigarette lighter between his fingers. He pocketed it now. "So he's nothing more than a good friend?"

"That's right. In fact, he was the one who suggested I try to get the art commission from Meta-Hellenic." Stefanos eyed her. "It's true. You can ask Julian yourself. He knows all about it and he'll be coming over soon. Maybe even today."

"No, he won't."

And you know everything, Stefanos Metadorakis? "He said he would, said he wanted a vacation. I felt—"

Stefanos took her hands.

"Why are you holding my hands?" she asked, and even she could hear the quaver in her voice.

He released them, and closed his eyes briefly.

"What do you know about Julian that you're not telling me?"

"He's dead," Stefanos said, his expression grim.

"Julian?" She stared at him. "Dead?"

"Yes."

"I don't believe that!" Molly exclaimed.

"It's true," he signed, then nodded.

"It's true," Molly repeated softly, studying the serious expression on Stefanos's face. My God! Julian was dead!

She turned into the corner of the couch, bringing her legs up to curl into a little ball. She thought she felt Stefanos's hand on her shoulder but wasn't sure. She wasn't sure what she was staring at on the end table. She wasn't sure what she was feeling, either.

Julian! He'd been such a good morale booster. She hadn't wanted to acknowledge it, but she'd actually begun to look forward to having his company, especially tonight when Stefanos had started becoming so unpredictable.

Stefanos's arm came around her shoulders to clasp her fingers picking at a loose thread in an upholstery seam. How long had she been pulling on it, she wondered distractedly, turning around to face Stefanos.

"Are you okay?" Stefanos asked, moving back slightly.

"I guess. It's just so incomprehensible. Was he in an accident?"

Stefanos shook his head and lifted his hands to sign. "He was murdered in his apartment. The police are still investigating."

Murdered. She felt the blood drain from her face. It was a good thing she was already sitting down. Her knees would have given way if she'd been standing.

She remembered the terror she'd felt when she'd been mugged last weekend. Lord, it must have been ten times worse for Julian. A sick feeling churned in her stomach and Molly closed her eyes and rubbed her forehead. Had the whole world gone crazy?

Stefanos said something. Molly sighed and opened her eyes, catching the concern on Stefanos's face before his expression went blank. Molly frowned. "But—but how do you know what happened to Julian?"

"We've been watching him."

Molly repeated his words, unsure she'd heard them correctly. "Who are you talking about?"

"The United States government," he answered.

Molly stared. What bizarre thing would Stefanos tell her next? "Why?" His mouth flattened, and he gazed across the room as if he'd forgotten she was there. "Why, Stefanos?" she asked again.

He looked at her, his jaw tight. She tensed. "I'm probably going to get my butt kicked for telling you, but Silver has been stealing classified defense information."

"Stealing?" The import of what Stefanos said dawned on her. Molly pressed a hand to her forehead. "That makes him sound like—like a spy."

"That's what he is. We believe his murder was connected with his illegal activities. You knew the work he was doing was for a sensitive defense contract, didn't you?"

"Government work, yes. But—he was selling the stuff to someone?" She sighed. Spying was so far from her normal range of experience, she didn't even know if her question made sense.

Stefanos nodded. "He was. Have you ever heard the name Topolac?"

Molly stroked her hand over the velvet of the couch and thought a moment. "He's the dictator people can't decide about. He's wonderful or terrible, depending on who's talking. You think he's terrible, don't you?"

"He is." Stefanos rubbed his palm. When he caught her watching him, he stopped and his gaze turned hard. "Silver had been selling Topolac vital new technology for almost six months."

"You're kidding!"

He shook his head. "Why do you want the money from the Meta-Hellenic commission?"

"I'm trying to buy Newpark School from the man who owns it now. You met him on Friday. Well, I am buying it now. That is, if I'm still going to get the award." Molly glanced at Stefanos and a sudden fear gripped her. "You think I'm working with Julian, don't you?"

"Are you?"

Molly blinked, then she straightened. "I can't believe you'd think that of me."

He grimaced but then his dark gaze found hers and she shivered. "You're not carrying any—?"

What was the last word? Molly took a deep breath. She had to try to stay calm. When she got upset, she couldn't understand anything people tried to tell her. "What did you ask? I'm not carrying what?"

"Microfilm," he spelled. "That's how Silver was sending the information."

Molly tried to think, but the little panicked messages flashing through her mind were getting in the way. "What does this microfilm look like? Could I have it without knowing?"

"Maybe. Though if you'd seen it, you would have known it wasn't yours."

Molly lifted her bag from the floor. How she held on to it, she didn't know. She felt so numb.

His hands settled on her shoulders, and she looked up at him. "Take it easy," he said.

"How can I? What if we find it in my stuff? You'll charge me with spying, too."

One corner of his mouth twitched. "Let's cross that bridge when we get to it. Okay?"

Yeah, easy for him to say. She knelt on the rug. He sat beside her, which made her feel marginally better. At least she wouldn't have to look up to him.

"Here's my camera." She handed it to him. He started to open the case. "I just put a roll of film in it today, so I know there's nothing else inside it."

He hesitated. "Did you take any photos yet?"

She shook her head. He rewound the film and opened the camera. She waited, gripping her hands together tightly, while he examined the film and the camera. Finally he set them aside and looked at her. The case with her spare hearing aid came next. It had two compartments, one in which she stored the aid and one in which she stored the batteries.

He glanced at the beige-colored aid, then frowned at her. "I thought you needed to wear only one aid."

She nodded. "I keep this old one in case something happens to the new one."

Stefanos nodded, and indicated the second compartment. "What's on the other side?"

"Batteries." She unzipped that side, and he glanced at its contents before picking up her passport wallet. "You don't seem interested," she said.

"Oh, I'm interested," he said, signing "I" and "interesting."

And thorough, too, she thought. He unzipped every compartment in her wallet, looked through the contents of her pencil case and coin purse. He even went as far as taking her hairbrush out of her toiletries bag before pausing and raising an eyebrow. "What else is in here?"

"Toothbrush, case with extra aid batteries, sanitary—"

Stefanos pushed the bag back into her hands and buttoned his jacket.

Molly raised her eyebrows. "You don't want to look through it?"

"I'll take your word for it." He gave her a rueful look.

She suddenly realized he'd been embarrassed. Well, how did he think she felt? she asked him silently, putting things back in her bag.

"Maybe it's in one of my suitcases. Julian was over at my apartment when I was finishing my packing."

"No. Tom didn't find it."

She frowned and caught Stefanos's gaze. "You had him search them?"

Stefanos placed a hand on her shoulder. "I had to, Molly. I had to know if you had it."

She stood. "Is that why you asked me to stay at your house? So you could search my suitcases?"

"No. I was worried about you."

"I'm surprised you would let that bother you." As soon as the words were out of her mouth she regretted them. In a minute he'd get mad and then what would she do? She couldn't leave. He'd follow her. She couldn't go to the embassy, either. He'd be there. Molly started to shake.

Stefanos stood and lifted a hand. Molly held her canvas bag to her chest, wrapping her arms around it. "Don't touch me."

Stefanos sank to the couch and laid his head back against the cushions. He closed his eyes so he wouldn't have to see the fear on Molly's face. He didn't want to hurt her. He . . .

In his mind's eye, darkness closed around him. He'd escaped, and he and Nikos were climbing the mountain. Night shadows swallowed the path ahead as they crept along, careful to stay hidden behind the rock outcrop.

"You will follow the path." Nikos pointed to a row of dark pines along the ridge in front of them. "The border is not far now."

Suddenly the shadows came closer. A soldier appeared before them, rifle in hand. Gunfire exploded into the night. Nikos crumpled to the ground, and Stefanos looked down to see himself holding the rifle. When he glanced up, Molly stood in front of him, terror etched in every feature. She was pleading with him, but he laughed and lifted the rifle to shoot her—

"Are you okay?"

Jolted, Stefanos opened his eyes instantly. Molly was bending over him.

He took a deep breath and wiped the sweat off his upper lip. "Would you ask the doctor's wife for a glass of water?"

She frowned, and he searched his mind for the sign for "water." Finally he remembered it and made the gesture, and Molly left the room.

Stefanos walked to the window. The dream usually came to him when he was asleep. He hadn't been shooting Molly in his dream, either. He slipped his hands into his pockets, not needing to ask why his unconscious mind had produced her image this time.

Molly could be innocent. He remembered her returning the incorrect change to the clerk in the Kennedy Airport newsstand when it would have benefited her not to notice. He recalled her insistence on paying for her plane ticket.

The evidence Leo had was mostly circumstantial. Leo knew Julian suspected he was being watched, so it was reasonable to think he might use someone else to carry the microfilm to Greece. Molly had been seen with Julian when he'd been supposed to meet his contact. She'd deposited money for him. She'd even taken him to his office one of the weekends he'd copied information.

Had Leo been so insistent on his accompanying Molly to Greece only because he also wanted revenge on Topolac? Leo had a good reason. Topolac's thugs had put a couple of bullets into him. Or maybe Leo was embarrassed because he'd failed to catch on to Julian Silver earlier.

Footsteps sounded behind him.

Stefanos turned, took the glass of water Molly handed him, and drained it. Lowering the glass, he gazed at her, taking in her loose-fitting jeans and navy crewneck. She didn't favor fancy clothes and her only jewelry consisted of a nylon-banded Mickey Mouse watch.

Appearances could be deceiving, but if he was to go on Molly's looks, he'd say she was just a woman trying to make a living for herself. Doing it by painting pretty pictures was no less honorable than tilling the soil as Nikos's father had done or shipping freight across the ocean as his grandfather did.

He realized he hadn't said anything since Molly had returned. Setting the glass down, he stepped toward her and brushed a finger across her cheek. Her warm, soft skin under his sent little nervous tingles through his fingers. "Thanks for the water."

She smiled shyly, her mouth parting slightly to give him a glimpse of her white teeth. He felt the corners of his own mouth turning up. Stefanos knew he should look away, but he continued to smile at her. Gossamer threads of warmth swirled around them, binding them together in a sort of glowing cocoon. He needed to stop staring at her, but he could not bear to break this beautiful thing happening between them.

Molly glanced away.

Stefanos stepped back mentally and sighed. "Molly?"

She looked at him. "Did you say something?"

"Why did you wait for me downstairs?" he asked aloud.

"Well..." She smoothed the flyaway wisps from her forehead. "I guess I wanted to give you another chance."

Stefanos took out a cigarette and lit it. "Another chance? Why?"

"I'm wondering if I misinterpreted the situation—the situation at your house," she continued speaking softly. "I do misinterpret sometimes because I don't hear everything. The questions I thought you were asking didn't make sense to me."

"If I confused you, why are you giving me another chance?"

Molly walked to the couch and sat, cupping her hands around her knees. "My instincts about people weren't very good when I was eighteen, but they're pretty dependable now. There was something about you in the beginning that made me feel I could trust you. Even when you annoyed me by being so nosy at my apartment."

"Thanks," he said, meaning it completely.

"If you suspected me of working with Julian, you had me followed, right?"

He nodded. He knew where this question was leading but was too tired to head it off.

"Why didn't you know about my burglary?"

He took a drag on his cigarette, then crushed it in an ashtray. "Because I was supposed to stay with you Friday night, Leo didn't put another tail on you."

"Because you were supposed to stay with me?" She frowned. "Oh, because you didn't want to drive back to New York. Well, I guess you could have stayed, but where would you have slept?"

He wondered if he really had misinterpreted her sexual interest in him that first night or if she was naive. He lifted a shoulder. "I would have slept with you."

Her cheeks colored. "What if I hadn't wanted to go to bed with you?" she demanded.

He gave her a rueful smile, and heard her sharp intake of breath. "It would have been my loss," he said.

"Your loss? Well, I—" She felt sick. Maybe his advances had been just a way to get close to her, just a way to gain information.

"Don't worry about it. What would have happened that night doesn't matter now. My house isn't safe anymore, so I'm going to the embassy. I want you to come with me."

"No, I can find a hotel. I noticed quite a few of them in this part of town. Maybe one is still open. The nightlife seems to go on pretty late around here."

Stefanos shook his head. "I can't let you do that."

"*You* can't?" Her expression turned mutinous.

He wished to high heaven she would just accept that he knew what he was doing and abide by his decisions.

She squared her shoulders. "I need some time alone to get my thoughts together."

"But you're in danger."

"Why? Apparently I don't have the microfilm."

"I want you to understand how dangerous the situation is," he said slowly and signed "very dangerous."

Molly let out a sigh but her mouth flattened. "How could Julian do this to me?"

"I don't know, Molly."

She rubbed her arms and looked away. "I wish I'd never met him."

"That still doesn't change things. Stefanos rubbed at the scars on his palms. "The people who work for Topolac are cruel and vicious. You don't want to know what they can do, believe me."

She caught his hands and held them out, palms up. "They did this to you."

Stefanos pulled his hands from her gentle grip and slipped them into his pockets. "What makes you think that?"

"It's a logical conclusion, don't you think?"

He shrugged a shoulder. "Not particularly."

"What did they do? Cut them up?"

"No, they poured burning oil on them."

"Oh, Stefanos. How horrible," she said, shocked, her face tight with sympathy.

He didn't want her sympathy. "I believe the man you saw at the taverna and my house must be one of Topolac's." Molly looked at him quizzically. He repeated until she nodded in understanding. "Silver was supposed to make one last transfer of data. It hasn't been made yet. We know Topolac is expecting to get it before the NATO conference taking place here in Athens within a few days."

Molly appeared to be thinking about that. "What if Julian never filmed the last batch of information?"

"Topolac would never believe that. Silver probably gave him a date for the handoff. The man following you could be Julian's contact or the man he was going to meet here in Greece."

"Do you think he's the one who killed Julian?" she asked, a furrow pulling her brows together.

"I don't know." Stefanos braced his hands on his hips. Molly's gaze dropped to the front of his shirt. He glanced down, saw the bloodstain and buttoned his jacket.

"Will he kill me?" she whispered, clasping her hands so tightly her knuckles turned white.

She was talking about the man following her. Stefanos lifted his chin in the direction of the doctor's examining room. "He didn't mind shooting Tom," he said.

Her gaze connected with his. "Okay, let's go to your office."

An empty bus lumbered along ahead of them on the broad avenue that would take them to the American embassy. Stefanos passed it, and the murky night once again closed around them. He glanced over at Molly, who sat with her head back, her eyes closed.

Tired or scared?

He hadn't wanted to scare her, but she deserved to know the seriousness of the situation. She'd handled it well, too.

He even admired the way she'd stood up to him at the *cafenion*, though it had been trying at the time. Thank goodness she'd waited for him.

She'd said her instincts had told her she could trust him. And he knew he'd gone with his, too. He would check her story out, of course. That was his job.

Stefanos rolled his shoulders. This was the way he'd felt so many times before his kidnapping. He realized for the first time that he'd gotten himself kidnapped in Lidacros not because his instincts had misled him, but because he hadn't listened to them. He felt his mouth pull into a little smile. He was going to listen to them now.

When they reached the embassy compound, Stefanos stopped at the gate to show the marine on duty his ID, careful to keep his jacket closed. He didn't want to arouse any needless curiosity. The guard nodded and opened the gate. Stefanos noticed Molly watching. He gave her a smile, hoping the marine's acknowledgment would add to his credibility. Maybe now she would accept his decisions without arguing. For the time being, he'd decided she should stay in his office. She needed some sleep, and he had to make some plans.

They walked through the maze of corridors. She preceded him through a door marked Consular, and he led her past a row of desks into his office. "You can sleep here. On the couch. I keep a pillow and blanket on hand for that purpose." He pointed out the door to the bathroom, then went to a chest and pulled open the drawer where he kept a few extra shirts. He took off his jacket and began to unbutton his shirt. "You'll be safe here." He stripped off the soiled shirt and tossed it into the wastebasket. "I'll tell security to post someone in the outer office."

She was staring at him. Stefanos absently rubbed a hand across his bare chest. She lifted her gaze to his and he saw her swallow. He couldn't hear her breathing from here, but she looked a little out of breath.

He reached for a clean shirt, unbuttoned it and pulled it on. "Did you understand me?" he said, signing the words "you" and "understand."

"You want me to sleep here. But what about you?" she asked. "You need to sleep, too."

"Is that an invitation to join you?"

"No." She pushed her canvas bag behind her and propped her hands on her hips. "It was just a question. Do you have to read a sexual meaning into everything I say?"

He knew it would be better if he didn't. "I'll get some sleep." He fastened the last button. "Don't worry about me."

"Are you going back to your house?"

"No."

"Because it's dangerous, huh? That's my fault, I guess. If I hadn't been staying with you, the man from the taverna wouldn't have followed me—"

Stefanos held up his hands. "I expected some danger when I took this job." She still looked upset, though, and he added, "We'll talk some more in the morning."

"Will I be able to get my clothes and things then?"

"We better leave them—" Stefanos stopped when he saw the distress on Molly's soft features. "Don't worry. We'll find some things for you to wear."

She looked disappointed, but she only shrugged. "Fine."

He noticed she hadn't said good. Stefanos tucked in his shirt and stuck his hands into his pockets. "Okay, I'll get them."

"Then I should go with you. You said it would be dangerous to return to your house."

"Are you going to protect me?" he asked, amused.

"Is that ridiculous?" Molly tucked a strand of hair behind her ear, then sighed. "I guess it is. But I don't want anything to happen to you."

He clasped her shoulders, drawing her close and stifling the urge to slip his hands all the way around her. "I've been told I'm a pretty good shot."

She gazed up at him, her blue eyes fierce. "You were shooting at the prowler at your house. You didn't hit him."

"I wasn't trying to kill him."

She gave him a knowing look. "You would say that, of course."

He smiled in spite of the seriousness of their discussion and let her go. "Okay, I'll take someone with me."

Stefanos left the office, shutting the door behind him and leaning against it. How had he let the situation slip away from him again? He'd been planning to act professionally for the first time all evening. Instead, he'd let her get to him, let her make him smile, let her make him want her. Wanting her was going to be a problem, especially if she checked out okay.

Moving from the door, he went in search of a phone. He needed to call the States and substantiate Molly's story. Flint's California office had confirmed the man's reasons for being in Greece, but now Stefanos wanted to know more about Molly's marriage to him.

And that was important? Stefanos curled his hands into fists. His mission was to keep Topolac from getting information to build sophisticated aircraft. It had nothing to do with Molly's emotional life.

Stefanos uncurled his fingers and let out a sigh. He still wanted to know.

The next morning Molly put her sketch pad on Stefanos's desk. If he were here, he'd probably center it in the middle of his pristine blotter, directly under the row of neatly arranged office accessories and beside the sculpted-glass ashtray and a model of an oceangoing vessel.

She hadn't had much inclination to look around last night, she'd been too exhausted—and scared. She lifted a hand to her aid to make sure it fit snugly in her ear, knowing she really had been frightened even though she'd tried not to let Stefanos see it. Why not? She could trust him now, couldn't she? Yes, otherwise she never would have agreed to sleep in his office of all places.

She scanned the office now, noticing her two suitcases near the door before turning back to his desk, taking in the framed baccalaureate and law degrees hung on the wall behind his desk. She could be standing in some lawyer's office back home, she thought, and her shoulders relaxed at the comfort of familiarity.

Her gaze dropped to the two photographs on the file cabinet behind his desk, one of a group of men in some ornate, palacelike room and one of Stefanos shaking hands with the President. He took pride in his career, but she knew that already.

Like his house, his office was personal and impersonal at the same time, as if he was afraid to show too much of himself. Stefanos's reluctance to reveal anything to her made sense now that she knew about his assignment to stop Julian's espionage. She still had trouble thinking of Julian as a spy—and getting killed because of it.

Julian might have dragged her to a similar fate. He still might. He might even have intended to let her take the rap. A shudder went through her, and Molly rubbed her arms through the cotton of her sweater. She had really misjudged Julian Silver, and she'd been trying so hard to make good judgments about people. If only she'd heard more—

Molly swallowed. If-onlys were a waste of time. She needed to stop agonizing over her gullibility and start thinking seriously about how she was going to get out of this mess.

Daylight glowed around the edges of the drawn blinds. She walked to the window and opened them. What a lousy view! Stefanos's office overlooked the parking lot and the guard station at the entrance. She gazed beyond the gate to the other side of the avenue where patches of various colors showed through the trees. Residences, she figured, though the area looked strangely unoccupied. In a residential neighborhood she would have expected to see more than one car parked on the street.

The awareness of someone else's presence suddenly rippled through her. Molly turned with a smile, expecting to see Stefanos. Holding a sheaf of papers, Stefanos's assistant stood just inside the door. Molly swallowed her disappointment and managed to say hello.

"What are you doing here?" Claire Green asked, walking toward her.

"What am I doing here?" Molly repeated. "Waiting for Stefanos, actually."

The brunette's gaze narrowed. "I thought you were supposed to be painting."

Molly pushed her hands into the pockets of her jeans. "I'm mostly doing sketches and taking photographs here to use back home in the studio." Did she really have a commission or was it just a setup?

Claire crossed to Stefanos's desk.

Molly could hear her saying something. "You remember I don't hear that well. If you could—"

The woman looked up. "How long have you known him?"

"Stefanos?" Molly shrugged. "Only a few days."

Claire smiled at her. "Oh, then you're not friends?"

Were they? Molly put her sketchbook in her canvas bag. She thought of the way Stefanos had kissed her on the plane, of the way he'd held her in the Rome airport. They'd been through enough to be friends, but a sexual awareness kept getting in their way. She couldn't forget he was a man. Ever.

Molly crossed her arms and lifted her shoulders. "No, I wouldn't say we were friends."

The other woman nodded. "I see. Do you want some coffee?"

"No, I—"

The office door opened wider. Stefanos sailed in and gave them both a smile.

His gaze lingered on her longer, Molly thought, noting his impeccably tailored gray suit. He'd looped a tie around his neck, and at the unbuttoned collar of his blue oxford shirt, dark chest hair curled toward his throat. With a flood of heat, she remembered how that hair spiraled across his chest. He had a magnificent chest, and—

Molly reined in her thoughts. She might not be able to forget he was a man, but she needed to think of him just as she would any other man.

He exchanged a few words with his assistant before she left, then placed two foam cups on his desk. "I made some calls last night," he signed. Molly tensed. "I talked with the director of Newpark School and also with your banker. Can you understand me?"

She nodded, but rubbed a hand down her hip, wishing he could speak faster to her for once.

"They both confirm what you've said."

"I'm in the clear now?"

"Based on what I've learned so far."

The diplomat again, Molly thought with disgust. She'd really appreciate it if he'd say something definite. Stefanos opened the bathroom door and started to knot his tie. She watched him. He caught her gaze in the mirror and smiled, and she felt somewhat relieved. "You look almost as fresh as a daisy."

"Don't feel that way," he said, and she read his speech from the mirror. In the quiet she could hear his voice, and the sound of it left her invigorated. She felt the same thrill from hearing anybody's voice so plainly, she told herself.

"I see you got my luggage. Thanks. Nothing happened at your house then?"

"No. No unexpected visitors."

Their gazes met in the mirror again. "You sleep okay? The street traffic bothers me sometimes. Not too noisy for you?"

"Too noisy?" She laughed. "If it was, I wouldn't have noticed."

The mirror reflected the wry flattening of his mouth. "I forget about that sometimes."

"About my hearing?" she asked incredulously.

"The implications of it."

"Really?"

Stefanos nodded, shifted the knot snugly into his collar, and came over to her. A mischievous smile brought his dimple to life. He touched his tie. "Is it straight?"

Molly held up her thumb imitating an artist judging perspective and laughed. This felt normal, she thought, wonderfully normal. She lowered her arm and became thoughtful. There was nothing ordinary about the current circumstances.

The teasing glint vanished from his eyes. "I brought us some coffee."

"Thanks." She took a sip from her cup, letting the hot, fragrant liquid warm her insides, then set her cup down and opened her sketchbook. "I drew a sketch of our prowler. Maybe it will help you identify him."

A serious expression settled over Stefanos's handsome face, and he took the book from her. Molly watched him study the drawing, wondering what he was thinking and mentally tracing the sweep of his dark lashes against his tanned cheek.

He lifted his gaze, unveiling his compelling, brown eyes again. "I need some copies of this."

She tore it from the book and handed it to him. "Take it. I don't want it."

"No, I suppose not." He left the office.

Molly walked to the windows and looked out again, wondering what would happen next. She wanted to get out of there, and she especially wanted to get away from Stefanos.

It would be so easy to let her emotions go, to really care for him, and she knew such a relationship wouldn't work out. She wanted a man who would long for her companionship and place his feelings for her above all else. Stefanos was too self-sufficient, too confident, too in control to ever need anyone.

Besides, she had a commission to do for Meta-Hellenic. At least she hoped she still did. Perhaps her getting the award had been a sham, too.

Someone came up behind her. Molly jumped, then turned to find Stefanos. "Hey, you scared me."

"Sorry." He reached around her and closed the blinds, his sleeve brushing her shoulder. In the dimness of the room, he seemed too close, and the moment too intimate. Molly stepped back from the window and pushed her hands into her jeans pockets. "Do I still have the art commission from Meta-Hellenic?"

"What makes you ask?"

"You thought I was involved in Julian's espionage. That's why you came out to New Jersey and why you escorted me to Greece. Right?"

He nodded.

She gave a little shrug. "I'm wondering if anything you told me is true."

Stefanos ran a hand through his hair. "Yes, you still have the commission. Anything else?" he asked, raising an eyebrow.

She nodded. "At the taverna when I told you about the man grabbing me, you seemed to believe me because you helped search for him. But then at your house afterward, you questioned whether or not I really had seen someone. Why?"

"I had to assume there was a man and look for him, but I wasn't sure you were telling the truth. At that time I still thought you were Julian Silver's partner."

Partner—in crime, she added silently. Stefanos had been doing a job, she told herself. It was a worthy job, an important one.

He'd been using her, too. She grimaced. "Did you lie to me about having to carry documents over to the ambassador?"

"I was carrying documents. They pertained to Topolac and the espionage."

"Okay," she said, then sighed. "I guess diplomats don't really lie." Stefanos's expression turned grim, but she couldn't stop. "They just twist things."

"Molly—"

"What about kissing me? Was that part of being a diplomat, too?"

"No!" he said, his gaze intense. "The kisses were not part of the job," he signed.

"You weren't trying to seduce me?"

His mood suddenly shifted, his gaze darkening. A ripple of warmth washed through her. Stefanos touched a finger to the tip of her chin. "Did you want to be seduced?"

Chapter 7

Stefanos imagined exactly how he would go about seducing Molly. He could do it here in his office. To start he'd slip that cotton sweater up, brushing his hands against her breasts and watching her blue eyes shimmer with the heat building inside her, the heat she felt—for him. Then he'd plant wet kisses along the smooth column of her neck and—

"I've never seduced anyone in my life," Molly said.

He doubted that. Stefanos lifted the lid from the coffee he'd brought in from the canteen. He was about to take a sip when he noticed her frown.

"Why did you think that?" she asked, her voice tight. "Because I went to your house after the hotel reservation mix-up?"

Stefanos set his coffee down. He'd meant to tease her, not embarrass her. "No. I knew you were uneasy about something. For all I knew, you might have been uptight about the possibility of running into your ex-husband again. I guess that's when I started worrying about you."

She stared at him and he signed, "Did you understand me?"

"You were worried about me," she murmured, nodding as she spoke.

She made it sound as if he cared about her. Maybe he had made it sound that way, but he had to get her mind onto another subject. "I don't understand something, Molly."

She sat down in one of the chairs facing his desk. "What?"

"You felt scared at the airport and at the restaurant last night." She nodded. He rested a hip on the corner of his desk. "Why didn't you say so?"

"At that time, I couldn't decide if you were like Warren or not. I thought if I let you know I was afraid, I'd be showing you a weakness. It would have given you a way to manipulate me. Warren did that. He was very good at it, too. You are definitely in his class as far as being able to control a situation."

He clenched a hand and pressed it into the desktop. He didn't want to be compared to her jerk ex-husband in any way. "I wasn't manipulating you."

"You were telling me only what you wanted me to know," she said.

"Of course."

"Forget it, Stefanos. I know that must just be part of your job."

What she meant was that she'd been honest with him and he should have been honest with her out of common decency. Stefanos stood and walked to the window with its drawn blinds, wishing her words didn't hurt so much.

"Tell me about Nikos." Molly had left her seat to stand beside him. "Is he a favorite nephew or something?"

"Why do you want to know?" Molly stepped back as if he'd struck her. "Sorry," he signed and rubbed a hand across his mouth. "I'm supposed to be a diplomat and yet I'm making a mess out of this conversation with you."

She chewed on her lower lip.

"Molly?"

He lifted her braid and tucked it behind her shoulder. He hadn't meant to make her feel responsible for his confusion.

She lifted her gaze to him, vulnerable and apologetic. "Did you say something?"

He took a breath, hoping he could find the right words to make her understand and accept his actions. "I came into this case thinking you were a spy. I wanted to hate you."

"Because you wanted to do something to get even for the torture?"

"Partly," he said and finger-spelled the word. Molly raised her eyebrows. He was not going to tell her what he owed Nikos. She'd never set foot out of the building with him then. "My instincts," he said aloud, making sure she followed what he said, "were telling me you couldn't be involved in this espionage, but I didn't think I could trust my instincts anymore. Besides," he said and shook his head, "even when I fought it, I found myself liking you and admiring you for the way you handled your hearing problem. I had to be doubly sure my own feelings were not misleading me."

"And so all this was terrifying for you, too," Molly concluded.

He shrugged. "About the boy," he said, bringing the conversation around to Nikos again. "I didn't mean to jump on you. I'd prefer not to talk about him. Okay?"

"Sure."

Good. They could get this relationship back on a businesslike footing again. He indicated her suitcases. "Do you want to change before we leave?"

"I suppose I better."

He glanced at his watch. "Why don't you drink your coffee and change? There's a C-141 flight coming in from Germany this morning, and—"

"A C-141? Is that what you said?"

"Yes," he signed and explained, "A C-141 is a type of military plane used for embassy mail and supply runs. This one will take us back to Germany, from which this embassy is serviced. When the microfilm is found and things settle down, you can return to New Jersey from there."

Molly crossed her arms. Stefanos started to cross his own but shoved his hands into his pockets, instead.

"You didn't ask if I wanted to go," she said.

"That's true. I had to make plans while you were asleep."

"I don't mind being asked my opinion, you know."

Why couldn't she just accept his protection? She was his responsibility. "I know," he said, trying for calm when he felt like throwing her over his shoulder and carrying her out the door.

She caught his gaze and made a vague gesture with her hand. "I thought I should do some work on the Meta-Hellenic award if I could. They wanted the commission finished this fall."

"They can wait."

"But—" she started, her blue eyes anguished.

"Molly."

"Did you say something?"

"Your name," he signed and smiled. "If we're going to catch this plane, we don't have time to discuss the decision in detail."

Her shoulders sagged. "Okay. I guess your plan is the best one for right now."

"Good," he answered.

"You sound like me," she said and gave him a smile back. "That's what I always say."

Stefanos straightened, feeling dismayed. He'd never picked up someone else's expressions before, certainly not since he'd become a professional negotiator. Well, there had been nothing professional about the way he'd handled this conversation with Molly.

Maybe relating to her in a personal way wasn't bad? He swore under his breath at his indecision. Of course it was bad.

Molly splashed water on her face, then reached for the hand towel, pausing as she wiped her cheeks. She held the towel away from her, then smelled it again. Yes, the terry cloth smelled like Stefanos—musk mixed with a tangy citrus smell that suited him and his background. She folded the towel, thinking about his heritage and wondering if he'd rejected a job with the family company.

Maybe he'd never been offered one because his family had found out what a difficult man he was to work with. He was certainly a difficult man to understand.

As she brushed her hair, she thought about Stefanos's defensive reaction to her question about Nikos. In fact, she'd introduced the subject only to take his mind off his embarrassment. And her questions about his honesty *had* embarrassed him. Why had she persisted?

She put her brush away and changed into a long-sleeved white shirt. She hadn't really been angry that he'd used her; it was more that she was disappointed in herself. She'd wanted him to like her and there lay the problem. Maybe it wasn't bad to want someone's appreciation and admiration, but a fine line separated wanting it from needing it so badly she imagined it in the other person's every word or gesture.

Molly resolved to keep any future conversations with Stefanos objective. That was only fair, really.

It wasn't solely his fault she'd come under suspicion. She could have confided in him more, she thought, stepping into the outer office, where several women worked on an impressive array of computers, fax machines and who knew what other kinds of high-tech equipment.

Stefanos stood beside his assistant's desk. When he saw her, he broke off his discussion and joined her. As he guided her out of the office, bags in hand, Molly caught the look of disgust on Claire Green's face.

What had she been thinking about, Molly wondered, stopping when Stefanos paused by a water fountain near the exit. "Your assistant thinks I'm connected with what Julian was doing, doesn't she?"

"No, she knows nothing. Unless you mentioned it to her." He raised one dark brown eyebrow. "Did you?"

"No." Molly watched him take a small white envelope from his pocket. He tapped two tablets from it into his palm. "Your hands hurt, don't they?"

"A little." He shrugged a shoulder, then crumpled the envelope and dropped it into a waste bin.

It was more like a lot, she thought, watching him toss the painkillers back and bend to sip from the fountain. "I'm sorry they hurt," she said, fighting the urge to touch him.

He smiled wryly. "I'll live. Why did you ask about Claire?"

"I think she's jealous."

Stefanos shrugged. "I told you back in New Jersey that I had no one," he reminded her.

Her pulse sped up. Did his insistence that she know mean he was interested in pursuing a relationship with her? Molly forced herself to calm down. Where was her resolve?

He was a strong man. He would have had to be to survive the torture he must have endured. And his emotions were intense, too. Sometimes she could see them positively burning in his brown eyes. They intrigued her, but she'd be safer leaving them alone. That shouldn't be hard to do. After all, they would be going their separate ways in a few hours.

In twenty-four hours at the outside, Molly would be gone from his life.

Stefanos glanced over at her in the car's passenger seat. The sunlight set her golden hair aglow and brought out the fragile pink color in her cheeks. He caught a trace of her delicate scent, and his body responded. It didn't matter what she looked like or what she smelled like, he reminded himself. All that mattered was getting her to safety.

He loosened his tie, wishing he'd worn jeans. The fold-down web seats in the plane's cargo bay would be anything but comfortable. He *would* have been wearing jeans if he hadn't needed the authority a suit and tie gave him when he'd finagled permission to take Molly with him.

Milair didn't like to airlift civilians who weren't U.S. government personnel, but he couldn't chance taking her on a commercial flight. He didn't even like the idea of driving her here and jockeying with the taxis and buses that always seemed to clog the airport entrance.

He finally pulled into the parking lot and let out a sigh. So far so good. Several heads of state were scheduled to arrive this morning for the conference. Their arrivals would add to the congestion. That could be bad and that could be good. The impending arrivals would draw attention away from him and Molly, but the crowd would easily hide anyone following them.

Stefanos glanced around the parking lot, hoping the man who had been after Molly was sitting back in Athens somewhere. The last thing Stefanos wanted here at the airport was to pull his gun. He would if he had to, though.

A click sounded inside the car as Molly pressed the door handle. He reached across to touch her sleeve and get her attention. "We have to walk a little ways. Be careful of the traffic and stick with me, okay?" He refrained from telling her that anyone could see them crossing the exposed parking lot. She already looked worried enough to follow his instructions.

"Fine." She smiled and reached for one of her bags in the back seat.

He shook his head. "We'll move faster if I carry everything." He shouldered the nylon athletic bag with his change of clothes and hefted both of Molly's bags despite her renewed protest.

Molly kept pace with him as they crossed the lot. They had just stepped up on the curb when a limousine pulled up, a small Turkish flag fluttering from its short antenna. Stefanos's pulse jumped. Topolac was due to arrive a few days early. Today?

"Stef—"

He shook his head, hurrying Molly inside and into an alcove near a car-rental booth. No one seemed to notice them, even though Molly's blond hair stood out like a beacon. They were probably fine. He was just overreacting.

Stefanos had just started them toward the main lobby again when he spotted the dark-haired man who had been following Molly.

Every fiber in his body tightened as he shielded Molly from view and watched the man with the skewed face pass them a mere fifteen feet away, his hands in the pockets of his buttoned black jacket. Did he hide a gun?

Stefanos felt Molly look up at him, and he put a finger to his lips even as he kept an eye on the other man, waiting for him to continue walking into the terminal proper. Suddenly the man stopped and scanned the flow of tourists and travelers. Stefanos felt his breath stall in his lungs. Finally, the other man started walking again, and Stefanos looked down at Molly. "He's here," Stefanos whispered.

"What did you say?" she whispered back, a furrow between her brows.

"We need to go outside," he mouthed, wishing he could sign. He wanted to do nothing that would draw attention to them, though. "Maybe we can get to the plane another way." They had no choice now but to find one.

The back of his neck prickled. Stefanos glanced over his shoulder. Molly's pursuer had stopped again. He swept his head around, his gaze passing over them, then coming back. He looked straight at them, and Stefanos felt the other man's spark of recognition.

With fear racing through his blood, Stefanos shifted both bags to one hand, took Molly's elbow and started to run, dodging around the incoming passengers. They ran across the vehicle ramp to the sounds of honking horns and screeching brakes. Molly stumbled. Stefanos steadied her and, glancing over his shoulder, saw the man with the skewed face coming out of the terminal.

Stefanos picked up the pace. They managed to reach the car before a bullet ricocheted off the front fender. Somehow he got them inside the car before another bullet glanced off the side mirror. Holding Molly's head down, he tore out of the lot. In the rearview mirror he watched a black sedan swerve into the lot and pick up the man chasing them, vaguely aware no one was noticing this drama. Why would they?

No one could have heard the shots, Stefanos thought grimly. Topolac's man was using a silencer.

"Where are we going?" Molly asked.

"Embassy," he said, glancing over at her so she could see his mouth. She'd be safe there, even if this guy knew where she was.

Ahead of them stretched a line of cars, their rear lights flickering as they slowed. Stefanos braked and checked the mirror again. The black sedan merged two cars behind them. They'd be okay as long as the traffic kept moving. The car in front of him stopped completely. Stefanos saw the motorcade for some conference dignitaries approaching from the left. He tightened his grip on the steering wheel.

They couldn't wait for the motorcade. In the time it took to pass, Molly's pursuer could be here beside him, pointing a gun at his head and demanding they let him into the car.

A horrible coldness gripped him. Stefanos shook it off. Just ahead an exit veered off to the right. He pulled into it, cutting off the car behind him. "Sorry, fella," he muttered. This would take them in the direction of Piraeus, the port of Athens. From there he could get back— His spirits sank when he remembered the ambassador's busy agenda. It would be impossible to get near the embassy all day.

Molly turned to look out the back window. "We're losing him, I think."

For the time being, maybe, but how much longer? He was going to have to come up with a plan. He glanced at his watch and made an instant decision.

Curling a hand around the warm metal railing of the ferry deck, Stefanos watched the island on the horizon grow larger and more distinct. He glanced at Molly's small, pale hand resting beside his and covered it briefly with his own.

She glanced at him. "That will be Paros," he told her. He looked at his watch. "We'll be there in about twenty minutes." She nodded and went back to watching their approach.

He rubbed the back of his neck, still having trouble believing he and Molly had managed to elude their pursuers. The black car had followed them to Piraeus, but he'd lost it before he and Molly had arrived at the ferry terminal. He hoped.

The little farmhouse he owned on Paros would be a good place to hide. Actually he hadn't been able to think of any other place to take her, not without involving his family. Plus, Takis—a boyhood friend and chief of the small police force on Paros—could help if Molly's pursuer found them.

Stefanos pushed the sleeves of his tan windbreaker up to his elbows, zipped it higher, and felt for the gun in the holster under his arm. He'd changed into jeans and a knit shirt after they'd left Piraeus, knowing his business suit would have made him stand out in the crowd of vacationers aboard the ferry.

Molly turned to him. The wind whipped several strands of hair loose from her braid. She held them back with one hand and shaded her eyes from the sun with the other. "You look worried. I thought you said we'd be okay?"

"I think so, but I don't understand how they figured out I was taking you to the airport," Stefanos signed to Molly.

"I've been wondering about that, too." She squinted as she peered up at him. He offered her his sunglasses, but she shook her head. "The prowler knows where you live. Could you be traced to the embassy from your address?"

"No, the ownership of my house is pretty well hidden, thanks to my family," he said. Topolac's agent—and as he'd told Molly, this man following them had to have some connection to Julian—could try to find him through his grandfather if he were smart enough. Stefanos swore under his breath.

"What did you say, Stefanos?"

"It was a nasty swear word and it's just as well you didn't hear it. Don't look so surprised."

"Why would I be? It isn't just men who use those kinds of words."

Stefanos felt his mouth pull up at the corners. "Do you?"

"Well, no." Her cheeks reddened, and Stefanos wondered if he shouldn't have teased her. She continued, "I don't know too many. Besides, I have to be careful because I don't always know if the words I'm hearing are nasty."

He let his gaze slide over her face and settle on her mouth. "You can say anything you want to me," he signed.

"Well, okay. Maybe someone followed you from your house when you went back to pick up my bags?"

Stefanos shook his head. "I didn't see anyone," he signed. "Nor did the man who was with me."

"But someone could have followed you. When I looked out your office window this morning I saw a car parked across the street. There was only one. That's why I noticed it." She frowned. "Now that I think of it, it could have been that same black car that followed us from the airport."

"Maybe you're right." He tensed, waiting for her to blame him. "I should have asked you if you'd seen anything unusual."

She smiled and her blue eyes softened. "You can't think of everything."

He shrugged. "I'm not afraid to take responsibility."

"That's very obvious."

"Is it?"

She nodded.

He stuck his hands into his pockets, unsure if he liked being so transparent. At least she hadn't blamed him for getting her into this mess. He wondered what she'd say when she saw the farmhouse. It wouldn't be long now.

The ferry had drawn close enough to Paros now that they could see the colors of the land. He swept a glance around the deck, then back to Molly.

She leaned against the rail, studying the view, and Stefanos felt a nervousness starting in his gut. Because he loved the island so much, it was as if Molly was scrutinizing something as close to him as—his hands. He rubbed the ridges of one palm.

She glanced at him, her blue gaze capturing his. He lifted his chin in the direction of the island. "What do you think?"

"It looks so barren, all browns and ochers. I don't remember Greece like this."

He raised an eyebrow. "In the summer it is always dry and brown."

"I was here in the spring," Molly said, catching back a windblown strand of hair. "Everything was green with wheat and hay, and oregano and red poppies were blooming."

"I can see why you liked it then." He thought about the way she'd yielded to him the last time he'd kissed her. "You are soft inside, like the spring."

Molly's mouth dropped open.

Stefanos had to force himself to hold her gaze. He should never have said that. Now she'd know he was thinking about her sexually. Oh, hell, she already did. Stefanos tried to smile. "You're going to catch a fly that way."

She closed her mouth. "I don't know how you can tease me. We're in a dangerous situation, you know."

Stefanos gripped the railing with both hands. *Here they come,* he thought. *Here come the recriminations.*

"Stef—"

He looked at her, mentally bracing himself. "What?"

"I don't know why I said that. I guess I'm just tense."

"It's okay." She wasn't the only one who was tense.

The ferry rounded a headland, and in front of them rose a stack of whitewashed dwellings glowing in the late afternoon sun. In one direction the gleaming white houses tumbled down upon each other to form a long line along the harbor.

He watched a motor scooter zip along the waterfront, then let his gaze lovingly follow the street on up the hill to where a round, whitewashed windmill rose, its triangular white sails stretching from its four arms. *Home,* he thought. It was good to be home.

The deck under his feet vibrated as the ship reversed its engines and started to back into the pier. Gears groaned and the back of the ferry lowered to provide a ramp for cars and passengers.

Stefanos looked down at the people on the pier: men with weather-beaten faces, dressed in black coats and caps; short, stout women in black with the traditional kerchief on their heads; tourists in shorts and sunglasses. Takis was standing with two other policemen, their white uniforms brilliant in the sun.

He touched Molly's arm. The warmth and softness of her skin felt like silk under his fingertips. He couldn't help wondering how *she* felt when he touched her. Did she really feel the same elemental pull he did or was that his ego telling him she did?

Molly lifted her gaze to him, her blue eyes mysterious and beautiful like the sea sparkling in the sun. Stefanos swallowed and spelled, "Takis is the one in the middle."

She glanced at where he pointed, nodded and picked up one of her suitcases. A few minutes later Takis strode toward them down the pier, looking all business except for the smile in his dark eyes.

Stefanos waved. "You are looking for someone, maybe?"

"*Yasou*, Stefanos," Takis said and embraced him. "It is too long you wait to come back."

"I was here two months ago," Stefanos responded in Greek.

Takis shook his head. "Sofia wants to cook her special moussaka again."

"I'm afraid she will have to wait a little longer." Stefanos stepped back, put an arm around Molly's shoulders and drew her toward Takis, noticing as he did so the nonchalant watchfulness of the other policemen. He made a fast survey of the dock, then introduced Molly.

Takis shook hands with her, then winked at him.

"I'm only protecting her for a few days," Stefanos muttered in Greek, looking down at the woman beside him. Her braid had started to come undone. A smile tugged at his mouth. She ought to give up trying to keep her hair tamed, and wear it loose.

One of the other policemen stepped forward and took Molly's bags. They followed him off the pier.

"We expected you two weeks ago," Takis said in a low voice as they all walked toward the street that would take them into the heart of the little town.

"I had to go to New York," Stefanos said, gripping the handles of his own bag more tightly.

"It is your grandfather, right?"

"How did you know?"

"Word travels. Do you want to come—" Takis stopped walking, as did the other policemen. Stefanos noticed a rapid, darting movement in the group of travelers clustered in the street and slipped his hand inside his jacket. A child burst through and ran toward him. Stefanos withdrew his hand and zipped his jacket. "He was not supposed to come here," Takis said.

Stefanos frowned. "Is he being too much trouble?"

"Oh, no," Takis protested. "But—"

"But Nikos will have to learn to mind better," Stefanos finished for him.

The boy raced up to him. Stefanos didn't want to encourage Nikos's affection, but he couldn't keep himself from dropping to one knee to accept the child's embrace. "Stefanos, Stefanos! How long are you staying? Can you stay until my birthday? Are you going to go with us to Pisso Livadi?"

"So many questions!" Stefanos held the child away from him so the boy wouldn't notice the holster and gun and ask him about them. He wanted to put on a stern face and scold the boy. Instead he laughed. "Look at you, growing so tall. And you are only nine."

"Almost ten, you forget."

"No, I don't forget." Stefanos ruffled the boy's hair, then stood. "Say hello to Molly."

Nikos stared up at her as if he'd just become aware of her presence. "She's nice."

"*Ne.*" Yes, Stefanos thought. She was nice, one of the nicest persons he'd ever had anything to do with. Stefanos caught Molly's gaze and spelled out the youngster's name.

"Nikos." She held out her hand, and Nikos shook it solemnly.

Takis patted the boy on the shoulder. "Go home now."

"Yes. Go home," Stefanos said. "We will talk later."

The boy ran off and disappeared in the grove of eucalyptus trees beside the village school. Stefanos let out a sigh and turned to Takis. "I'd like to get out to the house. Give Molly time to get used to it before dark."

And time to get used to the fact she'd be spending the next few days with him in a very small house, he added silently. He had the sneaking suspicion he was going to have a harder time adjusting to having Molly there than the other way around.

* * *

It was a good place to hide, all right. Molly shaded her eyes against the afternoon sun and looked across the small clearing to a one-story, whitewashed, rectangular house. Thick cane grew tall on either side of the wide dirt path they'd walked on from the main road. It also fenced off the area around the dwelling.

Boy, did the place feel isolated.

Well, what did she expect? It just wasn't the city, she told herself, glancing at Stefanos and the policeman who'd come with them. Though she'd seen several motor scooters in town, she and the policeman and Stefanos had walked, Stefanos having assured her that going on foot would be the least conspicuous way to get here.

An arbor graced the side of the house facing her, its beams green with the broad leaves of a grapevine. She could even see some small, ripening clusters of grapes. A low wall protected the arbor on one side of the open, paved patio in front of the house.

On the opposite side of the house stood several small structures. She pointed them out now. "What are those?"

He rubbed a hand over his mouth, then spelled, "The well and an old stable. The one toward the back is the—"

"Outhouse?"

He nodded, twisting his lips wryly. "Sorry about the lack of plumbing."

"If you can stand it, so can I." What she wasn't sure she could stand was the feeling of being defenseless. She gazed down the dusty track. "You pointed out the beach from the road. This is the way to the beach?"

"Yes," Stefanos signed. "It's not public, and there is no other road to it."

"Someone could still get to it, I'll bet."

"The water is very shallow there and the hills are too covered with rocks and brush." Stefanos looked as though he'd say something more, but suddenly held a finger to his lips.

The policeman seemed to be listening, too, and she strained to hear something unusual.

What was that? The wind in the cane behind them? The waves on the beach Stefanos had said was close? Were they close enough to hear that? Molly waited nervously for the men to move again, telling herself Stefanos would never have brought her here if it wasn't safe.

The policeman finally spoke again, then made a circuit of the clearing. Molly's heart pounded at the thought that someone might be lurking close by. The officer returned, smiled, and shook Stefanos's hand.

Molly watched him start down the dirt track back to the main road, already feeling isolated. Stefanos touched her arm. "Come on, I'll show you the house," he said.

"Okay." Molly lifted her art bag and followed him toward the entrance, its narrow double doors painted blue, a darker blue than his shirt.

She glanced at him walking beside her. The shirt contrasted nicely with his tanned skin, the color enhancing his vibrantly male presence. His open collar exposed the slight bump of his Adam's apple in the strong column of his throat. He looked dangerous, especially with the darkening shadow of his beard.

A shiver slipped through her at the thought of staying out here alone with him. He'd talked about her being soft, his gentle voice and steady gaze raising goose bumps all over her. She knew what sort of softness he'd been referring to.

That he found her attractive now when he had nothing to gain from it filled her with a new excitement. Well, not exactly new. She'd felt this sexual nervousness as a teenager, but not for a long time, not since she'd failed to make Warren happy.

Warren was in the past. Yes, she knew that. What she didn't know was whether or not she'd fail with Stefanos. Excitement was one thing and a man's expectations another.

She set her bag down to hitch her shoulder bag higher and regarded the little flat-roofed whitewashed house. She must be crazy to be even thinking about making love with Stefanos. They were on the island to hide.

She hoped he was right about their being safe here.

Chapter 8

Later that evening, Molly was still worrying about their safety. She'd tried to tell herself she was letting her overactive imagination run wild. She'd reasoned that Stefanos wouldn't have brought her there if he hadn't thought it safe, but he might not have had any other place to take her.

She glanced at Stefanos standing at the small, butane-fueled, two-burner stove and studied the way the light from the kerosene lamp caught the reddish highlights in his hair.

Maybe Stefanos worried, too. He'd been very quiet since they'd arrived at the farmhouse. Oh, he'd said a few words when he'd handed her the thick blue-and-white striped sheets from an old leather suitcase in the back room, but then silence had descended, a silence that made the ringing in her ears sound so much louder.

They really hadn't had a need to talk, she supposed, watching him pour hot water from the copper hourglass pot he'd called a *briki* into the top of an old, drip coffeepot. She'd made the beds, one in each of the house's two rooms, while Stefanos had gotten water from the well and made a simple dinner of omelets, bread, fresh apricots and figs.

With every passing minute, though, he seemed to withdraw more. Maybe he was just tired or maybe— "Are you afraid?" she asked.

"No," Stefanos signed behind his back, then faced her. "I'm not afraid. Are you?"

Molly paused. He was speaking, and she needed a minute to be sure she understood him. When she did, she glanced first at the recessed window, its strong inside shutters closing out the night, then at the double doors across which Stefanos had placed a long, flat, steel bar. Both the window and doors looked as if they could provide solid protection. So why did she feel fear quivering through her?

"Cold?" Stefanos asked.

"It's because of the walls, I think. They must be three feet thick."

"Probably. The coffee will be ready in a moment, but..." Stefanos took his windbreaker off a nail in the wall and draped it around her shoulders.

"Thanks."

He rested his hands on her shoulders a moment, and Molly couldn't keep from reaching up to touch his hand. The hair between his knuckles slipped beneath her fingers like hot silk, and a shiver of another kind shimmied through her.

He squeezed her shoulders, then walked back to his chair. She wanted to tell him to come back and put his hands on her shoulders again, wanted to tell him to stroke her neck where a knot of tension had hardened. It would feel so good, but that would be asking for trouble, trouble she wasn't sure she was up to handling.

As soon as they finished their coffee, she should call it a night. Even if her worries kept her awake, at least she wouldn't have to also be on guard with Stefanos. He'd made a definite point of telling her they both needed their sleep . . . but he'd taken liberties with her before.

Molly glanced around the room while Stefanos tended to the coffee. Besides the table at which they sat, the two chairs and Stefanos's bed, the room contained a built-in corner cabinet and a makeshift table on which rested a stove and a plastic dishpan. Two lighted kerosene lamps hung from nails in the whitewashed wall, the only decoration except for the small, plastic-rimmed mirror hanging from another nail.

Never in a million years would she have matched this farmhouse with Stefanos. With his expensive tastes, she could more easily see him in a villa on the French Riviera.

She hadn't pegged him as someone who liked being alone, either. Though she'd noticed some other farmhouses up in the hills behind the road, they'd passed none on the coast side before reaching Stefanos's.

"I'm surprised you don't get lonely here." Molly propped her feet on a rung of her chair. "Away from the town and everything."

"Loneliness is a condition of life, at least for me." He set the coffeepot on the table and took two white porcelain mugs from the cabinet. Light gleamed on their shiny finish when he came back within the lamplight. "I take it you would not want to be alone."

"I'm used to being alone, even when I'm with someone. It's a condition of my hearing loss," she said, paraphrasing his words. "But I'd rather be around people."

He turned his chair around and straddled it, leaning over it to cradle his mug. He would have looked totally relaxed if he wasn't lightly tapping the side of his mug.

She tilted her head questioningly. "You usually come here alone, don't you?"

"How did you know?" Stefanos frowned briefly, then ran a hand through his hair. "I mean, yes, I usually come alone. I'm surprised you could tell."

"I'm getting to know you," she said.

Molly took a sip of coffee and savored the warmth of it sliding down her throat. He obviously felt vulnerable. He wasn't comfortable with that feeling or with letting her know about it, but it made her feel closer to him.

She reminded herself that she didn't need to feel closer to him. Not now when the isolation of the little house seemed to be spinning a cocoon of intimacy around them, an intimacy in which every word, every gesture, every breath they drew sparkled with possibilities.

Stefanos stared into his mug a moment, then looked up. "You know why I like it here?"

"No, why?" She propped her chin on her hand, pleased he made an effort at conversation.

"I can be myself. I don't have to pretend to be anyone else." His chest rose and fell as if in a sigh. "I don't have to think about how I'm affecting others."

She added a spoonful of sugar to her coffee, stirring slowly. "You have to do a lot of role-playing in your work, I suppose."

"Yes."

Molly regarded the tight lines at the corners of his mouth, and a similar tension pulled in her chest. He could be himself when he was alone, but she wanted—no, needed—him to be himself with her. "Are you playing a role now?" she asked, holding her breath.

He raised one eyebrow, and Molly couldn't keep from tracing the shiny, dark brown curve in her mind. His gaze snagged hers, "The proper host, I hope."

"Couldn't ask for a better one." She smiled, hiding her disappointment. "I don't really see that as a role, though."

One corner of his mouth pulled up shyly. The gesture sent tenderness spilling from her heart out into every pore. Molly started to reach across the table to touch his hand but caught herself in time. Half of her wanted to find and experience the warmth and intensity within Stefanos and the other half knew it would be a big mistake.

He seemed not to notice her hesitation and, in fact, gazed again into his coffee. She tried to ignore the disappointment still brewing inside her.

"I don't know if coffee was such a good idea. At least for me." He unbuttoned several buttons of his shirt. "It's pretty warm in here, isn't it?" The shirt gaped open, giving her a glimpse of his chest, his hair a dark contrast to the soft blue fabric. Molly swallowed and curled her fingers through the handle of her mug.

"I don't find it uncomfortable in your farmhouse." She paused. "You know, I can't picture you as a farmer."

He laughed. "No. We are sailors," he said, spelling out the last word when she couldn't understand his speech. "I will soon be going back to the ships, too."

She raised her eyebrows. "Back to the ships? What do you mean?"

"I'll be working for Meta-Hellenic again soon. Probably in New York." He looked at her.

She smiled, not sure what he was thinking. Perhaps he wanted to see her after all this was over? Her heart skipped a beat and then another one. If he was going to be in New York, maybe she could persist in this attraction. No, she reminded herself, Stefanos was too sophisticated, socially and sexually, for the likes of her. That was the bottom line and she needed to remember it. It would be too easy to fail his expectations, and she wanted at least a fighting chance with the next man in her life.

"Anyway," he interrupted her thoughts, "my family rents the fields here to real farmers." Stefanos smiled wistfully, then turned his chair around and sat again. He stretched his long legs out beside the table, crossing his running-shoe-clad feet at the ankle. "This house comes to me from my father's grandmother. Her family were the farmers."

"Do you ever see your family?"

"Sometimes."

"You mentioned your mother?"

"No," he said and signed it with a sharp gesture of his hand, his face hard. "No, I never see her, which is fine with me. She's married to a lawyer in San Francisco."

"Well." Molly stood and draped Stefanos's windbreaker on the chair. His stony expression made her uneasy. It suggested he disliked all women or all mothers. That couldn't be true, could it? "You have your own life," she said and picked up her plate and mug. "I'll do the dishes."

"No." Stefanos pushed back his chair.

"We've had a long day, Stefanos, and you haven't slept since who knows when."

He cupped her chin in his broad hand. Molly let her plate slide into the water of the dishpan and held her breath, watching Stefanos's mouth. She willed him to say something so she could stop thinking about his kissing her. "You couldn't have slept very well in my office, either." He released her chin. She expected to feel relieved; instead she felt anxious—anxious for him to touch her again. He hooked his thumbs in his belt loops. "We'll have time to do the dishes tomorrow."

Tomorrow, she thought, glancing around. The shadows in the room seemed to grow larger with every passing second. She didn't want to think about going into the back room. Stefanos would be close, though. Very close, in fact.

Molly watched him clench one hand into a fist. She tensed and laid her hand on his chest. "Is there something you're not telling me?"

He raised an eyebrow but merely signed, "No."

The heat of his skin came through his shirt. She could even feel his crisp chest hair under the soft cloth of his shirt. Why was she touching him when she'd been trying not to all evening? Because, she told herself, she needed to know—really know physically—that he existed, that he was strong and capable, that he wouldn't desert her.

"So you're not worried now?" she asked, thinking the question a formality, but needing to hear his assurance again.

His brown eyes held hers, their orange specks glowing in the lamplight. "I will worry until we know you are safe."

"Right," Molly said and smoothed a few errant wisps of hair from her forehead. They weren't safe yet because someone was still chasing them, the someone who'd been shooting at them at the airport. Suddenly cold, she rubbed her arms without looking at Stefanos. "Well, I did want you to be honest," she said. "May I take one of the lamps?"

"Yes," he signed, "that's fine. By the way, Takis will come out later. He's going to make sure our prowler isn't staying here on the island at any hotel or camping site."

"Takis would come out tonight?" she asked, her voice trembling as she thought of walking down the dirt track to the house in the dark.

Stefanos took her by her shoulders. Molly looked up at him. He smiled at her, and his hands slipped down to her hands. "You don't like Takis?" he asked.

"It's not that. He's very nice. I was just thinking about us being so far out of town."

"It's only about two miles, and people can run a mile in less than ten minutes. Don't worry." He tugged her hands around his waist, pulling her against him.

She lowered her cheek to his chest, wondering what it would be like to hear his heart. She'd heard people say they could hear someone's heartbeat. Stefanos's would be strong, steady, dependable. Did it beat a little faster because he was holding her? She didn't really want to know, she told herself.

"I don't want to worry, but—" she started to say but stopped when his hands urged her back. She automatically looked up at his mouth, waiting for his words.

"I want to—" he said.

"You want something?"

"To kiss you. May I?" he said, lowering his mouth until it was only a few inches from hers.

He wanted to kiss her. A fever rushed over her. Molly told herself to step back. She'd be sorry they were rushing things. She hadn't known him long enough. It was just a kiss. Just one kiss, then they could go back to avoiding this sort of thing.

"Yes," she answered him and, rising to her toes, clasped his shoulders.

His arms tightened almost instantly. Before her eyes drifted shut she saw a smile on his wide mouth, a wicked, tempting, satisfied smile. Molly told herself she didn't care. Not now. And later it wouldn't matter because there weren't going to be any other later times to worry about.

His lips touched hers. He must have still been smiling for she could feel the curve of his mouth. She tried to smile, but he slid his mouth along her jaw, leaving a trail of moisture and sensation. Her breath caught in her throat at the shimmering wonder she felt, and when his mouth moved to hers, she didn't care if she ever caught her breath again.

The first delicate touch of his lips quickly became more urgent. Like a well drawing water from deep in the earth, his kiss pulled a hunger from her very center. It was as if they'd been storing all their aches, all their hopes, all their desires since the last time they'd kissed.

His hands moved feverishly over her back, and she slipped hers past the collar of his shirt to tunnel into the hair at his nape. He pulled her closer, snuggling her hips against his. They fit so well, surely he could tell— His hand glided over her hips and her mind stalled. This was getting to be much more than a kiss.

Molly twisted away from his mouth. "Stef—" She drew a breath and started again. "We—we better stop now."

He lifted his head and leaned back to look down at her. "Yeah, I know."

Yeah, he knew, she repeated silently. "Does that mean—"

"That means if we don't stop I'll take you to bed."

His words brought the fever back. He'd meant to do that after their first dinner together. He'd resisted then, too. "Do you want to?" she heard herself ask and worried at her audacity.

He laughed. "Of course."

Did he realize how good that made her feel? She smiled at him. He held her gaze but pushed a hand into his pocket.

"I guess going to bed together would be one way to get over being afraid, but you said—"

"We both need our sleep." He smoothed her hair back from her forehead.

She let herself relish the tenderness of his gesture a moment, then caught his gaze and shrugged. "You're right. I just wish I didn't feel so much like a sitting duck."

He looked about to speak when a thunk sounded. Molly went rigid. Stefanos looked toward the door, and her heart slammed into her chest. Another thunk reverberated through the silent room, then a voice called.

Stefanos's expression relaxed and he touched her cheek. "Takis. Maybe he'll have good news," he said, his fingers lingering on her skin. "So soft."

Sinking onto her chair, Molly watched him walk to the door. He was talking about her skin, but she couldn't help remembering when he'd told her he thought she was soft inside, like the spring.

Did he mean feminine? She had felt distinctly feminine when he'd kissed her. His kiss had been hungry, and that hunger scared her. More accurately, the way she'd responded to the kiss scared her. She'd felt like a runaway train barreling down the tracks.

Maybe later she would be comfortable with her response to him. *Maybe* was the operative word because Molly couldn't remember ever feeling quite this way with a man before.

Across the room, Stefanos stood at the window ledge, his back to her, the smoke from the cigarette in his raised hand lazily etching spirals in the air.

It was after midnight. What was he doing up? Molly tightened her grip on the muslin curtain. "Is something wrong?"

He half turned at her question.

Molly let the curtain slip from her fingers, almost unaware that it rippled back into place in the doorway between the two rooms. She couldn't take her eyes off the sculptured curve of Stefanos's bare shoulders, gilded with light on one side, shadowed with darkness on the other.

She watched his gaze travel down to where the bottom of her shirt circled her thighs. Her skin tingled there as if he had touched it with his fingers. Molly tugged on the hem, realizing too late he would know *she* knew what he was thinking about.

His eyes seemed to darken, but he said nothing, merely pressed down on the hand bracing open the pages of a book. It looked like the sign language book. Unexpected delight twirled through her. She stepped to the foot of his bed and gripped the tall, iron bed frame. Would she ever again meet a man who was willing to spend so much time learning to communicate with her?

He turned to face her completely now, and the light reflected off the metal waistband button of his jeans—the unfastened metal button. She bit down on her lower lip. Nothing separated them but a few feet of empty space. He could bridge that gap in a second.

Instead he placed his cigarette in a cheap, alizarin crimson ashtray like the ones she'd seen at taverns and cafés, and sat on the bed, reaching over his shoulder to pull the pillow up behind his shoulders. She liked the way his biceps bulged when he did that, wondering a little at herself. She had seen lots of other men's muscles in life drawing classes.

Looking at Stefanos's body made her feel womanly, made her want to lie down beside him, made her want to accept his lovemaking. Was she strong enough to handle this attraction, strong enough to handle Stefanos?

She'd stood up to him at the *cafenion* and demanded answers in his office. She hadn't let him steamroller her, but that didn't mean she could satisfy him.

"Did Takis come back?" she asked. When Stefanos's policeman friend had stopped by earlier, he'd brought no news and had stayed only long enough to be sure they were okay.

Stefanos shook his head and lifted his cigarette to his lips. "Sorry to wake you," he said and expelled the smoke. "I must have been making too much noise."

Molly smiled. "You keep forgetting. You could be playing rock music full blast in here, and it wouldn't wake me. Warren used to say it was one of the best things about our marriage."

A furrow pulled Stefanos's brows together. "Do you think about him often?"

"I try not to, and I don't know why I woke up. Maybe it was the smoke." She gestured to the ashtray.

"I couldn't sleep." He crushed the cigarette.

"Why not?" His brown eyes briefly filled with something she'd never seen in them. A sort of longing, she thought, but it wasn't sexual. He didn't say anything, or maybe he had and she'd missed it. Maybe he hadn't heard her question, either. "Am I talking loud enough?"

"Fine," he signed.

"I don't have my hearing aid on. Sometimes when I'm not wearing it, I don't talk loudly enough for other people to hear."

"You're speaking fine," he said and signed, too.

Something inside her heart melted.

Stefanos moved over and patted the bed beside him. She sat next to him without thinking about the consequences, and he lifted the hair back from her face. Molly studied the rapt expression on his face as he brushed his hand across the top of her ear. Little pulses of heat scattered through her.

He could be so intoxicating, she thought wonderingly, gazing at his bare chest. The areolas of his dark nipples nestled under swirls of dark hair. She wanted to reach out and touch them. Instead she ran a hand down her thigh. She ought to go back to her bed now, but she couldn't move, not when she thought about that strange longing in his gaze.

A frown darkened his brow, and his brown eyes held none of their usual fire or interest. Molly found herself leaning forward, frowning, too. "Now you know what woke me up, but I still don't know what woke you."

"Sometimes I have nightmares," he said.

Her heart turned over. "Oh, Stef. What sort of nightmares?"

"That's not important."

She doubted that. "You have them because of the torture?"

"Yes."

Most men would disavow having anything but erotic dreams. She wondered what she could do to help him, but she didn't want to seem nosy. Molly rubbed her hands down her thighs then glanced up at him. "Do you want to go back to sleep?"

"Eventually. I'm thinking right now."

"Do you have to think alone? I can sit here and think with you." She smiled. Stefanos's expression remained serious, and Molly felt her smile falter.

"We shouldn't even be here. You should be in Athens or wherever it was you wanted to do your sketching," he finally said.

She shrugged. "We won't have to stay here in the farmhouse long, will we?"

"I don't know," he said.

Nice of him to admit that, she thought, drawing one leg up and tucking her foot under the other leg. Funny, right now she didn't mind how long they stayed here. Stefanos rubbed a hand down her calf, and Molly found she didn't mind that, either.

"You remember this afternoon on the ferry?" he said. "I embarrassed you by telling you I thought you were soft inside. I wasn't just talking sexually." His mouth twisted at the corner.

He might not be thinking sexual thoughts, but his gesture filled the very air between them with vibrant heat. Molly knew she should do something or say something to dispel the mood but she couldn't think of a thing.

"You are kind," he continued. "Kind, as the spring is to the land. I need you, Molly. Will you—?"

"Will you..." It took her a few seconds to figure out what he said. *Will you let me make love to you?* Her pulse began to race. He needed her.

Could she risk not satisfying him? He'd risked a lot for her already. He'd tried to get her to confess in order to help her even when he'd still thought her the enemy. And hadn't he volunteered that he admired her and was attracted to her? Surely she had as much courage as he did.

He stretched a hand toward her, and she clasped it.

Stefanos pulled her close enough that the tips of her breasts touched his chest. Heat pulsed through her, heat like no other she'd ever experienced. Was it real?

Yes. She could never have fantasized exactly the way his breath skittered over her cheek and then her neck. Nor could she have imagined the solidness of his body beneath hers. Molly let her leg slide off his, hardly noticing the slight roughness of the cotton sheet clinging to her skin when she braced herself.

He placed his fingers on either side of her neck. She could feel the pad of each one as he drew them down, slipping them under the collar of her shirt. Molly closed her eyes and relished the exquisite sensations flowing through her. She felt herself shining as if she'd been polished.

Stefanos kneaded her shoulders slowly. The gentle pressure wore away the last shred of her resistance, leaving only instinct, the instinct to share with this man, share everything.

She cupped her hands around his arms, absorbing the heat radiating from him. It fanned through her in ever-widening circles until her whole body glowed.

He smiled at her now, a tender smile that plucked at her heartstrings. She lowered her hands and tried to slip her arms around him. He caught them and held them back. "I want to look at you," he said, scoring a finger down the buttons of her shirt.

Need coiled through her, and she raised her fingers to her buttons, watching his brown eyes darken and his brows lower as he watched intently, still as a cat when it sights its prey.

She'd only freed one when he brushed her hands away and undid them himself, slowly, his gaze holding hers. Molly felt herself sinking into the dark mystery of his gaze.

Her shirt fluttered down her arms, brushing tantalizingly past her breasts to expose her to the cool air of the house. Her nipples tightened, begging for his touch. He gazed at them. Didn't he know she ached for him? He gave her a mischievous smile that raised her pulse another notch.

Finally Stefanos touched a finger to one tip, slowly tracing a circle around it. When he slid his fingers to the other breast, she sighed. "You're driving me crazy," she whispered.

"That's what I'm hoping," he said, then lowered his head. She tensed, anticipating the delicious wetness of his mouth against her skin. The soft, warm flutter of his breath made her skin tingle and tighten, and then his tongue took its place, tracing an intricate pattern over her skin.

Molly sank her hands into his hair, loving the silky weight of it against her fingers. She urged his head down to its proper place—the tip of her breast. "I'm crazy now," she murmured.

"Not yet," he said and lowered her to the bed.

The sheet no longer felt rough, but smooth and satiny. It caressed her back even as his tongue caressed her breasts. She felt as soft and weightless as a feather.

He ran a hand down over her rib cage, then gradually slid it lower. Lifting the elastic of her panties, he stroked his hand over her skin. The yearning inside her, only a candle before, suddenly flared into a major fire. She would burn up if he touched her; she would burn up if he didn't.

He found her, his fingers gliding teasingly across the very center of her femininity. Everything blurred behind the delicate enticements of his touch. He made her feel so much she only half realized that he had stripped her, that she was lying beside him naked, that his jeans-clad legs were moving against hers.

She stilled. Stefanos raised his head and lifted a questioning eyebrow. She traced it with a fingertip, loving its silky springiness. "I want to make you feel good, too."

He shook his head.

"Yes, I insist." He might deny it, but she'd learned the hard way that she needed to think about the man and what he might want. She knew what she wanted. She wanted him to remember this night with her always.

The frown Stefanos had been wearing disappeared, and he leaned back, giving her access. Her gaze dropped to the fold of denim across his zipper. She peeled it back, then caught the tab and guided it slowly down. The little metal teeth pulled apart, exposing the shiny nylon of his royal blue briefs.

He said something. She glanced up at his mouth. He ran a finger under the waistband of the briefs. "You didn't expect these?" He smiled at her mischievously.

"I will get to you," she teased and stroked a finger down his fullness. He closed his eyes. She slipped her hand under his waistband and over his hair-roughened skin, marveling at how natural all this was with Stefanos.

He lifted his hips and slipped off the rest of his clothes. After tossing them to the floor, he turned to her and ran both hands up her thighs. "I want to take this slow," he said. "You haven't been with a man in a long time, have you?"

"Does it show?" She looked down. Her hair fell over her shoulder, and she pushed it back with a sigh of resignation. She glanced up, surprised to find Stefanos leaning so close.

With one finger, he lifted her chin. "I'm sorry, Molly," he said. "I only meant I don't want to hurt you."

She smoothed her hand across his whiskered cheek. "You could never do that."

He bent his head, and she opened her mouth to him in welcome, pulling him closer. He kissed her until she ached with its promise then nudged her back against the pillow.

Molly smoothed her hand over the tight muscles of his shoulders, and he rose over her to press his hips to her. He filled her slowly and completely, then lowered himself, resting on his forearms beside her shoulders.

"Stef..." She touched her fingertips to the line of his jaw. "You—" He placed a finger across her lips. "You make me feel like a candle," she said around his finger. "Make me feel as if I could burn like one."

"Good."

"That's my word," she teased.

"I know."

His hips pressed into her again, then he withdrew. The flame within her flickered. Molly lifted to meet him, and Stefanos slipped his hands under her shoulders. She closed her eyes and gave herself up to the heat and light.

She could see a candle in the distance, beckoning to her. She reached for it, and it grew brighter. Stefanos was with her, urging her to try harder, to move higher, to reach out farther. She suddenly touched the burning flame and became one with it.

Stefanos gripped her shoulders, shuddered then stilled. Molly sighed and let herself float. She felt like a bubble of light. No, nothing so concrete, she thought wonderingly. She hadn't melted, but it had been a near thing.

Stefanos shifted to draw her under his arm, and she snuggled against his side, nestling her head in the hollow of his shoulder. She opened her eyes, looking down at where he rested a hand on his stomach.

She traced the outline of his thumb, then let her gaze drift along his strong wrist to his forearm, where his dark hair glowed in the light of the lamp. He was a beautiful man, and he'd made such beautiful love to her.

He'd made love to her, anyway, but had he felt any satisfaction... or just release? Maybe release was all he'd wanted or expected from her. A slow spiral of discouragement unwound inside her. Molly tried to block it out of her mind, but the question nagged her. She grew more uncomfortable, noticing for the first time how the buttons of the mattress bit into her legs and back.

Under her cheek the rise and fall of Stefanos's chest had slowed as if he'd fallen asleep. "Are you awake?" she asked, immediately wishing she hadn't. If he'd already fallen asleep and she woke him, he might get annoyed.

Stefanos lifted his hand and caressed her shoulder briefly. Molly eased up into a sitting position. The arm he held in back of her slid to her waist. He smiled up at her, his brown eyes dark.

She smiled back and waited. He didn't say anything, but he didn't look annoyed, either. Instead of feeling relieved, Molly's nerves only tightened. She tried to tell herself Stefanos wouldn't consider this a performance test, but she wanted to know his thoughts about what they'd just done.

He began to draw lazy spirals on her back. She tucked her hair behind her ear, waiting for him to say something and wishing she weren't waiting. She could ask him. No!

If he didn't want to say anything, she'd be putting him on the spot to ask. Maybe she should just offer to go back to her own bed. He might not like sleeping on his back with someone cradled in his arms.

She looked around for her shirt and finally spotted it draped across the iron railing at the foot of the bed where someone—probably Stefanos—had tossed it. Reaching for it now, she felt him watching her.

Maybe, now that their desire had been satisfied, he just didn't want to be bothered to get past the communication barrier with her. Molly held her shirt to her chest, covering herself as best she could.

He tugged on the shirt, and one corner of his mouth curved up. "You don't have to get dressed."

She forced a laugh but it sounded as unnatural as it felt, and she knew Stefanos would be able to detect her nervousness. "Putting on this shirt is hardly getting dressed," she said. "I thought I'd go back to my bed so you can get some sleep."

His brow wrinkled, then he signed, "Do you want to leave?"

She rubbed her thigh, looking down at where her knee touched his side. The warmth of their lovemaking lingered inside her, and it was as if *her* knee and *his* body connected with the same liquid glow, one she wanted to bask in a little longer. But what about Stefanos? She glanced at him, but his bland expression gave nothing away of his emotions. "Do you want an honest answer or the one I think I should give you?" she asked.

The sparkle in his eyes vanished as he lowered his brows. He looked as if he didn't understand why she would ask. "The honest answer. I always want the truth from you."

"Sometimes the truth can hurt."

"Yes." He ran his fingers through his hair. "I know that well."

"Well, back to your question," she said and touched the trail of dark hair descending his abdomen. "No, I don't want to go. I like being with you, but I thought maybe it might not—that you might not feel the same way."

"If I wanted to be alone, I would get out of bed and pull on my jeans just like you're doing with your shirt."

Molly leaned forward. Did he mean he'd enjoyed it? That she hadn't disappointed him? She felt the tightness in her shoulders relax.

He folded an arm behind his head. "I'm surprised you agreed to make love with me."

Molly stared, then frowned. She'd felt as if he'd been reaching out to her emotionally. He had, hadn't he?

"Don't frown. Please," he signed.

"But I don't understand. What are you talking about? Oh, please, Stef—don't confuse me now. I don't know if I can stand—" She stopped herself.

Sure she could stand it. She'd put up with a lot of things. Molly realized she still held her shirt. She pushed her arms into the sleeves now and started to button it.

Chapter 9

Stefanos took Molly's hand before she could fasten the rest of the buttons. He looked down at their joined hands, hers soft as a violet's petal, amazed that the simple action of folding his fingers around hers could bring with it such an intense awareness.

"Stef..."

He lifted his gaze and read confusion in her gaze. "I don't want to confuse you," he said. How could he not, he wondered. He wanted her to stay and wanted her to leave, both at the same time.

"Something's bothering you. Will you tell me what it is?" Molly leaned toward him, the expression in her blue eyes no longer confused, but challenging, as if she was daring him to answer.

"Yes, something's bothering me," he said, deciding she deserved some sort of explanation. He hoped he could find one to give her.

"Is it something to do with my being honest?" she asked.

He cupped her chin and dropped a kiss on her lips. "That would never be a problem."

The problem was *he* didn't want to be honest. He needed to face the fact that, if he didn't get her to step back now, they might both be sorry. And wasn't she trying to do just that? Stefanos balled his fist. She had a right to be annoyed with him.

Molly touched his shoulder, and he felt the sensual repercussions of the gesture ripple down his arm. "Is it something to do with the nightmare, Stefanos?"

"Partly."

She crossed her legs. "You sound like a diplomat. You don't have to be one with me."

Stefanos didn't know about that. They'd just had sex, the most intimate activity a man and woman could share, but for some reason she seemed nervous. Molly twisted her hair in one hand, then let it fall behind her shoulder. She was waiting. Stefanos fingered a strand of her golden hair, smiling at her. Maybe letting her go back to her own bed would be the best thing, but he couldn't do it. If she stayed, she had to know the score, though.

"I don't feel much like a diplomat at the moment," he said, letting his fingers slip from her hair.

"What do you feel like?"

Confused, restless, eager to make love to her again, he thought, knowing he couldn't tell her that yet, maybe never. "Wait a minute." He rolled off the bed, lit a cigarette, then set it in the ashtray while he tugged on his jeans. "I didn't intend to back you into a corner and make love to you," he said.

She tilted her head. "I know that."

He waited for her to lay the blame on him. He'd been waiting for it all evening. It bothered him that she hadn't said anything about their enforced intimacy at the farmhouse.

Stefanos put the cigarette between his lips and inhaled. A bit of tobacco burned his tongue, reinforcing his bitter thoughts. "This isn't coming out right," he said.

"Do you really want to talk, Stefanos?"

He propped his pillow up behind him and leaned back, facing her. The lamplight made her face look even more fragile than usual. He wanted to reach out and slide his fingers along her cheek, but he couldn't let himself do that—for her sake. "It's my fault you're here."

Molly shook her head. "You've been doing your job. It's a job that I respect, too, Stefanos."

"If I'd been doing my job instead of being so keen to get revenge, I would have paid more attention to my first impressions of you."

"I don't see you wanting revenge." Molly frowned, then shook her head. "You're too willing to be fair, to try to understand. You tried to do that with me."

"Not soon enough. I should have seen you were too honest to be involved in espionage."

"Why are you going back over this?"

"There are a few things you don't know about me," he said. There, that ought to make her worry a little.

She smiled. "There are plenty of things I don't know about you. I do know that you are honest and honorable. You're kind and patient. And very good with children."

Stefanos closed his eyes. "I shouldn't be allowed around them."

"Why?" Molly laid a hand on his chest. "I can see that your friend's little boy, Nikos, adores you. You must care for him, too. You have a photograph of him at your house."

He stroked a finger down the back of her hand, knowing any minute she'd shudder at the thought of his touching her.

"You two look like you're very close."

A heavy weight rolled onto his heart. He took Molly's hand. She squeezed his. He put her hand back into her lap. "It's the least I can do for Nikos. But I should try to discourage his friendship."

She stared at him. "He loves you."

"No, don't say that."

"Why not, Stef?" He grimaced and rubbed a hand across his mouth. Molly leaned toward him. "You look so upset."

Upset? That was a nice way to describe what he felt. Stefanos took a deep breath. "First of all, Nikos is not Takis's son. Second of all, he does not adore me, as you say."

"I can see it with my own eyes." Molly leaned forward, her blue eyes fierce.

"No," he said, resisting the urge to touch her. "I take care of him because I'm the reason he lost his family."

"The reason he lost . . ." she repeated before straightening and apparently understanding. "I don't believe that."

"You wanted to know, right?" he signed patiently and spoke, too.

She nodded.

"I went to the island of Lidacros two years ago," he said, speaking slowly, pausing after every few words for her to catch up. "You may remember that Topolac and his army had invaded the island then. Most of the islanders are Greek, and Greece got involved. Threats were exchanged and there was real danger war would break out." Stefanos finished his cigarette and stubbed it out.

"Anyway, NATO stepped in and I was sent to negotiate a peace settlement that would get Topolac out. I'd always had a certain feel about people. Instinct, if you will. You need that if you're any kind of negotiator. I though I must have been reading everyone right because we did come up with a compromise. All sides got something they wanted. No one would look really bad. We'd all be friends again. But then I was kidnapped and the whole situation fell apart."

Stefanos glanced at Molly. "Want to know why? Because I made a stupid mistake."

Molly pressed her lips together. Stefanos waited for her to raise her gaze from his mouth. When she did, he nodded. "What do you mean?" she asked.

He looked down at his hands, wishing he could undo the disaster he'd caused by his carelessness. "It was the last morning. I thought everything was in order, but one of the Turkish delegates asked for additional explanations and reassurances from NATO. Since I was leading the negotiating team, I stayed behind to do that. After that, I was handed a message from my boss to get home as soon as possible. If I hadn't believed that message and hadn't been so anxious to please my superiors, I wouldn't have walked into the trap. The whole thing—the need for further explanations and the message from my headquarters—had been fabrications. Topolac just wanted me in a car alone."

Stefanos rubbed the bridge of his nose, wondering why Molly didn't look more disgusted. "The driver stopped along the road and picked up soldiers. They took me to a village where they tried to convince me to repudiate the agreement that had just been signed."

Molly's blue eyes seemed to melt with sympathy. Stefanos cupped her cheek, and she lowered his hand to gaze at the scars. "That's why they tortured you," she whispered.

He nodded, watching her, realizing he should never have touched her. She needed to be thinking about his mistake, not his hands.

"Where does Nikos fit into this?" Molly asked.

"They took me to the village where Nikos and his family lived and allowed Nikos to bring me a meal every night, never thinking Nikos would be able to help me. He did, though. With the aid of his family and the other men in the village, Nikos got me out."

Stefanos gazed across the dimly lit room. He might be looking at the simple wooden table and the butane stove of his own farmhouse, but what he really saw were the boulders and trees of one particular Lidacros mountain.

"We ran into some of Topolac's soldiers. They shot up Nikos pretty badly. I got him safely off the island, but his family and a number of the others in the village were executed as punishment for their part in helping me get out." Stefanos rested his head against the pillow and closed his eyes.

"They killed his mother, too?" she asked, her voice full of horror and disbelief.

He couldn't look at her and merely signed yes.

"I can't imagine someone being so cruel." Stefanos felt her gaze on him. He was sure she was disgusted and angry with him now. "It wasn't your fault."

He snapped his head up and glared at her. "How can you say that? I made a mistake. We'd been told to be wary, and I was just the opposite."

"You couldn't have known it was a plot, Stef. You were doing your job, a good job. You should be proud of what you tried to accomplish."

"Right. My accomplishments include helping Topolac rise to power. He was only an army colonel two years ago. Nikos, a mere child, was hurt. And it was bad, too, Molly. He needed a number of operations. The doctors didn't think he would live." Stefanos looked away, biting down on his trembling lower lip. "His parents wouldn't have been killed, either, or the other villagers. I shouldn't have tried to escape."

"Any self-respecting man would have tried to escape," she said, planting her fists on her knees. "You did it for your country, too. The villagers took a risk. Nikos did, too."

"You don't understand." He said it aloud then signed. Why had he thought she'd understand? Molly was just like everyone else. He let out a sigh.

"I do know what it means to feel guilty," Molly said.

She got off the bed and walked to the table where they'd eaten dinner, picked up a chair and brought it back. She'd never told anyone this, and she couldn't even tell Stefanos now and sit as close as she had to him on the bed.

Stefanos swung his feet over the side of the bed as if he meant to leave. "Wait. I think you should hear me out," she said, setting the chair down and sitting on it. "Maybe it will help, though I don't propose to hold myself up as a good example of anything."

She tucked her hair behind her ears. "Warren didn't love me." There! She'd said it aloud. "I didn't know that in the beginning, of course. I thought he was madly in love with me. It seems he married me because of some screwy provision in his father's will. To inherit the estate, Warren had to be married for at least two years before he turned thirty, and he was running out of time when he met me. Apparently he never intended to stay married to me."

Molly lifted her shoulders and let them fall in a resigned shrug. "After a year I could tell something was wrong. He didn't pay me as much attention as before, didn't desire me as often." She laughed. "That really is funny because I don't think he really desired me at all, except as a body. What sort of satisfaction can a person get from that?"

Her heart suddenly stopped. She didn't know for sure that Stefanos had wanted *her* because she was a woman or because she was Molly Light. Well, that was water over the bridge, or whatever the expression was. "At the time, I thought it was my fault, that I wasn't 'lovable' anymore. I felt badly that I couldn't make the relationship work."

Stefanos said something.

"Pardon?"

He leaned forward and ran a hand up her bare thigh.

Molly caught her breath. "When you do that, Stef, I can't think."

"Proves my point," he said and lifted his hand. "I don't know how any man could find you undesirable. You're very sensitive to touch."

"Isn't everyone?" Stefanos shook his head, and a lock of hair dropped toward his eyebrows. Molly pushed it back. Stefanos took her hand and brought it to his mouth. The moist heat of his tongue sent ripples of excitement up her arm. "Stef. Let me finish."

He let her hand go, but a very masculine smile played across his lips. Her body responded with a very feminine shiver of delight.

"Warren told me our marriage was disintegrating because of the difficulties my hearing problem caused, and I felt guilty for that. I couldn't do much more to cope with it than I already had. It wasn't until Julian told me about Warren's father's will just last year that I stopped feeling guilty." She tucked her hair behind both ears, wishing she'd taken the time to fasten it back.

Stefanos had been looking at her face. His gaze drifted down now to where her shirt collar parted, and something inside her tightened.

"Anyway..." She gestured in an effort to get him to look up at her face again. "Even though I finally realized he was using me, I still wonder if I'm inadequate." She swallowed. "I know in my mind making love has nothing to do with whether or not I can hear very well, but inside," she said, pointing to her chest, "it's like I haven't quite accepted it. I was married to Warren for only two years. But I guess I grew up thinking my loss made me less than normal and I still feel inadequate sometimes."

She wanted to tell him that he, too, should try to put his past mistake behind him instead of dwelling on it, but she didn't want to sound pushy. Still, the only reason she'd told him her story was to try to help him. She smiled. "I'm trying to get past that now. I think that's the important thing."

Stefanos leaned forward, and his male scent wrapped around her, enticing her, lulling her. "Is that why you're taking birth control pills?"

Did she understand him correctly? "Birth control?"

"I noticed them when we looked through your bag. Don't you remember? You actually wanted me to paw through your sanitary supplies."

Molly felt the heat rise to her cheeks. "I didn't think anything there would embarrass you."

"Are you taking them because you're trying to prove to yourself you can have any man you want?"

A little laugh escaped her. "Are you trying to be funny?" He looked as solemn as Abraham Lincoln. "No, I guess you're not." Molly rubbed her hands up and down her arms, feeling unaccountably chilled.

"I took them when I was with Warren. He didn't want kids. That makes perfect sense now. He didn't even want to be saddled with a wife. After we split, I just kept taking them. I guess I was hoping to find some man I was attracted to, some man I wanted to share myself with who wouldn't think about my hearing."

"Your hearing loss doesn't bother me, you know." He cupped her face, and the ridges on his palms felt almost soft.

"Stefanos, you—" She had to stop as his hand slipped over the sensitized skin of her neck. "Will you hold me?" He pulled her to her feet and slipped his hands under the hem of her shirt. He cupped her bottom and tugged her closer, then pressed his face to her stomach. Molly slipped her fingers into his hair. "I love your hair. It's like you. Unpredictable."

He grinned up at her. "Why don't I show you how unpredictable I can be?" he asked.

It must have been nearly dawn when Stefanos woke. He could feel Molly beside him but could see nothing. Without the lamp, which he'd blown out earlier, the room was pitch-dark.

He closed his eyes and listened to the steady sound of Molly's breathing. Strangely enough, the nightmare hadn't awakened him. Usually when he dreamed it, it replayed three or four times during the night, whether or not he was sharing his bed with a woman. He always awoke after each time, almost always in a cold sweat.

Pinpricks of pain stabbed his left hand. So that was what had awakened him! He wanted to rub the palm, but he didn't want to let go of Molly to do so. He didn't want to wake her, either. The weight of her head in the hollow of his shoulder pleased him. Thank goodness she hadn't talked about going back to her bed again. He'd been a little worried—*say it, Metadorakis, you were hurt*—when she'd started putting on her shirt.

Okay, he'd been hurt, but now he felt wonderfully weightless and disconnected from reality. That was all right for the time being. He didn't need to take control of anything at the moment.

At first, he'd had trouble finding the words to tell her about his kidnapping and the consequences. Gradually the story had gotten easier and easier to tell. He'd even actually had to work to keep up his own indignation. Her words and her hands had soothed him, but he'd actually wanted them to, which was not good. He didn't need to find ways to connect with her—just the opposite.

He didn't regret making love to her. He didn't regret concentrating on making Molly feel good or making sure Molly knew she made him feel good. Good was an understatement. Sex with Molly had been an almost out-of-body experience for him, though he wasn't sure why. He tried to tell himself it didn't matter why sex with her had been different. After all, Molly would probably be out of his life in a few days.

He folded an arm behind his head. It was nice not to have to explain his every action. He'd miss it. A sense of loneliness wound through his mind just at the thought of not having her around. He tucked in his chin to look at Molly.

The sheet had slipped off her shoulder. He slid it back into place, relishing the way her hair draped across his chest, soft and silky. Molly was soft and silky, too, and so loving, so warm. That she hadn't known this had astounded him. That she'd felt inadequate because of Warren Flint had angered him.

She stirred. Stefanos stilled. She needed her sleep. They both did.

Her voice, gentle and low, brushed across the intense darkness of the room. "Am I keeping you awake?" she asked.

"I don't mind."

She groped for his hand. "What did you say?"

He grimaced, belatedly remembering she wouldn't be able to understand him in the dark. With her hand resting lightly on his, he signed what he'd said.

"You don't mind?" she asked. Her leg slipped over his. His body tightened. "No."

"In that case..." Molly murmured. Her hand glided down his chest, and his breath caught. Molly's small hand found him.

He told himself to resist. Her hand moved on him, and a tide of exquisite sensation swept through him. He could handle one night with her, he told himself, rolling her onto her back and kissing her deeply.

Her hips sought his and he touched her, finding her wet and ready. A tide of sensual excitement tugged at him, threatening to pull him under. He hadn't wanted her to go back to her bed, right? So enjoy this.

Finding the center of her womanhood, he teased her, smiling as he listened to her sighs of pleasure. "Stef—"

He stilled. The sound of his name chimed in the darkness, calling to something deep inside him, something he rarely gave anyone, something he hardly acknowledged anymore. He blocked the thought. He didn't want to think about anything, just this...

Slowly, carefully, he entered her. Her breath fluttered across his collarbone. He slipped his hands under her, lifting her and drawing them more deeply together.

Come with me, he told her silently, moving in time with his words. *Come with me.*

They moved together until, suddenly, completion rippled through her. He wanted to draw out her pleasure, bring her to that burst of feeling over and over, but she shifted against him. The rising crest of sensation exploded inside him, shattering him as if he were the sun broken up and scattered into the sky.

Molly kept her eyes closed when she woke later that morning. She didn't want reality to distract her just yet. She wanted to savor the tingling lightness of having been thoroughly loved. She hadn't felt like this since her honeymoon. No, not even then.

There had always been the nagging worry of whether or not Warren would consider her adequate. He'd never been as unselfish as Stefanos, and Stefanos had actually praised her. With her eyes still closed, she patted the bed beside her, encountering nothing but air when she hoped to find a warm body. Where was he?

She opened her eyes and sat up, wiping the perspiration from her upper lip. The sun traced the bottom of the window shutters with yellow, and in the dimness, Molly could see that the room was empty. The metal bar that had been across the inside of the double doors last night stood on end against the wall. Stefanos must be outside.

Molly threw back the sheet and got up. She pulled on jeans and a sleeveless knit top and thought about the previous night. She'd never been so bold with a man.

She brushed her hair, catching it back in an elastic band before sitting to put on her tennis shoes. Her cheeks heated at the memory of her fingers on his fly. She'd not only helped him undress; she'd touched him. It had been the most natural thing in the world. Stefanos hadn't seemed to mind, either.

Halfway to the door, she stopped. Something was wrong. Fingering behind her ear, Molly confirmed her guess. She'd forgotten to put on her hearing aid—for the first time in her adult life.

Just the thought of going around without it usually set her nerves on edge. Not wearing it was sort of like going out for a drive without her driver's license.

A laugh bubbled up inside her now, surprising her. She went in search of the hearing aid. Slipping it on, she wondered how she could have forgotten it. She'd been thinking of Stefanos. That must be the reason, for he was endlessly fascinating. But she didn't want just to think about him. She wanted to see him and talk to him and tell him how she felt.

Hurriedly she stuck her camera, pencils and sketch pad in her canvas shoulder bag. Her battery would need changing soon, and she made sure she had her spare batteries. If it had been safe enough for him to be outside for the last few minutes, maybe it would be safe enough for her to sit and sketch for a while.

Molly reached the door but paused with her fingers on the handle. She wished she knew how Stefanos felt this morning. Had their lovemaking affected him the same way it had her? She'd thought so, but she couldn't be sure she didn't see some nonexistent emotion because she wanted to see it. Besides, asking might get her the wrong answer.

The seconds ticked by. She didn't want to rush things, but she and Stefanos would not have much more time together. Or would they? Maybe they would be here for weeks. Her stomach knotted at the thought. She wouldn't be able to resist him, yet it would be better if she did, at least until she knew if his heart was involved.

Slinging the bag over her shoulder, she tugged on the door. It resisted. She pulled harder. The door yielded suddenly, scraping across the flagstone floor.

Outside, the morning hung like a finished painting in the clearing, complete and motionless. In front of the house, a tall thicket of cane with its pale green, spiky leaves blocked her view of everything except the clear sky.

Molly looked down the path leading toward the beach and saw Stefanos. Her heart smiled. He was bending over the well, his arms extended down into it as he pulled up a bucket. She started toward him. By the time she reached him, he'd hauled the plastic bucket up to the rim of the well. As he set it on the ground beside another, Molly caught the dazzle of the sun on the clear water inside.

The sun also glinted off the handle of the gun stuck in his shoulder holster. She ignored it, shading her eyes to smile up at him. "Hi." He wiped his hand on his bronze-colored polo shirt, leaving a darker swatch of color. "I thought since you were outside, I could do some sketching."

He smiled and lifted a hand. She thought he meant to touch her. Instead, he stopped and looked down the dirt path toward the road, his face a mask of concentration. A sudden spasm of alarm gripped her. Molly glanced toward the path but saw nothing. She told herself to relax. Whatever he was hearing didn't have to be bad. He said something.

"Other shooter?" She thought she heard a humming sound—an engine, maybe. Had he said motor scooter?

Stefanos dumped the water from the buckets back into the well, then grabbed her arm and ran toward the stable building. They ducked behind it, and Stefanos set the buckets to one side. Her blood pounded in her ears. Beside her, Stefanos appeared calm. He lived with danger, she told herself, watching him ready his gun.

Stefanos glanced at her, an intent expression settling on his face as if he was listening to something. What did he hear? She opened her mouth to ask him when he caught her gaze and held a finger to his mouth. Had the motor scooter stopped?

They crouched lower, and Molly sagged against the rough, whitewashed wall of the stable. Across the clearing in front of them, tall cane delineated a field, a field that went down to the water, Stefanos had said. There would be no escape that way. Her throat tightened, and she gripped Stefanos's arm more tightly.

He mouthed, "In the house."

She nodded. Whoever had come on the motor scooter was in the house now. Stefanos's muscles moved under her fingers, and she forced herself to release his arm. They were only being cautious, she told herself, rubbing her sweaty palms on her jeans.

Besides, whoever had come was not looking for them, because it would have taken two seconds to determine they weren't in the house. He must be looking for something, maybe money or—her mind stumbled over the possibility—Julian's microfilm. What would he do when he didn't find it?

She thought she heard something. A man stepped into view. She caught only a glimpse of his back before Stefanos pulled her head down against his chest. She thought she heard a roar start up, and Stefanos straightened. Molly wondered exactly where the scooter was. Sometimes their noise was worse behind them, but—

Stefanos grabbed her hand and sprinted toward the cane barrier behind them. Her canvas bag banged against her side, and she thought her lungs would burst if Stefanos ran any faster. Suddenly, he stopped. She slammed into him. He steadied her, then stepped away from her and held back the cane. She went through the break and found herself in a vineyard. Stefanos joined her, and the stalks closed together behind him.

Gasping for breath, Molly let her bag slip off her shoulder to the ground. She should have taken some of the stuff out of it, she thought, amazed she'd managed to hang on to it during their dash for cover.

Stefanos looked up from adjusting his gun and raised an eyebrow. "Don't get too comfortable," he said slowly. She leaned closer and adjusted the volume of her aid. "We don't want our friend to find us."

"Friend?" Molly frowned, confused. "If this was a friend, then why did we run away from him?"

Stefanos grasped her shoulders with both hands. She looked at his hard expression and shuddered. His grip softened, and his hands whispered down her arms. "This guy isn't a friend."

Her heart leapt into her throat. "That was the man from Athens, wasn't it? The one who tried to break into your house."

Stefanos signed yes and wiped his forehead with the back of his hand.

"Oh, Stef, you're bleeding." She caught his forearm and turned it so he could see the long, thin red line.

"From the cane. It's nothing. Come on, we need to get into town." He pointed across the field. "If we go across here, we might make the road before he does."

Chapter 10

Stefanos brought her to a stop at the junction of two narrow, flagstone-paved streets in the town of Parikia. They were well away from the sea breeze here, and Molly wiped away the perspiration on her upper lip. "I know we can't be far from the ferry dock. Why isn't anyone around?"

"Lunch," he signed. He rubbed the palm of his hand. "And the tourists are in the waterfront cafés."

The stillness still felt creepy, Molly thought, watching Stefanos cock his head attentively toward some sound. She looked over her shoulder for the one-hundredth time since they'd left the farmhouse, wondering if she would ever really feel safe again. A lot would depend on whether or not Stefanos and the police caught the man on the scooter.

Stefanos started off again, and she hurried to keep up with him. In a few more minutes, they reached the police building, stepped under the blue-and-white Greek flag and opened the door. Molly let out a sigh, relieved not only for herself, but because she hadn't wanted any shooting to take place in town. Like Stefanos, she didn't want any innocent bystanders involved.

The policeman who came out into the hallway was one of the officers who'd met them yesterday. He frowned now as he listened to Stefanos. Stefanos looked over at her, his mouth pulled taut.

She touched his arm. "Did you tell him about the man at the house?"

Stefanos nodded.

"What did he say?"

"That he would round up some others and wait for orders." He nudged her in the direction of the stairs.

"Takis is here, then." Molly turned to look at Stefanos behind her for his answer.

"No, he's across the island, but Leo is here."

"Who?"

Stefanos spelled out the name. "Leo Rollins. I'm working with him to catch Julian's contact."

"And stop Topolac from getting the classified information."

Stefanos's brown eyes crackled with some dark emotion, but he merely nodded.

"Is this Leo guy from the embassy in Athens?"

"He's working on the Silver case. From New York."

Molly gripped the balustrade. "He thinks I'm working for Julian, doesn't he?"

Stefanos pried her fingers from the railing and held her hand between his two. "I've straightened him out on that already," he said. "Don't be afraid of him, okay? He's on our side."

She liked the sound of that—"our" side—and felt the warm glow of being included.

They climbed the stairs, and Stefanos knocked on a door. Someone must have answered, for he nodded to her and reached around to open the door. Molly took a deep breath and entered. A tall, beefy man in a white shirt and tan jacket rose from behind a gray metal desk and came toward them.

Stefanos shook hands and introduced her. The man said something to her.

"I'm sorry, I don't hear very well. Could you speak slower, please?"

Leo Rollins patted Stefanos on the shoulder and exchanged a few words with him, then looked at her. He didn't say anything to her, though, and Molly put a hand on Stefanos's arm. "Does he know about the man at the house?"

Leo's eyebrows rose. Stefanos explained what had happened. She presumed he did because she was too tired to follow his conversation. Anyway, Stefanos would tell her anything important.

Her legs felt weak from running over the uneven ground, and she started for a chair. Suddenly she felt an incredible tension charge the air, and Leo left the room. Molly glanced at Stefanos. He looked almost pale. Her stomach knotted. "What is it?"

"Leo went downstairs to talk to the police. We have to move fast." Stefanos rubbed his palm.

Molly watched his thumb slide over the center of his hand and felt the cold chill of premonition. "What else did he say?"

"Leo has identified the man who flirted with you in Athens," he said slowly, and his mouth twisted.

"Ismet," he spelled out. "He was the man in charge of my torture on Lidacros."

Molly stared. "Tell me you're joking."

Stefanos looked as upset as she'd ever seen him. "I wish I were. I didn't recognize him because I was usually blindfolded in Lidacros. But I heard his name." He grimaced.

Takis came into the office. Molly smiled at him. He returned her smile, put his hat on the desk, and spoke with Stefanos before leaving again.

"He's going to help Leo," Stefanos said. "They've organized a search."

"Good." She walked over to one of the windows and leaned against the sun-warmed frame, careful to stay hidden from anyone passing in the street below. "Why are you talking to the Greek police now, Stefanos, when you didn't back in Athens?"

Stefanos ran a hand through his windblown hair. "I couldn't do that without the go-ahead from Leo," he said slowly, finger-spelling Leo's name. "We couldn't be sure what action the Greeks would take. They might have been angry that the espionage had even taken place. They might have publicized it, and then we really would have had egg on our face."

"What about us?" she asked.

He looked at her, clenched his jaw, then shrugged. "We're going to wait here."

Five hours later, Molly put her sketchbook on the chair beside her. They were still waiting in Takis's office, or rather she was waiting and Stefanos was keeping her company.

He strode past the windows, pivoted and started back toward the metal file cabinets on the other side. She couldn't draw him, not when he was roaming around like a caged animal. Stefanos passed the desk, and her gaze skated over the ugly black gun resting there beside his holster. He came to a stop beside the file cabinets, his broad back to her.

"Why didn't you go with them?" Molly asked. "I would have been all right here with one of the Greek policemen."

Stefanos spun around. "You're my responsibility."

She straightened and tightened her jaw. She could accept his conviction that he had to protect her from Ismet. What she didn't like was his insinuation that she needed a baby-sitter. He was as bad as those darned bankers who'd refused her loan application.

Molly laid her pencil down and brushed the flyaway wisps from her forehead. Getting annoyed wouldn't help. "You wanted a personal hand in catching this Ismet, didn't you?" she asked. He stopped and propped an elbow on top of a file cabinet. His stalling attitude made her edgy, the way she'd felt with him when they'd first arrived in Athens.

Stefanos ran the flat of his hand over the cold metal of the cabinet, wondering why he didn't just answer Molly. He knew her well enough to know she'd persist until he did. Annoyance perked through him. Did she really need an answer? She already knew he wanted revenge. If she put two and two together from what he'd told her last night, she'd know why, too.

"They'll catch him," he finally said aloud and stalked back across the room, unsure if he believed his own words. He sure wanted to believe them, though.

"Pacing isn't going to help them catch the man sooner," Molly said.

Stefanos laughed. "No. It's only going to wear a hole in the floor," he signed, knowing she sat too far away to be able to understand his speech. He wondered how Leo planned to find Kemal Ismet. Anyway, the man chasing them had an identity now. He rubbed his palm and caught Molly watching him.

She held a pencil poised over the open sketchbook in her lap. He walked over to her chair and waved his hand toward it. "At least you've been doing something productive."

She smiled. He stared at her mouth. A totally irrational urge to kiss her rushed through him. It didn't come from desire, though that still lingered even after their intensive lovemaking last night. Where did it come from and even more importantly, why couldn't he stop thinking about being with her? An uneasy sensation moved through him. He crossed his arms, mentally slamming the door on his thoughts. He didn't want to pursue them now.

Stefanos looked down at what she'd drawn. "Who's that?" he asked, gesturing to the man's face on her pad.

"You."

His chest felt tight. "I would think you could find plenty of more interesting subjects."

Suddenly he heard voices in the hallway. Stefanos stepped to the desk and picked up his gun, holding it beside his leg.

Leo entered, looking disgusted, and Stefanos laid his gun down again. "Don't tell me you didn't find him."

His colleague pulled off his jacket. "That's what I'm going to tell you. We found the scooter abandoned on a beach, Paros Poros, I think Takis called it."

"That's the next beach down the road from the one at my house."

"Close then. How convenient. Looks like he had someone waiting for him in a boat."

Stefanos clenched his fists. "He's not going to stay gone. Topolac is probably putting lots of pressure on him."

Molly touched his arm. "I got that they didn't find him, but what else?"

Stefanos explained what Leo had said, then grimaced. "I want you to go back to Athens."

Molly's mouth dropped open. "Just like that?"

"Leo will take you back. If you go back with him, you'll be safer. I'll stay here and set a trap to catch Ismet. I would have done it before if you hadn't been with me." She crossed her arms. He ignored her gesture. "You'll be better off at the embassy in Athens. You can stay in my office. You felt safe in my office, didn't you?"

"I want to stay."

He shook his head. "That's not a good idea."

Molly turned toward Leo. Stefanos could see her about to involve his colleague in this discussion. Taking her arm, he steered her into a corner so they could talk privately. "So what are you going to do if you stay here?" he asked.

"Help."

He shook his head. "You can help by staying out of this. Ismet is clever and very dangerous. He'll be feeling desperate right now, too. It's Thursday evening now, but Topolac will be expecting him to get the microfilm before the international conference on Saturday."

"Okay, I understand that, but..." Molly paused and squared her shoulders. "It's my fault this is happening. If I hadn't had anything to do with Julian or had used a little more judgment with him, all this would have played out in the States." Stefanos didn't agree with her logic, but there was no point in going through the what-ifs. He started to speak, but she held up her hands. "Tom, your friend or colleague in Athens, wouldn't have been hurt. We wouldn't be trying to hide here in this village where people might get hurt."

Stefanos felt a muscle working in his jaw. "I've thought of that. That was one reason why we didn't stay in town." He took her by the shoulders, rubbing his thumbs over the ends of her collarbone. He didn't want Molly to get hurt, but he couldn't take her back to Athens himself.

She crossed her arms. "I want to see this finished. Resolved. I want to be able to go on with my life without looking over my shoulder all the time."

"And I want to go on with mine. You could get hurt. I've got enough guilt on my hands now. I want to get over it, not add to it."

"Why do you still feel guilty about my involvement? I thought we cleared that up last night."

He wouldn't get it cleared up until he'd either captured or embarrassed his old enemies. Molly looked up at him, her expression tough, probably as tough as she could make it, but not tough enough to handle this situation. He wasn't patronizing her, just being truthful.

Stefanos touched her cheek. "I don't want to say this."

"Then don't."

"I have to," he gritted out, hating that he might be undoing the self-confidence he'd tried so hard to give her last night. "Your hearing loss might be a problem. It would hamper you in a dangerous situation. One in which you might not be able to face me or whoever is talking. Do you understand?"

"Yes, Stef," she said patiently, her gaze never leaving his. "I do understand, and I appreciate your telling me." Leo stood up and Molly glanced in his direction. "I want you to hear this, too," she said, gesturing for Leo to join them.

Stefanos's frustration jumped a notch higher. She was going to see if Leo would take her side. Leo wouldn't want an American citizen killed, but he wanted to foil this espionage. He could be very single-minded about what he wanted, too.

"Look at this from Ismet's point of view," Molly said. "He probably saw Tom in New Jersey, probably knew he was a federal agent. He probably knows you're from the embassy, so he must think that you are holding me captive."

"That doesn't make sense, Molly," Stefanos said. "Why would I be doing that if I thought you had the microfilm? Why wouldn't I have taken you back to the States?"

"He must believe I still have it or else he wouldn't be here trying to find it. Besides," she continued, "what is he going to think if I disappear now? Isn't he going to go looking for me again?"

"She has a point, Steve," Leo interjected.

"Great. Agree with her."

Leo stared at him. "Why not?"

Stefanos slumped into a chair and rubbed his palm hard against the chair arm. Pain shot through his hand. He winced. Everything he'd done so far to protect Molly might count for nothing now.

"Steve?" Stefanos met Leo's gaze. "She'll have to stay with you," Leo said. "Can you handle that?"

No, not really, he said silently. Stefanos closed his eyes and raked his aching hand through his hair. Why was he letting Molly Light get to him? All he had to do was tell himself that she had nothing to do with him. *So let go.*

"If you can't," Leo was saying, "I'll stay. We have to catch this man."

"No. She doesn't understand you very well, and you can't sign. I can."

"Okay. We'll have to come up with a plan." Leo twisted his mouth in thought.

"Stefanos?" Molly's soft voice asked, drifting over him like the subtle scent of violets she wore. Jeez, how could he think about that now? He must be losing his mind. She walked across the room and stopped in front of him. "Do you want some aspirin?"

Concern radiated from her blue eyes. Flattening his mouth, Stefanos thought about the way he'd accepted her concern last night. It had brought them closer, but he didn't want to feel any closer to Molly than he did now. His guts were already turned inside out worrying about her safety.

"Stef . . ."

He met her gaze. "Why would I want aspirin?"

"You've been rubbing your palm for hours."

He looked down to see the thumb of one hand on the puckered palm of the other. Looking up again, he shook his head. "Aspirin isn't strong enough."

"Then why don't we get something at a pharmacy? Would they give you a painkiller without a prescription?" Stefanos nodded before he realized he was only encouraging her solicitude. "Can we go then?" She looked at Leo. "Didn't you say the man has left the island?"

Stefanos stood and answered for Leo. "It's only an assumption. Ismet is not a man who will give up."

Molly took his hand. He flinched. She raised her gaze, and the cool blue of her eyes splashed over him. Maybe if she just held on to him for a while, he wouldn't feel any more pain. No! He didn't want her holding on to him in any way.

"Isn't there a pharmacy or something like that on the island?" She raised her blond brows.

"Yes, of course."

"Go on, Steve," Leo said. "Let her play nurse. We've got some time before Ismet gets back. Go get something for the pain. You don't look like you can even pull the trigger of your gun."

That was true. Stefanos disregarded the holster and pushed his automatic into the back of his waistband, trying to ignore the pain pulsing all the way to his elbow. "The gun's going to show."

"No one saw it before?"

"We came through during lunch. I can hear people in the street now."

"Take my jacket." Leo tossed it to him. "Take one of the police with you, you hear? Just as a precaution."

Molly glanced out one of the open doors of the combination grocery-pharmacy where they'd come after leaving the police station. She didn't see the policeman who'd accompanied them, but knew he stood out in the street, which was crowded with tourists and locals now that the afternoon heat had started to wane.

Stefanos stood a few feet away talking to the pharmacist. He hadn't said anything to her since they'd left Leo. Was he embarrassed about his pain or annoyed with her? Perhaps she should have given in to him and agreed to leave the island.

She'd always been the one who had compromised in her marriage. She'd always been willing to accept a certain inequality because of her handicap. Not any longer, though. She knew she wasn't unequal now. Hadn't Stefanos taken away every last shred of doubt last night?

Stefanos glanced at her and raised a finger as if to ask her to wait a minute. She nodded, and he stepped behind the counter and out of view.

Molly walked across to the grocery side, careful to keep her distance from the entrance. No one knew the whereabouts of the man who kept following her. Ismet, Stefanos had called him.

What would she do if confronted by him again? She'd told Stefanos back at the embassy in Athens if that happened she'd just tell Ismet she didn't have the microfilm. Now she wasn't sure if she would do that, but she doubted she'd have to worry about him. Not with Stefanos and the policeman guarding her.

She walked toward the grocery counter where several customers were standing. She passed an aisle, only vaguely aware of its tall shelves stocked with canned goods. A single light bulb hanging from the ceiling illuminated the counter, and Molly watched a small woman dressed all in black with a basket on her arm negotiating a purchase.

She looked as though she'd been arguing with the grocer, but he laughed suddenly. A smile filled the woman's sun-wrinkled face with warmth, and their friendship made Molly smile, too.

Something metal and hard jabbed her in the back. She started to turn, thinking she'd backed into a shelf. The combination of black hair and intent black eyes made her heart stop. It was him! Ismet!

Panic rooted her to the spot.

His lips moved, and she heard bits of his speech. "I can't understand you. I have trouble hearing." She started to lift her hand to her ear as she always did when explaining her loss, but the metal pressed harder into her side.

She had to be careful. Really careful. Molly lowered her hand slowly. He nodded to her as if she'd followed instructions, then reached over her shoulder and dangled a folded piece of paper in front of her.

Looking over her shoulder, Molly watched his thin, pinched mouth, telling herself to stay calm. She had to in order to understand him. "Read," he said plainly.

She took the paper from him, and he moved his hand to the back of her neck. "Let go of me, please," she said, hoping the man understood that much English. Ismet left his hand where it was.

Molly unfolded the note. "I will take the microfilm off your hands now," she read. "They will kill you for it if I don't kill you first."

Her blood turned to ice as her brain frantically searched for a way out. Ismet poked the hard object—she knew it had to be a gun—into her side. The gun barrel didn't hurt nearly as much as the cramp in her neck.

"Kill," he said, prodding her. "I will kill you."

Was that really what he'd said? Molly blocked the words from her mind and turned slightly so he didn't stand directly behind her anymore. "You will be better hidden this way from the man guarding me. Understand?"

He nodded and pointed to the note again. Half-turned as she was, Molly could see into the pharmacy part of the store. Ismet wouldn't have a direct view. She hoped not, anyway, glancing toward the empty counter.

Where *was* her guardian angel? If only Stefanos—

Ismet jabbed her and said something.

Say something! You have to answer him. Yes, talking was the best way to gain control, she thought.

"I have it," she said. Sweat trickled down her temples. If she couldn't carry this off, she'd be dead. "You will take it to the man, won't you? Of course. Maybe you are the man I want, and I just didn't know it in Athens. It's in my bag."

Ismet started to pull her canvas bag from her shoulder, but Molly tugged back.

"No," she whispered. "You better not take the bag. Everyone knows this is mine. If they see you with it, they will be able to identify you. Wait. I will give you the film. I hid it in my camera."

She bent her head but slid a glance to the pharmacy side of the store while groping in her bag for her camera. Stefanos had come out from the back, thank goodness. He stared at her. She let her hand slowly fall and quickly signed "go" and "out," hoping he'd be able to read the last since it normally took two hands to sign. *Go,* she told him silently. *Go outside and wait.*

Ismet pressed closer now. She froze. He hauled her back into the shadows of the aisle. Terror clawed at her. Had Ismet seen her signaling? Would he kill her now?

"Come on." She stuck her elbow out as she took the camera from its leather case. "Give me some room. I don't want to take all day. The man guarding me will be back."

Ismet moved to stand slightly in front of her, and she saw him glance around the store. Her heart skipped a beat. Had Stefanos made it out of the store? She didn't dare look.

Ismet must be getting impatient, though. Molly began to rewind the film. "Ju-Julian made me carry it this way so that I could get it through customs undamaged."

He leveled his ugly gun at her, frowning darkly. Molly tried not to look at its long barrel. "What are you doing?" he asked.

"It's in the back." Her mind stalled. She'd thought about giving him the film in her camera, but now knew she couldn't. Microfilm wouldn't look like regular photographic film, and this man would see through her ruse. She pushed the camera at him hurriedly and looked around the store. "I don't have time to get it out. Here. Take it."

"If you are lying," he said and took the camera, "I will come back for you." Ismet glared at her a moment, then shoved her out of the way to disappear beyond the end of the shelves. Molly slammed against the hard edge of the shelf, but managed to grab hold of it to keep from falling. Ismet had vanished.

An outburst of noise came from the street. She stumbled out past the shelves and noticed the pharmacist frozen in the action of putting something away.

What had she heard? A gunshot?

People rushed around outside, but the dread growing in her kept her from moving. Suddenly a man loomed in the doorway and came directly toward her. Ismet? No, Stefanos! Molly's knees finally gave way, and she slipped to the floor.

Stefanos knelt beside her, his dark brows drawn together. "Where do you hurt?" he signed, then placed a hand on her shoulder.

"Nowhere. I'm not hurt. Did you—what happened to Ismet?"

"We caught him. He's on his way to the police station," Stefanos said. Tension tightened his expression and his brown eyes turned hard. "I told you how dangerous Ismet was, Molly. Didn't you believe me?"

"Yes." She smoothed her hair back from her forehead, wondering why he was so upset. She was safe. He was safe. They'd caught Ismet. "Of course I believed you."

"Why didn't you let me help you? I could have gotten you away from him."

She clutched her hands together in front of her. "But I wouldn't have heard what you were saying," she said. "I mean..." She shrugged awkwardly. "I thought you'd realize that."

He helped her to her feet. "You should have trusted me to come up with the best situation instead of signing to me to leave."

"How was I supposed to know what you wanted me to do?" she demanded. Molly looked away and rubbed her forehead. "I'm sorry, Stef. I—"

"We can argue about this later," he signed.

"I'm not..." Molly saw Stefanos glance toward the store entrance, and she looked over that way, too. Curious onlookers peered inside. "Okay. We can—" She stopped when Stefanos put his arm around her. She looked up into his eyes.

"Molly." He shifted his arm lower and steered her toward the pharmacy counter. "Remember when Takis came into the office, I was talking to him?"

"Come to think of it now, I remember you both gave me a funny look."

"He had spent the morning with a Hollywood producer showing him around the island." Stefanos rubbed a finger under his nose, then continued speaking slowly. "The man was looking for movie locations."

"Movie locations?" She suddenly figured out why he hadn't wanted to tell her. "Warren?"

Stefanos nodded. "We might run into him. I think I saw him outside just now."

She peered around him. "You thought I'd be upset, didn't you?"

"The last time you saw him, you were."

"I know."

Stefanos turned. A number of people had come into the store, among them a tall, red-haired man. He headed straight toward them. Warren first spoke to Stefanos, then grasped her arm. "Did you see what happened?" he demanded, or she thought that's what he said.

She extricated herself from his grip, surprised she felt none of the usual pain and humiliation his presence brought. "Yes, I saw what happened," she answered. "Interesting, huh?"

Warren looked as if he wanted to say something else, but she turned her back on him. "Come on, Stefanos. Let's get out of here."

Chapter 11

"Hold the pencil like this," Molly said. She leaned over Nikos's shoulder to gently position his fingers on the pencil. They sat together at the table in the kitchen of Takis's house after dinner where the aroma of cinnamon from Sofia's special moussaka still lingered in the air. Sofia sat across the room and a policeman stood outside the door. Stefanos said it was just a precaution. They weren't expecting trouble.

She'd been with Stefanos so constantly the past four and a half days, it seemed strange not to have him right beside her. She missed him, and yet it couldn't have been more than two hours since he'd brought her here from the pharmacy.

And why should he be concerned with her now?

He thought of her as just part of a job. His job had been to get the microfilm from her. That had led him into protecting her when he'd discovered she didn't have it. Now that she no longer needed protection, he didn't have to stick to her side.

She'd told him at the police station she'd wanted to get on with her life. Funny, she couldn't imagine a life without him. She'd better start trying, she thought, trying to ignore the sadness creeping around the edges of her heart.

He'd warned her about seeing Warren, though. If he'd just been doing his job, he wouldn't have cared about her feelings.

Nikos shifted beside her.

Molly blinked, realizing the child was waiting for her to continue. "Okay." She smiled at him and cupped her hand around his. "Move the pencil like this." She made several sweeping circles on the page. "There you have the basic face shape." Nikos looked up at her, his dark eyes dancing merrily. "Do you understand?"

"I understand. I do, I do. Stefanos teach me good English, and in school, too, I learn."

The boy settled into drawing, and Molly found herself glancing often at the door, wondering when Stefanos would return. She knew he and Takis had driven Leo Rollins, the Defense investigative agent, to the small airport on the southern half of the island. Leo and several of the island policemen were taking Ismet, her pursuer, back to Athens.

When Stefanos returned, would he still be angry with her over what had happened at the grocery-pharmacy? He had flustered her then. Maybe he would have done a better job than she had, but his needing to be in charge irritated her. She'd tried to explain to Stefanos her reasons for controlling the situation with Ismet, but she wasn't really sure why she had. She'd been stalling. Why? Because she'd wanted Stefanos to succeed in catching the man. Why had Stefanos's success mattered so much?

Because she loved him.

Her mind turned the words over wonderingly. She loved him. Was she rushing things? She'd known him only a week.

"This is the *Elli*. You see?" Nikos held up a drawing of a ship.

"I do." She recognized the island ferry on which she and Stefanos had arrived. "That really looks like the ship."

"I will add the—" He stopped and shrugged. "I don't know the English word. You will see."

She watched him add the pier to his drawing, wondering if she should do anything about her newly discovered feelings. First she had to see how Stefanos felt.

Nikos had just finished his pier when Stefanos and Takis came into the house. The room seemed brighter, as if Stefanos had brought the sunshine inside with him. He looked tired and happy and handsomer than she could ever remember. He relaxed against the doorjamb, bracing his hand on his belt and slipping a finger under a belt loop of his jeans while he looked across the room at Nikos.

It seemed to Molly the time passed as slowly as if it were hours instead of seconds. She waited, her heart in her throat, for Stefanos to meet her gaze. When he did, she smiled. One corner of his mouth curled upward, bringing out the dimple. Dare she hope *her* smile had brought out his?

Nikos jumped up and started chattering in Greek. Stefanos glanced at the boy, who carried the sketchbook over to show Stefanos what he'd drawn. Molly watched him bend over the tablet, attentive to the earnest explanations of the child. His brown eyes positively glowed with affection, yet last night when they'd discussed Nikos, Stefanos had denied loving the child.

Stefanos laughed now and ruffled the boy's hair, telling him something. Nikos nodded and returned to her, closed the tablet and held it out. "Why don't you keep that one?" she suggested. "I have another."

The child gave her a charming smile. Molly hugged him, noticing over his shoulder Takis returning from the patio. Takis said something to Stefanos. Nikos drew back and looked at Stefanos expectantly. So did Takis. Stefanos shook his head.

"What is it?" she asked.

"Takis is taking the family across the island tomorrow," Stefanos explained, his brown eyes steady on her. "But Nikos doesn't have to go. I can have him for the day, if I want."

Nikos tugged on her arm, and she looked down into his pleading dark eyes. "Please, please help. It is good for us to be together. No?"

Molly caught Stefanos's gaze. "You would enjoy that," she whispered, not sure if Nikos could understand her.

Stefanos shoved a hand through his hair and studied Nikos solemnly. Molly held her breath. What would it hurt him to acknowledge his affection? Stefanos spoke to the child. Shrieking with pleasure, Nikos skipped across the room and flung himself into Stefanos's arms.

Once Nikos calmed down again, Stefanos arranged for them to meet the boy in the morning. It was time to say goodbye then. After thanking Takis and Sofia for their hospitality, she and Stefanos left.

Stefanos paused in the small enclosed courtyard behind the house. Moonlight danced off the whitewashed walls enclosing them in a silvery stillness. She hitched her bag higher, unsure whether to speak or remain silent, step toward the gate or stay still.

Stefanos was watching her, and his dark gaze sent a shiver of excitement through her. Molly tensed. She didn't want to feel that sort of excitement until she knew for sure she could build on it. But how to go about finding out if she could?

She hooked her thumb around the straps of her shoulder bag and stuck the other hand in her pocket. "I think you'll be glad you agreed to see Nikos tomorrow. It will be good for both of you."

"Maybe," he signed. In the moonlight she saw his hand movements plainly.

She waited for him to say more. When he didn't, she looked down, tracing the edges of the paving stone at her feet, restless but also determined not to lead this conversation. The yellow flame of his lighter blazed, and she looked up, watching smoke rise from the end of the cigarette he'd just lit.

"I hope I'm not making a mistake with Nikos," he signed after pocketing the lighter.

"Why would it be a mistake to spend time with him?"

Stefanos shook his head. "He could become attached to me."

"He already is."

Stefanos held out his hands in a gesture of resignation before signing, "I think you're right."

Molly touched his arm. "I'm really curious, Stef. If I were in your shoes, I'd be thrilled to have his admiration and friendship."

She knew Nikos's feelings went beyond friendship, but Stefanos had never used the word "love" to describe any relationship—not to her, anyway. Surely he believed in love, though.

"I hope he won't hang his happiness on what I do," he signed, his gestures sketching a smoke design in the air. "That was nice of you to give Nikos the tablet."

She smiled, pleased Stefanos would notice and go to the trouble to tell her so. "He enjoyed our drawing lesson."

"You did, too. I think."

"Yes. I like teaching children. That's why I wanted to buy the school."

Stefanos turned and his face fell into shadow. Molly knew he was thinking about her words, and she wished she could see the expression in his dark eyes.

"Will Nikos have the opportunity to do more art, you think?"

"Why not?" Stefanos drew on his cigarette. "If he has talent, I want him to develop it."

"Then you do think about his future?"

"Yes." He crushed his cigarette in a small metal can on a worktable beside him.

The gesture had a sort of finality about it that brought the beginnings of discouragement. If he couldn't admit to loving Nikos, she doubted he would ever tell her he loved her. She didn't know that, she reminded herself, but because of what had happened with Warren she needed to hear the words—from the man this time, not herself.

"I was thinking of Ismet," Stefanos said without preamble.

Molly smoothed the flyaway wisps from her forehead. "If Takis is taking time off tomorrow, and, I mean, isn't that business all taken care of?"

Stefanos shrugged. "Ismet may not have been here on the island by himself. He could have ditched the motor scooter at the beach and then hitched a ride into town ahead of us, but he had help in Athens and probably did here, too."

Molly wrapped her arms around herself and glanced around. Would Stefanos hear if anyone walked past in the street on the other side of the wall? Stefanos put his hands on her shoulders, the gesture strong and tender at the same time. He was full of contrasts, she thought, intriguing but very confusing contrasts. He dropped his hands to sign, and disappointment washed over her. She'd been hoping he would slip his arms around her and pull her close. He had when he'd comforted her before.

"The police are being cautious and we will be, too," he signed. "Even if Ismet was working with others, he was probably calling the shots. Anyway, the focus will shift from you and me to Ismet now. Topolac will try to get him out."

"Get him out?" She stared at him.

"Don't worry. I don't think he'll manage it."

Molly nodded. Stefanos said nothing more for a moment, but his jaw tightened and his fists clenched. "So why are you frowning?" Molly asked.

"I won't be able to show the world how dangerous Topolac is without the microfilm for proof," he signed, stopping to spell out several words, his movements jerky with suppressed anger.

Molly cupped his bare forearm gently—soothingly, she hoped. He didn't pull away. Encouraged, she slipped her hand down to mesh her fingers with his. "Maybe Julian never had time to make that last film."

"Maybe," Stefanos signed, letting go of her.

This conversation wasn't going anywhere, she realized, certainly not in the direction she wanted it to. Molly suddenly felt tired, physically, mentally and emotionally. "Look," she said, drawing his gaze. "Should I stay here in town tonight?" He gazed down at her, and even in the moonlight she could see the quizzical expression in his eyes. She cleared her throat a little nervously, conscious now she couldn't retract her words. "I saw a hotel when we first arrived. I could probably get a room there."

"That's not necessary. I think you should come back to the farmhouse with me just in case. Do you want to?"

"What do *you* want?" she asked.

He touched a finger to her cheek. "I'd like to be with you again."

Fiery sensations spiraled through her, settling low. She pressed a hand to her abdomen. He still wanted her. She wanted him, too. No two ways about it.

He'd said nothing about feelings, though. Making love with him would only add to the pain she already felt, the pain of loving a man who might never be able to return that love. Did she need to go through that again?

"Did you understand me?" he asked, stroking her cheek softly.

"You want a one-night stand."

"We've already had one night. This would be the second." He smiled and she could sense the mischievous sparkle in his eyes even if she couldn't see it.

She returned his smile halfheartedly, looking away from him. The night breeze moved through the bougainvillea that dipped low over the wall, scattering a few blossoms across the flagstones. Eventually all the blooms would fall. Time passed. Tonight would fade into tomorrow, and tomorrow they'd probably be saying goodbye. Would she ever forgive herself if she didn't go with him tonight?

Molly reached up to smooth his crumpled collar, smiling. "I'd like to be with you, too."

Stefanos led Molly along the waterfront where they picked up the main road out of town. At the top of the hill he stopped her. "Let's take the footpath. It's prettier than the road and will be safer."

They walked in silence, Molly slightly in front of him. Stefanos looked out over the landscape, picking out the white rectangles of the farmhouses scattered across the hills. The moonlight blessed the countryside with a quiet peacefulness. Usually the island nights calmed him, but tonight his thoughts would not be still.

Why hadn't he let Molly stay in town? Takis had offered to let her stay with them. Was he being a fool? What was making love to her again going to prove? He didn't intend to have their relationship go beyond tonight. Hell, he hadn't meant it to go beyond that kiss back in Athens at his house.

She'd said he wanted a one-night stand, and he should have cut things off right there. Molly wasn't like the other women in his life. They knew he only wanted a casual relationship. So why hadn't he warned her away? He could easily have told her he never made promises—not of a personal nature. Was it because she hadn't blamed him for getting her involved in this dangerous situation?

It *was* his fault, but it seemed fairly certain the danger had passed. He would be content to be with her tonight, he decided. He would not worry about tomorrow. Hadn't she sounded as if she planned to do that, too?

He hoped he would be happy with her, anyway. He had the feeling he'd upset her with his remarks about what she should have done at the pharmacy with Ismet. The fact that they'd both gotten out of the situation alive was the only thing that mattered, and he knew it. Deep down, he'd known it then, too.

Stefanos looked over at Molly now, watching the moonlight in her hair. She'd braided it again, he thought with a sigh. Still, her blond hair glowed silver in the moonlight, making her seem more like a fantasy creature than a real woman.

They came to a place where the wall along the upper field had fallen apart, littering the path with rocks. He took Molly's arm to help her around the obstacles. The feel of her under his fingers reminded him she was flesh and blood and not some elusive night image.

Her hand felt good in his. Good. She'd been so good to Nikos. His heart filled with an emotion he could never remember having for a woman. He admired Molly. Was that why he wanted her when his better judgment told him he shouldn't? His gaze fell to her slim hips as they rounded a bend in the path, and his body tightened with the primitive male longing never very far beneath the surface when he was with Molly.

Molly halted, and Stefanos, sensing her fear, pulled his gun. She pointed a trembling finger at a family chapel next to the path ahead of them. "There's someone inside," she whispered.

His breath stalled in his lungs, and he quickly released the safety. "What?" he signed with his other hand.

"That light. See that light."

Stefanos realized now that she was pointing at the soft yellow glow in the small window of the apse. He'd seen it, of course, but hadn't thought twice about it. "Candle," he spelled after putting the automatic away. He tucked a strand of hair behind her ear before continuing with speech and signs. "A candle is always burning inside this chapel. I see it every time I come back this way at night."

"Doesn't it ever startle you?"

"No." He regarded the light in the small window. He always felt safe here at night—peaceful. Tonight he felt restless. They still needed to be careful, but just being with Molly gave him a sense of living dangerously. Danger had never bothered him, and tonight it gave an edge to his perceptions.

"I'd be scared even if I expected to see it," Molly said, referring again to the votive candle in the chapel. "Until I'd actually seen the candle, anyway."

"Sorry. Can't show it to you. It's a private family chapel. You probably noticed some others. There are a lot of them on the island. I look forward to seeing this candle, as a matter of fact. I'll tell you why when we get back to the house." He put an arm around her shoulders.

She relaxed against him, and her trust filled him with a warmth. Stefanos led her on around the hill and down to the road and the dirt track to his farmhouse. When they reached the clearing in front of the house, he pointed toward the beach. "The beach would be a good place to talk. Would you like to see it?" He raised an eyebrow in question.

"Sure." She smoothed her hair back from her forehead as if she was nervous, but smiled and let him take her hand.

Looking out at the strip of sand curving around a little bay, Molly thought the beach was exactly as Stefanos had described it when they'd stood in the clearing yesterday.

Could it have been only yesterday? She felt as if she'd lived a lifetime since then. Certainly she felt wiser and more confident. In some ways, she amended. She felt nervous right now, not about herself or her sexual abilities but about Stefanos's mood.

He started toward the water and Molly followed him, feeling the light breeze tease the loose strands of hair about her face. The open space between land and sea seemed boundless, and she opened her arms as if she could embrace that freedom.

At the water's edge, he stopped and swept out an arm to encompass the bay and beach. "What do you think?"

She caught the little furrow between his brows, and it reminded her of his nervousness about his farmhouse. His vulnerability had touched her then. It touched her now, making Stefanos less of a super government spy and more of a man, a man who might be able to love her. "It's really lovely." Molly sat on the sand and reached back to free her hair.

Stefanos pushed her hands aside and finished unbraiding her hair. He combed his fingers through the strands, and her tension slipped away, carried off by the soothing sensations his movements evoked. Coming with him tonight had been a good decision.

"Why is it you feel so wonderful when someone does something with your hair?" she asked, thinking aloud.

He moved to sit beside her. "It's the animal in us." She glanced at him, startled by his answer. One corner of his mouth lifted. "Are you afraid of our animal legacy?" he asked, finger-spelling most of the question.

"No." A chill passed through her, though. "It just seems that there should be more to it than that."

She'd wanted him to say something romantic, she realized, even though she knew she ought to stop thinking romantically about Stefanos. For him this was just a one-night stand—two-night stand, she corrected. She could still back out of it, she supposed. Doing that now would be embarrassing, but she could.

She tilted her head. "Did you want to talk?"

He faced the sea, sifting a handful of sand through his fingers before looking at her. "I was terrified for you today."

"Oh, Stef." Molly put a hand on his arm. "Thank you for saying that." He clasped his hand over hers and gave her a crooked smile. Her heart flip-flopped.

"I would have felt so guilty if anything had happened to you." Stefanos stared at the mass of broken shells and dried seaweed at his feet. "You were very cool under fire. It surprised me."

"I've been around men with guns before."

He frowned. "Your ex-husband?" he signed.

"No. One of my foster brothers used to get a little wild. Warren kept a gun, but I don't think he ever could have used it. He never did, anyway."

"I see," he both signed and spoke.

Molly smiled inside, amused by his words. It didn't sound as though he "saw" or understood anything.

"You were going to tell me about the candle in the chapel. The moon is pretty bright. I can see your mouth well enough to understand what you're saying if you want to speak."

Stefanos removed his gun and holster and folded his legs Indian-style. "When I was kidnapped, I was kept in a dark room. Sometimes I was blindfolded, too. But every night Nikos would bring me something to eat. He would always light a candle first, and I thought about that candle all day. It was the only thing that got me through, I think."

She took his hand in hers. It seemed an inadequate gesture, but the way they sat made it awkward to twine her arms around his shoulders for a real hug. Had he positioned them this way on purpose? She looked down at his long fingers lying against her palm. "You don't have to think about it anymore."

Stefanos tossed a broken shell into the water with his free hand, then glanced at her. He looked as though he was thinking about her—hot, erotic thoughts. Mesmerized by his gaze, she felt him loosen his fingers and slip them up to encircle her wrist. "I'm not thinking about Lidacros now," he said.

His vibrant energy thrummed through her, bringing to life a sharp physical yearning. She longed to know if Stefanos also felt a special desire for her. Maybe he would tell her, if not in words, then in actions. "Do you know what I'm thinking?" she asked, referring to his last remark.

He lifted an eyebrow in question.

"I'm thinking that if you and Leo hadn't thought I was involved in this espionage scheme, you never would have followed up on my note." She laid a hand on his thigh, needing to experience his heat and wanting to let him know.

He turned to her, spread his legs, and drew her within them. "I would've been a fool if I hadn't."

She cupped his face, rough now with a day's growth of beard, and he leaned into her hand. His skin's distinctive scent drifted to her, overwhelming the smell of the night that clung to his shirt and playing on her senses. She stroked her thumb down to the corner of his mouth and felt her own pulling into a smile.

He kissed her palm. Gazing into his dark eyes set a thrill fluttering in her heart. It began to beat harder as he leaned forward and lightly brushed his lips across hers. Molly licked her lips, and her tongue brushed his mouth. They hovered so close, but not close enough.

She narrowed the distance. "Stef—"

He kissed her. Joy and desire blended together and she lifted her mouth to his again. This time his arms came around her, and he kissed her deeply. Molly started to press herself against him, but he lifted his head.

She looked up to see him smiling. The moonlight shimmered around them, painting Stefanos's hair and eyebrows silver. Molly marveled at the power he had over her, a power she now willingly gave into.

He gestured to the water. "I want to show you something."

"Show me something?" She laughed. "Now?"

"I plan to get back to kissing you, don't worry." He gave her a sexy smile, then tossed another piece of broken shell into the water. "Did you see that flash of light in the water? I'd forgotten we could see it at this time of the year. Watch." He pitched a third shell into the water, and she saw what he was talking about. Bits of gold rode the ripples he created. "It's plankton in the water," he spelled.

"Plankton?"

He nodded his hand for yes. "Microscopic animals," he spelled before reverting to speech. "I remember as a kid how I thought I was making the water light up when I was swimming. I want you to see it, too." He traced a finger from her shoulder down over the tip of her breast.

Molly caught her breath. It had to be a sin to feel this good, or a sin to let him make her feel this good.

He unlaced one of her tennis shoes, slipped it off, and caressed her ankle.

"We don't have to go into the water, do we?" His only answer was to trace a finger down the top of each toe. "I guess we do," she whispered.

He laughed. Gently tugging on her hair, he drew her forward and outlined her mouth with the tip of his tongue.

"Stef—"

He slipped his hands down over her shoulders and asked, "Can you swim?"

She nodded, too aware of his hands to speak.

He stood, pulled her to her feet and reached behind him to pull his shirt over his head. He dropped it to the sand, then leaned over and popped the button of her jeans.

Molly gripped his hands.

He stepped back. "What is it?"

She glanced over her shoulder toward the road. She couldn't see it, but she knew it was there. "Someone will notice us."

"No one will." He kicked off his tennis shoes and pushed his own jeans down, baring his long, muscled legs. "There are no other houses, and all the farmers are home now. They're not traveling down the road."

She gazed at him. He had such a perfect body. He felt at home with it, and he'd tried to make her feel comfortable with hers, too. He definitely had, and she wanted to show him she now felt the same confidence he did.

Molly grasped the hem of her knit top and pulled it over her head. Dropping it to the sand beside his, she felt his gaze on her. The heat suffusing her from within made the night air feel that much cooler, but she didn't shiver. "Have you gone skinny-dipping before, Stefanos?"

"Only alone."

A new wave of heat rushed over her skin. Now he wanted to experience it with her.

He stepped closer to bring his chest mere inches from hers. Her nipples chafed against the satiny fabric restraining them. She wanted to press them into his warmth, wanted to feel his springy chest hair caressing her sensitive skin. He slid his fingers along the bottom of her bra to the fastening at her back. Molly impatiently wound her arms around his waist, resting them on the hard ridge of his hipbones.

The clasp gave. Molly sighed. He slipped the straps off her shoulders and brought their bodies together. For a long moment, neither of them moved, then his breath fluttered across her shoulder.

"Umm. What did you say?"

He stepped back, letting his hands slide to her hips. "I love the way you feel."

"That makes two—" She gasped, her breath caught in her throat.

Stefanos had unzipped her jeans and was pushing them down. She'd been naked with him before, but something about being outside made everything more exciting—and scary. It was as if he could see her more clearly, and surely tonight he'd notice the appendectomy scar and all her other imperfections.

He knelt on the sand and looked up at her. He'd brought her jeans down her ankles, and she knew he was waiting for her to step out of her clothes. She hesitated, feeling shy.

"You're beautiful," he said, signing the words, too.

Did he really think so? A sweet shudder of anticipation turned her knees to jelly. She braced her hands on his shoulders, and he freed her from her jeans. Still kneeling, he skimmed his hand up her leg, brushing the thatch of hair at the top of her thighs.

"If you continue like this, I'm not going to be able to walk to the water."

He laughed and stood.

She placed her hearing aid deep inside one of the pockets of her jeans. He took her hand and led her to the water's edge. Soon the sea lapped at her toes, then her ankles, then her knees and thighs. She sank lower to let the warm Aegean lap around her shoulders. Where she broke the surface of the silky sea, rings of dull gold phosphorescence flashed. "It's like finger painting with light," Molly said.

"I've always thought of it as fireflies locked in the water," he said.

He gestured for her to follow, then swam to deeper water where he stood and waited for her. When she reached him, he slid a hand up her hip and over her rib cage, stopping just shy of her breast. Molly's blood raced. He pulled her close, kissed her, then let her go. She caught his shoulders, moving her body against his, and kissed him back.

The plankton choreographed their movements with light. Just as their movement drew light from the dark water, his mouth on hers plucked something bright from their dark insecurities and doubts. She could almost see it when she closed her eyes.

Stefanos lifted her in his arms. Cool air against her wet skin made her feel new and fresh, yet hot inside, heavy, yet insubstantial as the moonlight. He kissed first one breast then the other, and Molly ran a hand through his wet hair, letting the heavy strands fall through her fingers. Stefanos lowered her and buried his head in the hollow of her shoulder. The solid feel of it in that vulnerable place sent shivers of delight all the way to her toes.

"We can capture some fireflies of our own, you know," she said.

"I know," he signed.

He took her hand, guiding her toward the beach. Excitement washed through her, lapping and tugging at her like the heavy, glittering Aegean pulling at her legs.

Stefanos rose from the water beside her. She glanced at him, taking in the glistening strength of his strong, male body and the very definite evidence of his desire—for her.

Chapter 12

Stefanos listened to the night. Around him, the languid waves lapping against their legs, the breeze, and even the stars all seemed to sigh—the way he wanted to hear Molly sigh when they made love.

The sand became firmer beneath his feet now, and as they left the water, the night air warmed and invigorated him. Stefanos glanced down at the beautiful woman walking beside him. She was everything he found desirable, he thought, and every nerve cell in his body chorused agreement.

Molly's wet hair flowed across her shoulder. He lifted a strand, twirled it around his finger, then rubbed it across his lips.

She turned her gaze on him. The moonlight shone on her wet face, but her expression glowed with something else— the heat he hoped was building in her. He wanted to ask how he appeared to her, but something held him back. Besides, words weren't important. Their need was all that mattered right now, he thought, pulling her close and nuzzling her neck.

She smelled of the clear, blue Aegean, and his hunger for her was like that of the land for life-giving water. He couldn't imagine being anywhere but in her arms, couldn't imagine doing anything but making love with her.

"Oh, yes, do that," she said, her voice breathy and urgent.

"I've hardly done anything yet," he murmured and felt a tremor move through her. His groin tightened at the thought of all the things they'd do tonight.

She rose on tiptoe, and he caught her mouth, seeking and searching, all the while drinking in her intoxicating taste. The kiss lengthened and intensified, bringing their hunger to the edge. Stefanos urged her away and led her up the beach to where they'd left their clothes. He spread his shirt on the sand and lowered her to it, then knelt in front of her, barely aware of the soft fabric or the coolness of the sand against his legs.

Molly gazed at him, her blue eyes dark now, magical and mysterious as the night. He felt as if he stood on some precipice with a deep, unexplored valley below. It would be dangerous to go—especially without a candle. She lifted her head and kissed his neck. Light burst within him, and he smiled. He didn't need a candle now; he had Molly.

He lowered his head to capture her mouth. Her kiss should be salty, but all he tasted was honey, sweet and thick like the hunger pouring through his blood.

He filled her with one long, smooth thrust. Together they explored the edge of that dark valley carefully, slowly. Suddenly, without warning, she pulled him over.

The valley was no longer dark. It shone full of radiant light. He could see into the corners of the world and of life, and he wanted it to go on forever.

He held her afterward, and when she grew chilled, they dressed. He took her back to the house, where he made her a cup of tea and tried to ignore the disorder Ismet had wreaked in his quick search. It brought back the question he'd pushed from his mind, the question of how Molly saw him.

Stefanos found his cigarettes and lit one. He'd tried to live his life so that he felt proud of his actions. He didn't want to care what someone else thought. Somewhere along the line, though, Molly's assessment of him had become important.

His chest tightened. He took a long draw on his cigarette and waited for the tension to dissipate. He wanted to know her feelings about him, but he couldn't risk asking her now. Perhaps he never could. It would mean facing something he'd put out of his life forever.

Molly sat on the bed, peering at him over the mug she held. She looked as though she expected him to say something. He wanted to say he was glad she'd come home with him. He wouldn't mind telling her in great detail just why he'd enjoyed that last hour at the beach, either.

She wasn't like the other women in his life, he reminded himself. He needed to start stepping back emotionally and helping her to do that, too. He tapped the ash from his cigarette. He could compliment her, he supposed. That might lessen any awkwardness she felt at saying goodbye.

"You know, Molly, I really admire what you're trying to do with your life. Buying the school. A lot of people want things, but they're not willing to do what's necessary to make their dreams come true." He smiled.

"Thanks for the compliment."

"It's not a compliment. It's the truth."

She blessed him with a glorious smile, her blue eyes limpid. He shouldn't have said anything, he thought, curling his fingers around the cold steel of the bed frame.

Molly studied the way Stefanos's long, tanned fingers gripped the headboard. The fire they'd shared at the beach had dissolved into a comforting warmth when they'd returned to his farmhouse, but it seemed to have disappeared now.

Surely she was wrong, she told herself, and she settled the warm mug in her lap as if to reassure herself. "You mentioned you'll be going back to work for the shipping company. In New York?"

"Yes." He raised an eyebrow.

Molly hesitated. Should she take the lead after all? She took a sip and caught Stefanos's gaze. "I want to see you again."

"Why? We've been together only a week." His grip seemed to tighten on the bed rail. "What do you really know about me?"

"I know what I feel and how you make me feel," she protested. He rubbed a hand across his mouth in a weary gesture. "I'm only saying I think we should get to know each other better." She gestured, her palms out. "We could spend some more time together. That's not a commitment."

"Yes, it is. It's a commitment in time and a pledge to be willing to compromise because of the relationship. It's also a sort of promise that I am interested. I'm not going to give you that promise."

She leaned forward, a fierce desperation eating at her. "But I care about you, Stef."

"Don't say that," he demanded.

"What's wrong with saying I care about you?"

"Nothing, I guess." Stefanos sank onto the bed, and turned to face her. "Not as far as you're concerned."

"And what about where you're concerned?"

"I don't have permanent relationships with people."

Her heart plummeted, but she refused to give up. Hadn't he just told her he admired her persistence and drive? Yes, and at the moment, conquering his fear or his guilt or whatever it was took priority over everything else she'd ever wanted, even the school. "You could start now. I'll help."

"No!"

She flinched as if he'd hit her.

He took her hands and rubbed his thumbs across her knuckles a couple of times. "I mentioned something way back last week. About how my grandfather and mother used to fight over me. At least, I think I mentioned it. We were talking about flying and I was certainly thinking about those two." He paused.

She nodded her understanding.

"I'd like to tell you a story. After my father died, I used to fly to Greece every summer to see my grandfather and the rest of my father's family. That's when I used to come here to this house."

She watched his face, not sure she was going to like the end of this story.

"I thought the world of both of them. My mother was the most beautiful, sophisticated woman on earth. My grandfather was the most wise man on earth." He laughed, his mouth twisting bitterly.

"The summer I was ten years old, my mother was seeing a man—seriously. In fact, she let me stay here several weeks longer because she and her lover went to London. My grandfather took advantage of that. He told me he didn't want me to go home. He wanted me to stay with him all year."

Stefanos grimaced and took a drag on his cigarette. Molly wanted to take his hand, but he might stop. She wanted him to finish his story. Talking about the experience might help him get beyond it.

"My grandfather told me he needed me, and my mother didn't need me. He explained that my mother had kept me after my father's death only because she wanted to use me as a bargaining chip. Apparently she'd married my father for his money. When he died, she'd agreed to let me visit in the summer only if my grandfather supported her in style." Stefanos finished his cigarette and put it out.

"I would have been happy to stay in Greece, but I hadn't figured on my mother. When she came to get me, and I told her I wanted to stay, she looked crushed. Maybe she really did love me, I don't know. But she accused me of trying to hurt her. Made me feel so guilty. So did my grandfather. I felt like some sort of criminal, and all I did to deserve that was care about them. Actually they'd been treating me like that all my life, but I hadn't noticed it until that incident."

Molly took his hand now. She saw him look down at her fingers intertwined with his before extricating himself.

"I don't put myself into that sort of position now," he said, his mouth flattening.

A position in which he might start caring for someone, Molly added silently. A painful coldness cloaked her, heavy and suffocating. She drew her knees up, wrapping her arms around them, wondering how she could feel anything. She told herself she should have waited until they'd been on their way to Athens to discuss their future. She told herself she should have waited for him to bring up the subject.

No! Timing wasn't the problem. She'd been mistaken again. Once again she'd misinterpreted a man's feelings.

She rose, her heart a heavy stone in her chest, and went into her bedroom, hardly aware of the shambles it was in. She cleared her bed and stretched out, staring into the dark and telling herself to admit the painful truth. She hadn't been wrong about Stefanos.

They'd shared something wonderful and unique, and she knew with every fiber of her body he'd felt the same. Stef was the only one who'd ever made her feel whole and worthy. He had patience where she had impetuosity, sophistication where she had laid-back naturalness.

They both had a high sense of honor, too. It was too bad Stefanos didn't want to honor his own heart. He wouldn't admit his feelings to her. He wouldn't be able to until he wanted to, and he didn't want to now.

Tears stung, and she blinked them back. She'd die if Stefanos heard her crying.

The next morning when she woke, Molly felt she'd hardly slept at all. She hadn't for a long time, anyway. She hadn't cried, either, but she'd lain awake a long time thinking about Stefanos, about how sensitive of her feelings he was, about—

Molly took a deep breath and got up. She had no idea what time it was, but they'd promised to meet Takis and take Nikos to breakfast. She didn't like the thought of keeping them waiting. Stefanos might use her lateness as an excuse for not going at all. Even if he couldn't admit to caring about her and a future with her, he'd come pretty close to admitting the extent of his feelings for Nikos.

She looped her hearing aid over her ear and turned it on. In the dim light she could hardly see what she was doing. The window would allow in some sunlight, and now that they no longer had to hide, she could open it.

The shutter scraped against the stone ledge, and Molly paused. She hadn't heard any noise, and she knew in the quiet she would have if her aid was working properly. Suddenly she remembered that her battery had died last night on the way back from the beach. She must have been lip-reading Stefanos during their disagreement, though she hadn't realized it at the time.

She dressed in a blue chambray shirt and a fresh pair of jeans and looked for the case with her spare aid and batteries. There were two cardboard trays of batteries. No, one was empty as she'd told Stefanos two nights ago. When she'd changed the battery at the restaurant back in New Jersey, she'd put the empty package back in the case rather than leave it on the table. She pulled both packages out now, and a small, thin roll of photographic film fell onto the table.

She stared at it, terrified. Yes, eight millimeter film, that's what it was. She'd seen that type in a photography store once and remembered thinking the camera using that size would be very small.

Stefanos would want to see this. Her heart hammered against her chest at the thought of his reaction. Would he think she'd hidden it from him all along?

In the front room Stefanos leaned against the open door, his back to her. "Stef?" she asked and repeated his name, unable to determine how loudly she talked. He looked over his shoulder, then almost immediately turned from the jamb to walk over to her.

Molly tensed and told herself he wouldn't hurt her. He looked pretty upset, though. "What's the matter?" he signed.

"Is this what I think it is?" She held up the strip of film, letting it slowly unwind.

"My God." Stefanos took it by the edges and held it up to the light pouring in the door. "It looks like it contains about fifty exposures."

"Do you think this is Julian's microfilm?" Molly whispered.

"Yes," he signed. "where was it?"

"In the case with my other hearing aid and batteries."

He frowned. "We looked in there."

"I know." She swallowed against the tightness building in her. He probably thought she'd been hiding it all along. "But this is the first time since we left New York that I've had to change a battery. And when we were looking at them before, I just showed them to you. We didn't take them out of the case. That's probably the only reason I found it today. I took both packages out of the case."

Stefanos followed her into the second bedroom and examined her case, looking in the side with the spare aid, too.

"Do you think there's more?" she asked. He said nothing, just continued to turn the case around in his hands. "It must have been stuck behind the pocket flap so we didn't notice." She twisted her hair back from her face, wondering what else she could say.

"But how did it get there?"

Molly made a vague gesture. "If Julian really did make the film, he must have hidden it in there."

Stefanos raised an eyebrow. "Without your knowledge?"

Molly started to explain but stopped and took a deep breath. When she got nervous, her voice rose and she didn't realize it. If she didn't stay calm, Stefanos might not believe her. "He came to my apartment to take me to Kennedy Airport. I remember he followed me into the bedroom while I finished packing. He didn't help me pack; but he could have stuffed it into the case when I was standing at the closet trying to decide what to take."

Stefanos pursed his lips.

"I guess I should have mentioned all this, but he didn't have anything to do with my packing and he was never alone with my stuff. When we were looking through my bag—"

"It was my mistake," Stefanos interrupted to sign, then reverted to speech. "I should have been more thorough. I was feeling guilty because you looked so afraid."

"I'm scared now."

He pulled her into his arms. "Why?"

"You think I lied to you, don't you?"

The shock on his face appeared genuine, and relief washed over her. "No," he signed and sat on the bed. "I know you, Molly. Obviously Silver planted it on you. I think he meant to get the film from you here in Greece. Didn't you say he'd planned to join you?"

She nodded. He smoothed the bedspread beside him and gestured for her to sit, too. As she did, the old mattress sagged, throwing her against him.

"What are we going to do?" Molly put her hand on his thigh but lifted it hurriedly. She needed to start backing off from him, she reminded herself, and rubbed her palm down her own leg. "So what are you going to do now?" she repeated.

He stood. "I want to look at this film more closely. At the police station. If it's what we think it is, Leo needs to know immediately."

"Where are you going?" Nikos asked, jumping up from the white plastic chair he'd just sat down in.

They'd arrived at one of the cafés on the waterfront only moments ago, and Stefanos knew the boy expected him to sit down with him and Molly. Stefanos smiled and pressed gently on the boy's shoulder, urging him to sit again. "Nikos," Stefanos said in Greek, squatting in front of the boy, "I must make a phone call, and I am leaving you in charge. See that Molly eats some breakfast."

He glanced over at her. She stared out at the fishing boats bobbing in the water off the beach, sitting quietly, much too quietly.

He handed Nikos some drachma notes. "I will probably be back before you finish. If Molly doesn't order anything, you get her an omelet or yogurt. Understand?"

"*Ne, ne.* Yes, yes."

"*Kalo.*" Good. Molly's word, he thought sadly. He ought to be happy right now because things were indeed good—except between him and Molly. Stefanos stood and touched her shoulder.

She looked up at him, shading her eyes, but otherwise not changing her posture or expression. It was as if she was numb, he suddenly realized.

"I will only be a few minutes," he signed.

"Okay, sure." She gave him a smile that didn't meet her eyes.

Dammit! She'd wanted the mystery about the microfilm resolved, too. Why couldn't she be happy?

Because I rejected her and I know how much rejection hurts.

Confused and annoyed by that conclusion, Stefanos made his way through the tables to the arcade. He paused there and pulled out his cigarettes, thinking absently that he ought to give them up. He was smoking way too much these days. He ought to walk on and stop watching Nikos and Molly. That's what he ought to do. She was smiling at the boy now, and Stefanos felt as if he were being turned inside out.

After lighting a cigarette, he strode past the front of several more cafés to the winding street that would take him to the police station. Perhaps he didn't have to be on guard with Molly. His mind replayed the thoughts he'd had last night and again this morning. He'd revealed an awful lot about himself and she hadn't used this knowledge to manipulate him in any way.

Molly wasn't like his mother. She hadn't tried to make him feel guilty, and he'd certainly given her plenty of opportunities. She might never blame him, but he couldn't bring himself to chance it. He had tried to be fair to Molly and yet he'd wound up hurting her. He couldn't blame her for asking questions. He'd owed her the answers. After all, they'd made love together.

The smoke from the cigarette began to bother him, and he ground it out. He immediately wanted another but jammed his hands into the pockets of his windbreaker instead. Tension burrowed between his shoulder blades. Stefanos rolled his shoulders in an effort to work it out. He ought to be feeling relieved instead of regretful. He and Molly had finished the inevitable discussion. They were both free to get on with their own lives, and if he didn't stop replaying these thoughts he was going to drive himself crazy.

Out of the corner of his eye, he caught sight of the big, red-haired fellow who walked toward him. Stefanos lifted a hand in greeting but said nothing as they passed. Flint might ask about Molly, and he didn't want to discuss her with anyone. He wanted to start putting her out of his mind.

Ten minutes later, after first stopping by the bookstore that handled the island's air transportation, Stefanos stood in Takis's office talking on the phone. He'd just finished explaining to Leo about finding the microfilm. Now, he stuffed the envelope with the film back into his jacket pocket, the action pressing the butt of his gun into his flesh.

"Molly and I are taking a flight back to Athens." He gave Leo the arrival time. "Can you have someone meet us?"

"Will do. Want to hear what Ismet told us?"

Stefanos nearly dropped the receiver. "He talked?"

"Yeah. He's the one who broke into Light's apartment. It seems Julian Silver would give Ismet the film and he'd take it home or give it to someone else to bring home. Get this, though. Ismet never paid Silver. Someone else was doing that. We don't know who yet—that's another thing we're working on. Wait a minute."

Stefanos heard Leo speaking to someone else at his end of the line.

"Something's just come in, Steve. You asked one of the fellows here to find out what he could about Warren Flint, didn't you?"

"Yeah, I did." When he'd been obsessed with knowing all he could about Molly, thought Stefanos with a grimace. "It's not important now."

"Oh, but it is. We found out some interesting things."

The dawning of a premonition raised goose bumps on Stefanos's arms. He rubbed them while Leo continued.

"Seems Flint has received three big bank drafts in the last six months. Let me see..." He paused. When he spoke again, he sounded excited. "He got them each time after Silver's technical information arrived in Turkey."

"That doesn't have to mean he got the money from the Turks."

"Name of the originating bank would seem to confirm that it was from them."

The tension gripping Stefanos grew unbearable, and he could hardly raise his hand to wipe the sweat from his brow.

"Uh-oh, listen to this, Steve. My people have been asking around Julian Silver's condo building. They started including questions about Flint after your request for information on him."

"It was a personal request," Stefanos grumbled.

"Well, we disregarded that. Good thing, too. Seems some guy we'd never talked to—he was out of town before—identified Flint as someone whom he'd seen in the building. Said he remembered Flint because of the red hair. It was around the time of Silver's murder, too."

The air in Takis's office seemed to be disappearing. Stefanos took a deep breath. If Flint was involved, he'd be feeling a lot of pressure from Topolac to produce that film. Molly's ex-husband had been awfully anxious to get together with them in Athens, and out of all the islands in the Aegean, he'd turned up here on Paros. Because he thought Molly had the film?

"Leo," Stefanos said, "I just passed Flint in the street."

"You didn't tell me he was on the island."

Stefanos ran a hand through his hair. Warren Flint was all tied up in Stefanos's private feelings for Molly, but that was no excuse. "Well, he is."

"The Light woman could be in danger."

"Right! Got to go!" Stefanos jammed the receiver into its cradle, raced down the stairs and out of the building.

He'd hardly gone twenty feet when he saw Nikos running toward him, his face anxious. "Stefanos, Stefanos!"

Stefanos caught him. "What is it? Where is Molly?"

"A big man came and made her go away with him. I tried to stop him, but he pushed me away. I beat on him, but he just laughed. And—" Suddenly Nikos burst into tears.

Stefanos hauled the boy into his arms. "It's okay. He was too big for you to fight. Did he hurt Molly?"

Nikos shook his head. "But she didn't look happy."

Fear stabbed through him. Stefanos felt his whole body tighten. "Where did they go?"

Nikos sobbed and pointed. Stefanos smoothed a hand over the boy's head, fighting back his impatience. "Do you know where they went?"

"Up the hill—hill you go past to get to your house."

"I'm going after them. Wait here." Stefanos set the child down and ran to the waterfront.

Shielding his eyes with a hand, he could barely make out someone in blue near the spot where the road curved out of sight. Someone in bright yellow moved along beside the blue. He swore. Flint had been wearing a yellow shirt.

Stefanos started off in their direction but stopped before he'd covered ten yards, gulping for air. He'd never catch them even if he ran flat out. The best he could do was get close and call out. That wouldn't help. Molly wouldn't hear him, but Flint would be warned. Better to keep the element of surprise on his side.

Stefanos pivoted and ran back to the police station.

Chapter 13

The taxi screeched to a halt where the dirt track leading to his farmhouse met the main road. Stefanos stepped out into the hot midmorning sun, his gut clenching painfully. He prayed he wasn't going to be too late.

He could use a cigarette right now. Smoking calmed him, and he needed to be calm. Molly's life would depend on his remaining in control.

Before he'd gotten back to the police station from the waterfront, he'd spoken to Nikos again. The boy had confirmed his suspicions that Molly and Flint had come here, volunteering that Molly had said something about him and about his house.

The wind whispering through the cane sounded loud in his ears, and he shifted his weight while he listened to the policeman giving instructions to the driver. Stefanos hoped the man would stay out of harm's way and wished he hadn't needed to involve another civilian. He and the policeman with him had been forced to use a taxi, though. Takis had driven the only police vehicle on Paros across the island.

He mentally tried to calculate how long Molly might have been here with Flint. Anything more than a couple of seconds was too long for anyone to be in Flint's presence. Especially now. Topolac, an expert at applying pressure, would have Flint good and worried. Stefanos could only hope Flint wasn't yet at the point of being frantic.

Loose rock on the edge of the road slipped under his shoe. As Stefanos set foot on the cane-edged track to the farmhouse, he gestured to the policeman to follow. Together they ran down the path, and Stefanos continued to think about what might lie ahead. What sort of marksman was Flint?

Molly had said he owned a gun, but a lot of people owned guns they didn't know how to shoot. If he was a good shot, he wouldn't miss, and if he was a poor one, he might kill them all because he didn't know what he was doing. Either way, there wasn't much in their favor.

Stefanos picked up his pace. *Please let him get to the house before Flint can hurt her. Please!*

At the edge of the clearing, he stopped, panting. The house looked deserted, the front door closed. Stefanos studied the scene, his anxiety rising. Had Nikos misunderstood or had they stopped somewhere on the way? He hadn't noticed anything irregular along the road, but he hadn't been looking, either.

Voices—two voices—came through the half-opened window in the back room. A ripple of relief passed through him. At least Molly was still alive.

"I will go in," Stefanos whispered in Greek to the officer beside him. "We need to get the woman out," he said, checking the clip in his gun.

The policeman frowned and shook his head. "We should wait for reinforcements."

He was talking about the policemen who had been called to back them up. Stefanos had no idea how long they would take to get there. Only minutes, he hoped. He heard a voice again, this time only a male voice.

Stefanos's heart slammed into his chest. He could picture it now. Molly wouldn't be able to understand Flint, and he would yell at her. When she still didn't get his meaning, he'd get even angrier.

"We must act now," Stefanos insisted.

"I will go." The officer squared his shoulders and raised his weapon.

"No. Molly will not understand you." Stefanos shook his head and tightened his grip on the automatic. "Back me up. I will call to you when I need you."

He slipped forward, sensing rather than seeing the other man follow him. He would get Molly out of that house if it was the last thing he did. It might well be, he thought grimly.

The musty, pungent smell of the grape arbor closed around him as he stepped over the low retaining wall and under the trellis. He didn't know what he was going to do when he got inside, he realized. Maybe he ought to pretend he didn't realize she was in danger and make it look as if he'd just stumbled in.

He took off his holster and handed it to the policeman when Flint's voice rose again. No way could anyone not hear that—except Molly, and he imagined her crouching on the bed, frightened and confused. Cold crept over him even as he felt the heat of the flagstones under his feet.

Stefanos released the safety on the gun and ran to the door. He eased down on the handle of the latch. No click. Good. Slowly he pushed on the door and prayed it wouldn't catch on the floor. It gave easily for once, and he congratulated himself. He should be able to sneak in unsuspected.

"Hold it."

Stefanos froze. Across from him, standing at the entrance to the second room, stood Warren Flint. He held Molly against his chest with one beefy arm. The barrel of the small automatic he held to her head gleamed in the sunlight coming in the open door.

"Toss your gun out the door," Flint commanded.

Stefanos looked at Molly. Flint had her face twisted to one side. From the strain on her features, the position hurt. Stefanos snagged Flint's gaze. "Let go of Molly and tell me what you're doing here."

"The gun, lover boy."

Flint sounded like a villain from a cop action movie, thought Stefanos, his gut twisting. The kind with lots of shooting, car chases and people falling off roofs.

"What are you waiting for?" Flint demanded.

Stefanos tossed his gun outside. It made a sharp, metallic sound as it hit the flagstones of the terrace. Amazingly it didn't discharge.

Flint tightened his grip on Molly. Angry words sprang to mind, but Stefanos bit them back. He had to talk, though. Fast. He had to figure out the things to say to get Flint to let Molly go.

Stefanos flicked a glance at her, afraid to look at her too long for fear Flint would see his concern and capitalize on it. Molly watched him, her eyes ice blue with fear. He would get her out of this, he promised her silently.

"Follow instructions like a good boy, don't you?" Flint sneered.

"I try to." Sweat trickled down his brow. He hoped Flint would think it was from the heat, not from the very real fear beating through him. "Now let—"

"Shut up and close the door, real easylike." Flint jerked his arm higher so that it pressed against Molly's throat.

The look on her face made Stefanos feel as if he'd been slugged in the gut. Carefully he nudged the door back with the heel of his foot, leaving it open a crack so his backup could get in quickly when he called for help.

"All the way." Behind his glasses, Flint's pale eyes became hard.

Suppressing a sigh, Stefanos reached behind him and pushed the door until the latch clicked. He intentionally did not glance at the metal bar lying behind one of the chairs beside him. "Now let go of Molly."

"Not yet. Put the bar on the door, and don't try any funny business."

Stefanos's heart jumped into triple time. "I don't think that's a good idea."

Flint scowled, and for a moment, Stefanos thought he knew about the policeman outside, the policeman who wasn't doing him any good. He couldn't chance calling for help with Flint still holding Molly.

"You don't think I'm going to let you turn around and waltz out of here, do you?" Flint asked.

He sounded cocky, thought Stefanos. Flint's grip loosened, though, and his arm dropped down to Molly's shoulders once again. Stefanos said a silent prayer of thanks.

"Why not?" Stefanos asked. "What have you done?"

"Warren, let me go," Molly pleaded.

"Don't!" Stefanos signed before Flint could respond.

"So, you can talk to her. You like Molly, don't you?" Flint pushed her, urging her forward into the center of the room. "Then you'd better put the bar on the door."

Stefanos bit his lip, turned and slowly slid the heavy steel bar through the door slots. They were caught now, all three of them. No, he had an idea. First, though, Flint had to let Molly leave.

Flint abruptly released Molly. "Damn woman. She's no help at all." Molly staggered, and Stefanos started forward to help her. "Move, and Molly gets the first bullet. Get over there, Molly."

Molly stared at Flint. Stefanos urged her silently to look at him. She did and he beckoned with his chin. She took a step, then another and another, moving with agonizing slowness. Finally she was close enough that he could reach out and pull her close to him. They were making progress. At least he had her on his side of the room and could take the first bullet, he thought grimly.

"You're looking for Julian Silver's film, aren't you?" Stefanos asked.

Warren Flint raised his bushy eyebrows. "Yeah. Got to get it to the man who wants to buy it."

"Topolac," Stefanos muttered.

"Hey, you're smart."

"How do you know him?"

"You don't follow the movies much, do you? I made a movie in Turkey year and a half ago." Flint's mouth twisted. "We got to be pals, you know."

"How did you know he would buy this information?"

"I'm smart."

Stefanos could almost see the other man's chest puffing out. Molly brushed her fingers against his leg. *Yeah, I know,* he told her silently. They'd have to let him talk a little first.

"I figured the Turks wouldn't mind having a few fancy planes," Flint continued boasting. "And I knew who could get the information. Julian always did like the little luxuries of life." Flint's mouth twisted.

"So you helped him get them?" Stefanos asked.

"He didn't appreciate my help. The jerk got greedy. Thought he could double-cross me and sell it on his own." Flint laughed.

The sound sent a shiver down Stefanos's spine, and he slid a glance at Molly. She held herself rigidly, leaning forward slightly, trying to understand. Stefanos wanted to sign to her but didn't dare.

"You thought you had everything solved when you caught that guy last night, didn't you?" Flint asked.

Stefanos nodded slowly. Flint was talking about Ismet now.

"I didn't have to do a thing as long as that Turk was trying to find the film, you know. Too bad he couldn't have been a little more clever. I really thought he'd get it from you."

"Ismet didn't know you, did he?" Stefanos asked. He pretended to play the man's game while he searched for some lever to negotiate Molly out of there.

"Of course not. Like I said, I was clever." Flint motioned sharply at Molly with the barrel of his gun. "Come on, Molly, Silver said you had the film. I'll bet you've found it by now."

"We found it, all right," Stefanos said. "But she doesn't know where it is anymore. I do."

Flint's expression darkened, and he took a menacing step toward him. "Why didn't you say so before?"

Out of the corner of his eye, Stefanos saw Molly shaking her head. Either she didn't understand his words or she didn't understand his motives. "Let Molly leave," he said to Flint.

"She'll run to the police."

"No, she won't," Stefanos answered.

"I don't have time to talk. Hand it over."

"He's just talking, Warren," Molly said. "He doesn't have the microfilm."

"Molly . . ." Stefanos touched her arm.

She took a step forward. "I have it."

Flint's face flamed. "Which one of you is telling the truth?" he shouted.

"I am," Stefanos said.

Flint aimed the gun at him. Stefanos swallowed, knowing the other man's fuse was burning fast. Molly had to get out of the house now. Stefanos glanced over to find her watching him. Good. She was going to follow his lead this time. He would use her trick, he thought.

"D-o-o-r," he spelled. A flicker in her eyes told him she understood, and he looked at Flint, catching his gaze. "I'll give you the microfilm as soon as—" he reached for the bar on the door "—you let Molly—"

Molly stepped forward out of the way. It was just a tiny step, but it drew Flint's attention.

Almost as if it were in slow motion, Stefanos saw Flint's finger tighten on the trigger, saw him swing his arm toward Molly. Flint was too far away for him to lunge for the gun, but he could knock Molly out of the way. Stefanos threw himself at her.

The gun thundered, deafening him momentarily. Molly fell on him. He rolled her under him and leapt to his feet, ready to go at Flint.

The man cowered against the corner cabinet, his empty hands held high. Takis and two other policemen held him at gunpoint. How had they gotten . . . ? The window, the open window in Molly's—

Molly!

She lay inert on the stone floor, a red splotch spreading rapidly across her knit top. *No,* he screamed inside. This can't be happening.

Somewhere between Paros and Athens, Stefanos watched Molly open her eyes. She looked straight at him and her lips moved. He touched her cheek and bent close to hear what she said, trying to block out the whir of the emergency helicopter's blades.

Her breath fluttered across his cheek, but he couldn't quite grasp what she said. "Molly," he said and straightened in order to sign to her. "Will you repeat—" He stopped and dropped his hands.

She couldn't see him. She'd closed her eyes again.

Stefanos stared at her, feeling as if a heavy weight were crushing him. He'd heard one word clearly—the word "guilty."

Yes, he felt guilty. He felt as if he wore that guilt like a second skin. Stefanos took her hand, willing her to open her eyes, to smile, to do something that would tell him she'd be all right. Her eyes remained closed.

Stefanos only vaguely remembered their arrival at the hospital. He *did* remember every agonizing minute of the operation and the first time Molly opened her eyes afterward. She hadn't recognized him, and he'd died a little inside.

Stefanos swallowed the last of his coffee and walked across the hospital waiting room to dispose of his paper cup, wondering if Leo would come back. He hoped not. He was sick to death of talking about Ismet and Topolac and Flint.

"Do you think it looks like Molly?" a child's voice asked as he neared the bank of chairs again.

Stefanos glanced down at Nikos. Sofia and Takis had brought him to Athens yesterday because he'd been so upset about Molly. The boy now held up the tablet Molly had given him. On it he'd drawn a picture of Molly. While it was childlike, Nikos had captured the way her blond hair seemed to work loose and make a halo around her face.

"Do you, Stefanos?"

Stefanos nodded, sank into the seat next to the boy and, leaning back, closed his eyes. If Molly never regained the use of her arm, she wouldn't be able to draw anymore.

"You worry about her. I worry, too," Nikos said. "She is nice."

Stefanos opened his eyes and tried to smile. "That's what you said when I first introduced you to her." Molly was nice. Nice people shouldn't get shot, either. They should be protected, and he hadn't protected Molly.

"She is very sick, no?"

Stefanos was about to respond when the shuffle of feet and the sound of voices made him look up. Takis strode toward them. He shook hands and asked about Molly. Stefanos rubbed his forehead. "I don't know. I wish she'd just—" He stopped not sure what he wanted most. To see her smile? To hear her voice? To know she'd be okay?

Takis nodded solemnly and held out a hand to Nikos. "I will take Nikos home. He has bothered you enough."

Stefanos straightened. "No, no. Let him stay awhile yet." He looked down at Nikos. "Do you want to stay a little longer?"

Nikos nodded, and after a few more minutes, Takis left. Nikos did not go back to drawing, though, and Stefanos wondered, watching the child walk restlessly around the room, if he'd made a mistake in letting him stay.

The child came to stand before him and folded his arms. "Am I going to see Molly? Can I see her, Stefanos?"

"Let's find out." Stefanos checked with the nurses. At their okay, he led Nikos to Molly's room, where they found her still asleep.

"Is she going to be all right?" Nikos whispered.

"I hope so." Stefanos ushered the boy out and steered them back toward the waiting room.

"You should stay with her. She's lonely."

Stefanos wasn't sure he could stand to be next to Molly and see the price she'd paid for his mistakes. "She won't know I'm there."

"Maybe," Nikos said with a shrug.

Stefanos remembered when Nikos had been in the hospital after their rescue in Lidacros. "You were lonely in the hospital, weren't you?"

Nikos nodded. "I thought you'd be there."

Stefanos swallowed. He hadn't been able to sit beside Nikos's bed because he'd been in another room, doped up with painkillers. The child might never have known that, and Stefanos wanted to kick himself now for never explaining.

Nikos propped his hands on his belt, looked down at the tablet, picked it up and put it down again.

"Nikos?"

The boy's dark gaze found his briefly.

His heart twisted, and Stefanos gently drew the child into his embrace. "I love you, Nikos. Always remember that. You always make a happy place in my heart." Stefanos lifted the boy onto his lap.

"Is it true?" Nikos asked softly.

"Yes, it is true."

* * *

Molly thought she saw Stefanos, but he seemed to fade in and out of a soft, rainlike mist somewhere between daylight and night. Maybe she only imagined she saw him. Her right shoulder and arm throbbed with pain. That must be her imagination, too, because sometimes the pain also went away.

She couldn't even be sure where she was. It was a place full of strangers, and they were all bending over her, talking to her or poking at her. Stefanos was there, too, though she didn't understand why. He talked to her, but she couldn't hear him. When she tried to ask him to speak louder, he disappeared into the fog again.

The next time she saw him, he appeared clearly. She turned her head and studied him as he sat looking worn-out in a chair beside her bed. His eyes were closed, and for a panicked second she thought he might be dead. No, he breathed. His chest rose and fell.

Molly lifted her head and looked around. Hospital? Yes. Definitely. Probably in Athens, she thought. Her chin brushed something bulky and soft. She lifted a hand, felt the bandage on her shoulder and remembered everything that had happened at the farmhouse. Well, she remembered everything up to the point where Stefanos had knocked her down.

The fog in her brain cleared completely now, and Molly knew Stefanos had really been there beside her. It hadn't been her subconscious need conjuring him up.

Her throat clogged with gratitude. Molly swallowed and looked at Stefanos again. He might wake any minute, and she wanted to feast her gaze on him a little longer while undetected.

His dark eyelashes lay like little crescent moons against his cheeks. His russet-tinged brown hair in disarray, he looked innocent and cute, like a little boy, although his cheeks were darkly shadowed. She'd never seen him asleep, she realized. Would he have allowed her to see this vulnerability before? She thought not.

He wore a navy suit, white shirt and striped tie, as if he'd come from a day of work at the embassy. She glanced at the window behind him. The blinds had been raised, and she stared at a reflection of herself in the dark glass. Night again, she thought with discouragement, bringing her gaze back to Stefanos.

She remembered another night, the night he'd brought her back to the farmhouse from the beach. She'd mismanaged things badly then. She'd wanted so much for him to meet her halfway. He hadn't, and she'd pushed him. Regret twisted in her heart, and she sighed.

Well, he might not have been willing to say how he felt, but he'd shown her. She'd never expected to see him again after she'd left the café with Warren, but she had. He'd come to save her.

Was she searching for crumbs? she asked herself, feeling anguish tightening her mouth. Stefanos felt no anguish, not if the angelic look on his face meant anything.

His eyelids fluttered open, then his brown eyes stared at her. Molly tried to look away. He would see how she felt. He would—

Stefanos surged out of his chair to her side. For a moment, they only looked at each other. Molly took in the grooves on either side of his tight mouth, and the one that drew his brows together, but she hesitated only a second.

"Hi," she said as cheerfully as she could.

"Hi, yourself," he signed.

"Want to hand me my aid? I don't know where it is, but I hope I still have it."

"You still have it." He opened the drawer of the bedside stand and took out her hearing aid.

Molly watched his long, elegant fingers check the battery chamber. He gave the aid to her, and she looped it on her ear, wincing with pain.

"How do you feel?" he asked, his gaze shadowed with concern.

"Fine." He looked as though he didn't believe her. "I'm fine. What happened? I don't remember a whole lot about the argument with Warren." She thought she knew but she'd been so frightened at the time, she couldn't be sure now.

Stefanos cupped her cheek. "Can you understand me if I speak?" She nodded. "Flint shot you. I'm sorry he had to hit you. I was trying to get between you." He ran a hand through his hair, separating the waves so that one cascaded over his forehead.

"You're going to be all right," he continued, repeating his words with signs. "No nerves were damaged, so you'll still be able to draw."

Molly curled the fingers of her right hand. "I could probably do some now. I should, I guess. I have to—" He shook his head. "Stef—" She tried to sit up, grimaced and lay back.

Stefanos touched her cheek and shook his head. "Don't try. You have plenty of time."

His concern warmed her like spring sunshine. She wanted to tell him so, but he might think she was trying to pressure him. She'd take what he could give. It was enough for now that he'd stayed with her at the hospital.

"Where's the film?" she asked. "Warren didn't get it, did he?"

"No. It's safe. He's being extradited back to the States to face charges."

"Good. How did he know we were on the island?"

"Flint went to the embassy. He waltzed in and demanded to speak to me. When I wasn't there—" Stefanos paused and rubbed the bridge of his nose "—he pretended to be a relative of yours who needed to find you because of some problem at home. My assistant knew I had a house on Paros, and she thought we'd run off together when I didn't return as scheduled. I'd only told her I'd be away for a few days. I never told her I'd planned to take you to Germany."

Molly felt a smile play across her mouth. "We did run off together."

Stefanos grimaced. "She told Flint where you were."

"She was jealous."

He nodded. "That's my fault again."

Molly plucked at the sheet. He was still using guilt as a shield.

Stefanos stroked the flyaway wisps of hair from her forehead then signed, "Why did you tell Flint you had the film?"

"That's an easy question." Molly wished he would touch her forehead, just once more and she'd be satisfied. "Keeping it from Topolac was so important to you."

"Someone would have caught Flint," Stefanos said, signing as he went along. "Leo knew about him, too."

"But he would have killed us. Or if I'd left the house the way you wanted me to, he would certainly have killed you."

His gaze met hers, fierce and tender at the same time. The now-familiar longing wound down through her. She ignored it. She needed to know he'd stayed with her not because he'd felt responsible, but because he'd wanted to.

Stefanos pulled a string of amber-colored worry beads from his jacket pocket. Molly watched him twirl them around his fingers. She'd seen lots of Greeks play with worry beads, but never Stefanos. "I didn't know you had one of those."

"Just bought them. They're taking the place of my cigarettes."

"Oh?"

"You told me smoking wasn't good for me."

Had her opinion made that much of a difference to him? Her heart warmed, but she told herself not to read anything into his decision. She smiled. "I'm glad you're giving it up," she said.

He nodded.

Molly watched him swing the beads against his hand. He had really handsome hands, she thought. Her gaze traveled to the white cuff of his dress shirt. "Were you at the embassy today?"

"No. You have to admit I needed to change out of those jeans I'd been living in."

It sounded as if he meant to joke, but when Molly glanced up from his mouth, she found a troubled look in his brown eyes. "Stef, I told you not to feel guilty!"

Stefanos just stood there, motionless. "I told you on the plane, or wherever it was, not to feel guilty," Molly repeated.

The railing along the hospital bed fenced her in, and Molly glared in frustration at the IV attached to her hand. She wanted to stand up in front of Stefanos and give him a good shake.

Stefanos stared at her, his dark brows drawn together. Out of the corner of her eye she saw his fingers capture the beads in his palm. He slipped them into his pocket and smoothed the flap closed. "Is that what you told me?"

She nodded. "What did you think I'd said?"

"All I heard was the word 'guilty.' I thought you blamed me for your getting shot."

Her frustration evaporated and she lay back against the pillow, feeling a smile soften her mouth. "I would never do that, Stef."

Turning his back to her, he walked over to the window. Molly rubbed her cheek against the soft cotton of the pillowcase, and studied his broad shoulders. Now, if she could go to him, she'd put her arms around his waist and rub her cheek against his shoulder. "I wish you'd believe me."

He spun around and signed emphatically, "I do."

"Then what's the problem?"

"I'm trying to work up my courage to tell you something," he signed and walked back to the bed.

"That shouldn't be a problem. You have lots of courage."

"No, not always." He sat down beside her and clasped his hands together on his thigh.

Molly pushed herself higher, and Stefanos reached behind her to plump her pillow before urging her back gently.

The hospital gown dropped off her good shoulder, but she ignored it. He pulled it up, tucking it behind her neck. "Nikos was here," he said.

"Really?" She leaned forward. Pain stabbed across her chest but she ignored it. "Is he okay?"

Stefanos coaxed her back against the pillow again. "You must not hurt yourself."

She swallowed around a lump in her throat. He didn't want to know how much she was hurting herself just loving him.

"Nikos is fine, and he'll be glad to know you're fine, too." Stefanos smiled wryly. "He was almost as worried about you as I was."

"Stef, he loves you. You should—"

"I love him, too."

She stared at him a moment and was about to ask if he'd told the child this when Stefanos touched a finger to her lips. "Nikos helped me discover something about myself, something important. I had to tell him my feelings to make him feel better, and it made me feel better, too. It was like a boulder falling off my shoulders."

Stefanos slipped the tips of his fingers under hers. His heat telegraphed through her, and Molly shifted her hand so their palms touched.

He looked down at the bed, then raised his gaze. "Do you know," he asked, speaking and signing both, "all these years I've been trying to stay away from guilt, and yet I've been using it as a crutch, a defense mechanism? It worked fine until I met you, even up to the time I told you about Lidacros the first night on the island.

"I could admit to feeling responsible for something and feel guilty about it, but I couldn't admit to being afraid."

"What were you afraid of?"

"I was afraid of trying to make someone happy and risking failure again."

She brushed her fingers across his knee where it rested on the bed beside her and could feel the strong bone beneath the crisp fabric. "What about now that you've met me?" she asked, mentally holding her breath.

"It's not working with you. I tried to feel guilty, but you wouldn't let me. You wouldn't blame me."

"Are you still afraid?"

"Yeah, but I think I can face it now that I know it's there. When we talked at the farmhouse, I didn't want to try to understand what was happening to me. I wanted to sweep the subject under the table, but I tried to give you an explanation. I owed you that much."

Molly lifted her hand but couldn't reach far enough to clasp his. Stefanos seemed to know what she wanted, for he linked his fingers with hers. He was so perceptive of her moods, she thought, feeling a spark of hope inside. "I don't want you to owe me anything," she said. "Whatever you give me, I want you to give it freely."

He frowned. "What do you want me to give you?"

Love.

His gaze connected with hers. For a moment, she thought he might have read her mind. She thought he might even respond. He said nothing, though.

Well, she had something to say. She smoothed her hair back from her forehead with her free hand. "I was afraid, too, Stefanos."

"Anyone would have been in that situation."

He was thinking about their confrontation with Warren. "I suppose so," she said. "But I'm talking about when I insisted we see each other. I was afraid if I didn't open my mouth then, I would never see you again. I know now I wasn't being fair to you."

His gaze found hers, the little chips of burnt sienna glowing in the deep brown of his eyes. They reminded her of the phosphorescence she and Stefanos had seen at the beach the last time they'd made love. She wanted desperately for them to have a chance to make love again.

"Forgive me?" she asked.

He pointed to himself. "I'm the one who should be asking forgiveness."

Did that mean he was asking for it? From her? Would he really let her see him as vulnerable and needy? The hope within her began to burn steadily.

"We have to take turns," she teased, hoping her words were the right ones now.

Stefanos nodded, and his fingers squeezed hers as if he never meant to let her go.

"I love you, you know," she murmured.

Stefanos held her gaze but said nothing.

Molly closed her eyes. A pain that had nothing to do with her shoulder seared through her. The touch of his fingers on her cheek and the sound of his voice made her open her eyes again.

He smiled, a smile filled with hidden laughter and sunshine, a smile she'd never seen on his face before. "I'm glad you do. Because I think I love you, too."

"But you hesitated."

"I'll get better with time. I haven't confessed my love since I was ten years old. That's a long time ago."

"Oh, Stef." She pulled his hand to her mouth, disregarding the flash of physical pain from the movement.

"I thought we could get married as soon as you get home and start the fall session at the school. How does that sound?"

"Married?" she repeated hesitantly, unsure she'd really understood him.

He lifted her left hand and rubbed the base of her ring finger. "You've heard of that custom, I believe?"

Epilogue

Molly guided the little blond boy out the front door of the Newpark School of Art and into the summer sunshine. "Go along, Teddy."

Teddy patted her on the hip, and she looked down, cherishing the open affection the child showed her. "Your mommy's waiting. I'll see you in September."

The little boy skipped down the front steps and over to his mother's parked car. After they left, Molly looked out across the lawn toward the street, admiring the bold strokes of blue and yellow the bachelor buttons and nasturtiums made at the school's entrance. Things were working out pretty well.

She started back toward the school entrance when a blue Jaguar entered the driveway. A smile pulled at her mouth, and at her heart, too, the way it always did when she saw Stefanos. Yes, things were working out pretty well, indeed.

Funny, she had expected him to meet her at home. Home was another redbrick colonial filled with elegant English

furniture, which she and Stefanos shared with two cats and
sometimes, Stefanos's grandfather.

Her husband had brought someone with him, she saw
now. Molly removed her painting smock and folded it over
her arm, wondering who else might be in the car.

Stefanos occasionally left the Meta-Hellenic offices early,
but he rarely came to the school. He said he preferred to
have her all to himself.

Molly smiled as she thought of certain ways he liked to be
alone with her. The joy of that smile still lingered within her
when Stefanos pulled into the parking lot. She met him as
he got out and leaned on the top of his car door.

His brown eyes sparkled, and he dropped a kiss on her
mouth. "I brought someone to meet you," he signed.

"I see that." His amusement made her relax, and Molly
turned happily to the husky man who came up beside them
now. She hadn't spoken to Leo Rollins since that day in the
island police station almost a year ago, but he looked pretty
much the same. Molly held out her hand. "Hello."

Leo buttoned his jacket, pulled it down and said something in a serious voice. She frowned. He jerked his head
toward Stefanos.

"He's giving us his congratulations," Stefanos signed.

"Oh? On our marriage, you mean?"

Leo nodded.

"Thank you." She smiled at him and looped a hand
through Stefanos's arm. Stefanos pressed his hand on top of
hers. She gave him a smile, too, but her stomach knotted
anxiously. "What brings you out here, Leo? I trust it's not
another mission for Stefanos."

Leo shook his head. He said something, and Stefanos
disengaged himself to translate. "I never had a chance to
thank you for what you did last summer, but you were a
tremendous help. I'm just sorry I involved you in the first
place."

Molly stared at Stefanos's former colleague. Stef had been
recognized recently by the State Department for his part in

helping to foil a certain Mediterranean dictator's plan for
military dominance. He'd tried to get her recognized, too,
but Leo had objected because she hadn't been working for
the government.

She hadn't wanted to steal any of Stefanos's thunder,
anyway, but she would bet two nickels that Stefanos had
twisted Leo's arm to get him to come out today.

"Better say something." Stefanos's dark eyes danced with
amusement.

Molly patted Leo on the arm. "Thank you, Leo. I was
glad to help." She caught her husband's gaze, warm and
loving. The Greeks loved playing host, she'd discovered, and
Stefanos had turned out to be just like the rest of his family
in that respect. She gave him a little nod and turned back to
his old friend. "We would be delighted if you'd join us for
dinner."

After dinner, much later that evening, Stefanos helped
Molly clear the dishes away, thinking how much pleasure he
took in sharing even an ordinary task with her.

He set the plates he carried down besides the sink, slipped
his arms around her, and pinned her against the counter.
"Thanks for being so nice to Leo."

She kissed him quickly. "You're welcome."

He kissed her back, lingeringly. "Let's go upstairs."

"We have to do the dishes. Maria's not going to be here
tomorrow, or have you forgotten that your grandfather is
coming?"

Stefanos laughed. The housekeeper and his grandfather
did not get along at all. He draped his arms around Molly's
waist and pressed his hips against hers. He still felt like a kid
even after ten months of marriage. He needed to feel her, to
touch her, to know she wanted him. It was as if the emotions he'd dammed up for so many years overflowed now,
demanding to be expressed.

Molly looked up at him, her blond brows raised.

He stepped back, tucked a loose hair behind her unencumbered ear and explained, "My grandfather is going to meet us in Greece."

"Good."

Her favorite word, he thought. "Yes, it's good."

"I'll have time to paint the office at the school."

He shook his head. "I've already arranged to take the week off."

Her blue eyes widened. "You have?"

He nodded. Taking the dish towel from her hands, he tugged her toward the door. "I've never made love in the kitchen. It might be interesting, but the bed would be softer."

Molly laughed, and the sound of her happy voice sparkled through him like sun on water. "We'd better blow out the candles, then."

"Let's take one upstairs."

In the dining room he blew out one candle, took the other, and followed her up the stairs. In the bedroom, he set the candle beside the big four-poster and tossed back the spread.

Molly slipped off her shoes and came over to him, pulling her hair aside with one hand. "Will you get the hook, Stef?" He did her bidding, then let his hands rest on her shoulders. "Tell me." She glanced over her shoulder, and her blue eyes flirted with him. "Why are you taking off a week early?"

Stefanos unzipped her dress and slipped it off her shoulders, kissing first one side of her neck and then the other. She made a sound like a cat, turned and slipped her arms free. The soft fabric whispered down her legs to the floor, reminding him of the *meltemi,* the wind that kept the Aegean islands cool in the summer. It sounded like that when it rustled in the trees.

He smiled to himself. There would be no cooling breeze for him. Nor did he want one. He scooped Molly into his arms and carried her to the bed, where he sat with her on his lap. The scent of violets rose around him, and he imagined them lying together in a bed of soft purple flowers.

He kissed her impulsively, then drew back to gaze upon her. She seemed to grow more beautiful every day, though he didn't know how that was possible. "What would you think about our going back to the farmhouse for a few days before meeting my grandfather? We never really got to enjoy our stay in it before."

"I thought you didn't want to ever go back there."

"We could be alone." He massaged her hip. "Do you want a baby?"

"Do I want a baby?" she repeated and stared at him. "Stef, you don't just go out and buy one, you know."

He kissed the end of her nose. "I know. Do you want to have one, as in you and me?"

Her mouth dropped open.

"Going to catch a fly that way."

She laughed. "I thought you didn't want any children. When we got married, you said—"

He held up his hands. "I've been thinking about it and I've decided I want a child."

"Really?"

He nodded. "And I thought maybe we could bring Nikos back to live with us."

Her blue eyes warmed. "Nikos? Back to live with us?"

"I want to adopt him." Stefanos lifted an eyebrow, watching Molly closely. "If that's all right with you." She looked indignant. His heart sank. "We don't—" he started.

"Of course it's all right," she interrupted. "Oh, Stef, I'm so glad. It will be wonderful having him here."

Molly looped her arms around his neck, and Stefanos bent his head. The kiss ignited something fierce inside him, and he shifted her back against the pillows.

Sometime later Stefanos awoke. He glanced toward the night table and the candle there. He'd extinguished the flame long ago but it still burned brightly in his memory. He smiled, tucked in his chin and looked at his wife nestled against his side.

His wife! A year ago, he'd never thought he would ever use those words. He'd been surprised and relieved when she'd agreed to marry him. Even now, he felt amazed she'd loved him enough to do that. How could he have been so fortunate?

And how could their love grow stronger every day? It did, though. The loving and the sharing had grown easier, too.

Most amazing of all, the dream had vanished. He never woke sweating and afraid in the middle of the night anymore. Stefanos tightened his arm around Molly—his Molly. He'd done his best, and for once it had been enough. Because of Molly.

Molly was like the candle he'd looked forward to seeing every night of his captivity. Her courage and strength and honesty warmed even the darkest corners of his psyche.

She'd shown him someone could love and cherish him. She'd brought him out of the darkness of doubt and loneliness, had helped him discover his own light, had helped him nurture it. It had been a good decision after all—buying those watercolors of hers.

She stirred and lifted her head.

"I don't want to ever stop loving you, Molly."

"Stop?" she asked sleepily.

"L-o-v-i-n-g," he spelled and felt the light inside him change to fire.

"Good." She dropped her leg over his. "That's very good."

Stefanos pulled her closer and let the flames within him consume them both.

*   *   *   *   *

Dark secrets, dangerous desire...

Lovers DARK AND DANGEROUS

Three spine-tingling tales from the dark side of love.

This October, enter the world of shadowy romance as Silhouette presents the third in their annual tradition of thrilling love stories and chilling story lines. Written by three of Silhouette's top names:

LINDSAY McKENNA
LEE KARR
RACHEL LEE

Haunting a store near you this October.

Only from  Silhouette®

...where passion lives.

Is the future what it's cracked up to be?

This August, find out how C. J. Clarke copes with being on her own in

GETTING IT TOGETHER: CJ
by Wendy Corsi Staub

Her diet was a flop. Her "beautiful" apartment was cramped. Her "glamour" job consisted of fetching coffee. And her love life was less than zero. But what C.J. didn't know was that things were about to get better....

The ups and downs of modern life continue with

GETTING IT RIGHT: JESSICA
by Carla Cassidy in September

GETTING REAL: CHRISTOPHER
by Kathryn Jensen in October

Get smart. Get into "The Loop!"

Only from Silhouette®

where passion lives.

SILHOUETTE®
Desire®

Centerfolds

They're sexy, they're determined, they're trouble with a capital *T!*

Meet six of the steamiest, most stubborn heroes you'd ever want to know, and learn *everything* about them....

August's *Man of the Month*, Quinn Donovan, in **FUSION** by Cait London

Mr. Bad Timing, Dan Kingman, in **DREAMS AND SCHEMES** by Merline Lovelace

Mr. Marriage-phobic, Connor Devlin, in **WHAT ARE FRIENDS FOR?** by Naomi Horton

Mr. Sensible, Lucas McCall, in **HOT PROPERTY** by Rita Rainville

Mr. Know-it-all, Thomas Kane, in **NIGHTFIRE** by Barbara McCauley

Mr. Macho, Jake Powers, in **LOVE POWER** by Susan Carroll

Look for them on the covers so you can see just how handsome and irresistible they are!

Coming in August only from Silhouette Desire!

Don't miss the newest miniseries from
Silhouette Intimate Moments

Southern Knights

by Marilyn Pappano

A police detective. An FBI agent. A government prosecutor. Three men for whom friendship and the law mean everything. Three men for whom true love has remained elusive—until now. Join award-winning author Marilyn Pappano as she brings her **Southern Knights** series to you, starting in August 1994 with MICHAEL'S GIFT, IM #583.

The visions were back. And detective Michael Bennett knew well the danger they prophesied. Yet he couldn't refuse to help beautiful fugitive Valery Navarre, not after her image had been branded on his mind—and his heart.

Then look for Remy's story in December, as **Southern Knights** continues, only in...

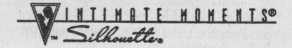

INTIMATE MOMENTS®
Silhouette®